CNAFR

T5-BYN-341

My Angel

First Chance Publishing

Cockeysville, Maryland

Copyright 2006 by Denise Skelton

Cover art by Kathy Harestad

ISBN 978-0-9790877-0-7
ISBN 0-9790877-0-8

First Chance Publishing
76 Cranbrook Rd.
Suite 232
Cockeysville, Maryland 21030
(443) 912-8719

Printed in the United States of America

To all the readers, thanks for the support and the encouragement.

Kathy and Sophia, thanks for all of your help.

My fantastic friends and family, thanks for always being there when I need you, I love you guys.

Special thanks to my assistant and daughter, Dominique. Not only do we have a ball working together, we make a great team.

And to my better half, James, each year your love and support make me a stronger and better person. I love you.

Prologue

Matt let himself into his parents' home with the same key he'd used since he was 9 years old. He walked through the house, heading toward the kitchen.

"Hey, Ma. Hey, Pop." Even his greeting had not changed.

Grabbing an apple from the fruit bowl, he took a bite and sat down at the kitchen table. His mother smiled at him. Standing, she moved to the cabinet to get a plate for him. "Hey. Did you have dinner yet?"

"No ma'am, I can wait till I get home."

"Are you sure?"

He nodded. "Wendy's waiting for me. We're going out to dinner, but I wanted to stop by and see you first." He took another bite from the apple. "So, you said you needed to talk to me about something?"

Marty looked from his son to his wife and back. "Becca, I told you to mind your own business."

She walked over to the table and leaned on the back of one of the chairs. "Marty, you know I can't. I can't just let this go."

"Can't let what go?" Matt asked. His mother sighed deeply.

Marty shook his head briskly. "Becca, as much as people say that they do, they really don't want to know something like this. I think you should just keep quiet."

"Quiet about what?" Matt asked as the realization of what she was saying slowly crept in.

Rebecca watched her son for a moment, suddenly unsure of her decision. She drew a deep breath. "Marty and I went to the mall today."

"Becca," Marty warned.

She waved her hand at her husband as she continued to speak. "And while I was there I saw Wendy."

Matt watched his mother, waiting for her to finish what she had to say. His stomach turned slightly. He looked at the apple, the sweet flavor in his mouth turning sour.

"She was with another man."

Matt glanced around the kitchen for a long moment, then he turned back to his mother.

"Okay."

"What do you mean, okay? Matt, she was with another man. She's having an affair with him."

"Ma, how do you know she's having an affair with him, or anyone else for that matter?"

"You know Rita Winston's niece, Dawn, who works for Wendy's friend Gail? Dawn said that she saw Wendy at Gail's house with another man, and she was hugging him and she even kissed him. Not a friendly peck on the cheek either. A real kiss."

"Ma, I wouldn't put too much stock in anything Mrs. Winston has to say."

"But I saw her with my own two eyes. They were holding hands ... her and this man."

"Did you talk to her? Did you bother to ask her who he was? It could have been anyone ... a family member or someone she went to school with."

Marty grunted, looking at his wife. "Told you so."

She ignored him, speaking to Matt. "Those are people that she would hold hands with?"

Matt knew the excuses that he came up with sounded lame even as he said them, but what could he do? His mother had told him on two different occasions that she thought that his wife was having an affair. Whenever he thought about it, the idea made him physically ill. He couldn't believe it. He would never believe that his Wendy would do that to him.

"Ma, I don't like you saying things like that about Wendy," Matt said, rising from the table and going to the waste basket to drop the apple inside. "She's my wife and I trust her. I would appreciate it if you and your friends stopped this witch hunt." Matt headed for the door to leave.

"Matt," his father spoke.

Matt turned back toward his parents.

"You know your mother better than that. She wouldn't bring something like this to your attention if she didn't honestly believe it was true." Marty looked up at his wife, who was now standing near the kitchen sink, tears pooling in her eyes. "Now, if you want to stay with Wendy knowing what your mother just told you, then that's your business, but don't go accusing your mother of something that's not true." He paused. "You know son, it takes a strong man to stay with a woman who's cheating on him, but it takes a much stronger man to leave her, even if he loves her." His father turned away, reaching for his coffee cup.

Matt looked at his father's back, then at his mother standing next to the sink. He quietly left their house, dropping his head as he walked out the door.

• • •

An hour later Matt walked into the condo he shared with Wendy. He had driven around for twenty minutes to clear his head before going home. He knew that his mother meant well when she told him that Wendy was having an affair, but she was wrong. He would be the first to know if anything was going on. He knew Wendy better than anyone. He went in search of his wife, finding her in the kitchen preparing a cup of tea.

"Hi, babe," he said, walking to her. She offered him her cheek to kiss as she glided past him heading toward the living room.

"Wendy, I talked to Nat today. He said that you changed the bathroom wall and floor tiles in the house. You asked him to order the Italian Terrazzo tiles instead?"

"Yes," her tone light.

Matt hedged a bit. "But they cost more then the ones we initially chose."

"Not much."

"Close to $4,800."

"Well, I suppose we can make it up somewhere else."

"Wendy, we're already $32,000 over budget as it stands, and the house is barely half complete."

"Matt, it'll be all right, stop worrying so much."

"Maybe we can install the Kraftmaid cabinets."

"No, I don't like those. I told you that I wanted to have them custom made."

"I know, but we can get the top of the line Kraftmaid cabinets, and it'll still save us quite a bit."

"I just said that I didn't like those. Matt, this is our dream house. Why do we have to cut corners?" Setting her cup on the coffee table Wendy moved around the room, running her finger along some of the furniture. "I think we need new furniture. We can start looking now. That way we can take our time and have it delivered when the house is ready."

Matt looked around the small living room.

"I like this stuff," Matt said, patting the back of the sofa. "Granted, it's dated, but we got it when we were struggling. It's — I don't know — comforting."

"Well, I sure hope it offers the next owner some comfort because it's gone as soon as I find something we like. Matt, everything we do to that house will show people your talent and let people know that you own a successful construction company. The more successful you are, the higher caliber clients you'll have. The higher caliber clients you have, the more money you'll make. It's that simple."

Matt blew out a heavy breath. "Okay, Wendy, I know you're right."

Wendy reached for the garment bag, opened it and pulled out a three-quarter length white mink coat. Matt stared at it for a full minute, his mouth open, before asking, "Where'd you get that?"

"Mitchell's Furs. Isn't it beautiful?" she said, slipping it on.

"Wendy, that had to cost a fortune. With the new house, we can't possibly afford that."

She looked up at him, her large eyes saddening. "Please," she eased close to him, wrapping her arms around him. "I love it so much, and when Gail let me borrow hers you said that I looked gorgeous in it."

He flinched as he looked at the price tag that read $6,300.

"Please, baby," she cooed.

He sighed and nodded. "Okay."

• • •

"This is a size 10. Maybe she needs a larger size." Simone's mother, Debra, said, tugging at the shoulders of the scarlet V-neck bridesmaid dress.

"No, she really doesn't," the seamstress assured her. "She definitely wears a size eight. The problem is that she's full breasted, so she'll need the next size up so I can alter it to fit."

Simone, standing on top of a white carpeted pedestal in Annapolis Bridal and Formalwear, fidgeted nervously and resisted the urge to bring her arms up to cover her breasts. She glanced at herself in the mirror. At 5'3" and 138 pounds, Simone had been told by one of the elderly men at the shelter where she volunteered that she reminded him of a black Jane Mansfield. Her father would often tell her that she was physically fit, while her mother complained that she was overweight. People of all ages and genders noticed Simone's gentle and vast beauty. But Simone didn't like to be noticed at all. She didn't like her hourglass-shaped figure or her voice that people described as soothingly sexy. She thought it was annoying, and it didn't help her combat the defiance that she sometimes met in her job as the Director of the Donnelly Youth Center.

"You know," Debra said to the seamstress. "I'm thinking that you might not want to alter Simone's dress just yet. She's been dieting and I'm sure she'll be losing weight before the wedding."

Simone glanced down at the woman putting pins in her dress. As the woman's gaze met Simone's, she smiled faintly, and continued pinning the dress.

Debra sucked her teeth slightly upon seeing the seamstress still pinning the dress, then looked up at her daughter. "Simone, Charles' wedding would be a wonderful opportunity for you to finally get a makeover and maybe have something done with that hair."

"Mother," Simone's sister René called. "I think I heard Tamara say that she didn't have a clue as to what sort of veil to wear with her gown. I'm not sure, but I believe I heard her saying something about white tulle with apple-red trim."

Debra gave René her "what would you people ever do without me" sigh as she headed to the front of the store. Simone looked over at her sister mouthing the word *thanks* and smiled.

Chapter 1

JANUARY 2006

"Everything is settled. I'll have one of my clerks send the final documents to your office in a few days."

"Whatever," Matt nodded quickly. "That'll be fine. Let her know that I'm going to need a little time. I have a lot of things stored in the house and I'll have them moved before the weekend. After that she'll be free to move in."

"No, that won't be necessary. She doesn't want the house."

"What — I don't understand?"

"She says she doesn't want anything. Not the house, the condominium or its contents. Nothing."

"I had that house built for her," Matt told him. "She can have it."

"What can I say?" Matt's attorney, Larry Frankie, hunched his narrow shoulders, his head moving toward his body like a turtle preparing to hide in its shell. "Everything is settled. It's all yours — free and clear." He turned, ready to walk away and then stopped, looking back at his client in disbelief. He shook his head slightly. "I don't understand you. Most men going through a divorce would give their soul to be in your position. Your ex-wife says she has hurt you enough, and now that the divorce is final she wants you to find happiness. Now you can finally move on. You should be elated."

• • •

Several days later, Mathew Turner was still playing that scene in his mind, repeatedly, like a DVD player — pause — rewind — play. He shook his head. That was three days ago, or was it four. He couldn't remember. He looked at the digital clock on the nightstand. The date read January 2.

"Happy Fucking New Year," Matt mumbled and then sighed.

~ 1 ~

He was astonished at how heavy his heart felt. At how sadness and despair were able to rip him apart and make him want his first drink at 8:45 in the morning. How it made him tired, dizzy and nauseated all at the same time. On the other hand, it could have been the half-bottle of whisky he'd drunk in the last two hours. He rolled over slowly, rose and sat on the edge of the bed holding his face in his hands.

"I'm free," he said in a raspy voice. Free to do what? For the last 10 years, his life had revolved around Wendy. He reached for the bottle of Jack Daniels and the glass on the nightstand. Pouring whisky in the glass, he raised it. "To the woman who was the love of my life. You were my reason for living. You were my world. But you ripped out my heart and squeezed all of the life from it, then watched as it dried up and blew away in the wind. To you, Wendy Kristin Turner," he said, his voice slightly slurred.

Then he chuckled bitterly, "No, I'm sorry, Wendy Kristin Warn. You don't want anything from me. Least of all my last name."

He set the half-full glass on the nightstand, taking a large swig from the bottle. The phone rang as he brought the bottle to his lips a second time. After listening to the greeting that he and Wendy had recorded on the answering machine, there was a short beep.

"Hey guy, where are you?"

Matt grunted at the yelling voice coming from the answering machine.

"I know you're there. Pick up the damn phone. Matt? Matt? Stop being a dipshit and pick up the phone."

"Shit," Matt cursed, as he snatched the phone up. "What?"

"It is about damn time," Matt's best friend, Josh Peterson yelled. "I've been calling you for almost a week!"

"Man, what the hell do you want?" Matt yelled back.

"Come on guy, you need to get off your ass and stop feeling sorry for yourself. You are not the first man who has ever gotten divorced and you sure won't be the last. You've had six days to cry about it. It's time to dry up your tears, pull your head out of your ass, and get over it."

"You just don't understand ... "

"Like hell, I don't. The world is not going to end because Wendy does not want your sorry ass anymore. You wanna be a wuss about it?" Matt was quiet. "Or do you wanna be a man?"

Matt let out a heavy sigh.

"Yeah, that's what I thought," Josh said smugly. "Meet me at my house around five o'clock. Oh yeah, and wear something decent."

Matt let out a loud moan and sighed again. "All right."

• • •

The second and fourth Sunday of every month at the Porter's home was always the same. Often the meal changed, sometimes the faces, but the atmosphere would always remain the same. The aroma of barbecued ribs greeted them as they entered the small formal dining room. Gathering around the table, everyone settled in, and after saying grace, they prepared to devour the meal that Debra Porter had cooked.

Looking across the table, Simone Porter smiled faintly at Alan Whitaker. Her mother's newest idea of what was the best thing for her daughter. He glanced back at Simone. He was handsome with dark eyes. His clean-shaven chestnut skin stretched over his high cheekbones as he offered her a bold smile.

"Go on everyone, dig in," Debra ordered, her voice demanding and tired at the same time.

Simone knew that tone all too well. It was her mother's "look at this magnificent feast I've painstakingly created especially for you people and you had better praise me before you even bother to put one bite in your mouth" tone that she used so often it's part of her personality.

"Everything looks wonderful, Mother," Simone whispered.

"Yes, it does, doesn't it," Debra beamed. "I've really outdone myself this time."

"Yes, honey, you have," Simone's father, Joseph, added.

Out of the corner of her eye, Simone saw her father pick up a large slice of cornbread, pass it to her sister René, and gesture for her

to put it on Simone's plate. René looked at her father, then glanced quickly at her mother before gingerly slipping the cornbread on the plate.

"There you go, baby girl," he announced.

Simone looked innocently at her father. "Thanks, Daddy," she said. Her voice, which was barely above a whisper, was fine and delicate like a perfectly tuned silver bell.

"Joe, don't give her that," Debra scolded him. "She doesn't need to be eating any bread. It'll go right to her hips."

Simone glanced uncomfortably across the table at Alan, then to her right, meeting her mother's disapproving gaze. She watched as everyone passed around the serving plates of green beans, potato salad and cornbread. When the plates were passed to her, she scooped out a tablespoon of beans and a tablespoon of potato salad.

"Simone, I made that rib just for you," Debra said, pointing to the lifeless, tasteless-looking piece of meat on the serving plate. "I steamed it first to get rid of as much of the fat as possible, then I used a new recipe that I cut out of some magazine." She paused as if trying to remember the name of the magazine, then waved her hand, dismissing the idea.

Simone groaned inwardly. Reluctantly, she speared the meat with her fork and placed it on her plate as far away from the other food as she could manage.

"Debra, let her have one of the other ribs. That one doesn't have any barbecue sauce on it ... " Joe said with concern.

"It doesn't matter, it's better for her that way .... Besides, you know I don't like to waste food."

"Why don't I just take Simone's rib," René said, reaching toward Simone's plate with her fork. "And she can have mine. That way nothing will go to waste."

"René," Debra warned, her voice low and stern. René looked at her mother, then sympathetically at Simone, saying *I'm sorry* with her eyes.

"Debra, leave Simone alone. Let the girl eat," Joe said, feeling embarrassed and sorry for his younger daughter.

"Joe, she's trying to lose weight. No wonder she's as big as

a house, with you sneaking her food all the time," Debra shot at her husband. "Now I," she said, proudly placing the tips of her fingers on her chest, "am trying to help her."

"You know, Mrs. Porter, everyone needs a person in their life like you," Alan said, smiling at Debra. "Someone to guide them, you know, and to lead them down the right path."

"You know, Alan, this is so true, and I have always been there for my family. To help them make the right decisions, even if they do not realize or appreciate it. And with Simone and her diet, I happen to be in that very predicament. Why just the other evening, Joe and I met her for dinner and ... "

Simone closed her eyes, willing herself to be anywhere but in the home where she had spent the first 19 years of her life, sitting across from the man her mother had hand-picked for her. A man who was intelligent, successful and very, very attractive. A man who was probably a great person. But something deep down inside Simone whispered that he was going to be the second most annoying person she had ever met. She crowned her mother with the title of "First Most Annoying."

She groaned. If God were merciful, then her latest diet would shift into high gear and she would shrivel up and fade away any minute. She opened her eyes, glancing quickly around the room. *Nope, it didn't work. I'm still here.*

"Excuse me," Simone said, rising from the table.

"But you didn't eat your dinner. I prepared that especially for you."

"I know, Mother, and I'm sorry. I'm just not very hungry." Simone averted her eyes from her mother's critical gaze. As she turned to leave the room, her mother's words followed her.

"Like I was going to say, I could not believe that she ate two whole pieces of fried fish."

Walking into the hall Simone took her coat out of the closet and went into the living room. As she opened the patio door, she stepped out into the frigid January weather. Taking a deep breath, she allowed the cold, crisp air to clear her mind. If she had known her mother had invited Alan to dinner, she would have made up

some excuse not to come. She would rather have gone to the movies or to the mall. She suppressed a moan. She would have even preferred cleaning her house from top to bottom than spending the entire afternoon with her mother when she was in her "can someone please take our pathetic daughter off our hands, I beg you" mode.

Simone walked across the yard, smiling at the sound of fresh snow crunching under her feet. Brushing off one of the lawn chairs, she sat down and stared into space as she contemplated a quick exit that would bring her the least amount of ridicule from her mother. She decided it might be better just to hang out in the back yard for a while.

For as long as she could remember her mother had made every attempt to change her. At the age of 7, Simone wanted to take ballet and her mother made her take piano instead. At 10, Simone wanted to play on the community co-ed football team. Debra had told her that she wasn't allowed to play or even associate with the children at the community center, because most of them were what she liked to call street urchins. At 16, Simone wanted to join the Young Democrats Club in school. Under threat of losing her driving privileges, Simone again bowed to Debra's wishes and joined the Republican club instead. After all, that was the place to meet unattached young men of stature and wealth.

Now, at the age of 28, Simone still felt she was ruled and bullied by her mother. Debra never threatened. She didn't have to. She just had a way about her that made people do exactly what she said and when she said it.

"Hey baby girl," she heard from behind her.

She glanced up at her father's smiling face.

"I brought you something. Follow me."

She rose and followed her father across the yard to the garage that doubled as a workshop. Once they entered the garage, Joe crossed the room and lifted a napkin on his workbench to reveal a plate with a regular-size portion of food on it. He reached inside his shirt pocket to pull out a paper napkin with a fork wrapped inside, and held it out to Simone. She looked at the plate and back at him.

"Go ahead, take it. She didn't see me bring it out."

Sitting down on a stool next to the bench she reluctantly took the plate, carefully placing it on her lap. Joe pulled up another stool to sit next to her.

"Simone, your mother means well, really. She just goes overboard with almost everything she does."

"I know, Daddy, and I'm trying to lose weight. It's just not that easy."

"Simone, you're not overweight."

"Daddy I'm five-foot-three and ... "

"You still go to the gym a few times a week, don't you?"

She nodded.

"You take good care of yourself. You're in good shape."

"But Mother's the same height and she's barely 100 pounds."

He shook his head as she spoke. "You and your mother are two different people."

"But ... "

"No, you are different people and you are going to look and act different. And I'm glad of that." He sighed. "I love your mother dearly, but I don't think the world could handle another Debra Porter."

• • •

Matt inhaled the sweet fragrance of apples from the hair of the woman in his arms. It reminded him of Wendy.

Wendy had beautiful hair, he thought, closing his eyes and inhaling deeply the intoxicating aroma. An image of Wendy flashed in his mind, and the realization hit him that this was not Wendy. He would never hold Wendy in his arms again.

Cassie, the blind date that Josh had set him up with, snuggled closer, as they leaned against her car in the restaurant parking lot. Matt held her in a light embrace and loosened his hold a little more.

She stroked his back, slowly moving her hand along to his side and down to his belt. She ran her index finger along the top edge

of his belt to the buckle and then traced her finger down the fly of his pants.

His breathing became ragged as he slowly licked his lips.

Drawing back, she tilted her head upward, allowing her lips to brush his.

"After all the things Josh has told me about you, I'm really glad we were finally able to meet," she purred, meeting Matt's gaze.

"Yeah, me, too," he said, trying to keep his voice even.

"Maybe we could do something? Go to my place if you like?" she said. He removed one of his hands from her waist, raising his arm as he squinted at his watch.

"I have to be going; I have an early appointment tomorrow."

She stepped back from his embrace and smiled at him.

"Now, that was a blatant lie," she said, her voice flat.

He flinched, not realizing that she could see through him.

"I'm sorry. It's been a rough week."

She laughed at the startled look on his face, and then said, "No, I'm the one who should be sorry. Josh told me about everything you've been going through." She looked around hesitantly, then back at him. "Do you want to talk about it?"

He could tell from her demeanor that she was just being kind. She did not want to hear his problems. He shook his head.

"No, not really, I just need to put it all behind me."

She nodded and pulled her coat tight to block out the cold air.

"Well, I'd better be going," she said as she reached in her pocket for keys and unlocked her car door. She turned back to him, "You sure you won't reconsider. I'm told I'm very good company?" she teased.

He watched her closely. "I'll bet you are, and that sounds like a great offer, but I wouldn't be very good company right now."

She smiled broadly. "I'm good enough for the both of us."

He looked down at her. With help from a nearby streetlight, he could see the sparkle in her green eyes.

"Yeah, like I said, I'll bet you are, but I think I'd better head home." He leaned forward, letting his lips brush hers.

" 'Night," he whispered, reaching around her for the car door and opening it.

She slid in and rolled the window down after he closed the door.

"Why don't you give me a call on Monday? We can get together next week. I could make dinner. I make a mean lasagna."

He smiled down at her.

"Sure, sounds good. I'll call you. Drive safe."

He stepped back from the car and watched as she backed out of the parking space and drove away from the restaurant lot.

"Nope. Not Wendy," he whispered before he walked to his car.

• • •

"I've been waiting months for this," Jamison Cartwright said as he watched the tall figure walk across the parking lot and get into his car. "That son of a bitch has been a thorn in my side for more than a year."

"I told you to let me take care of him," his companion said, stretching his legs as he tried to get comfortable inside the cramped Porche. "I could have just as easily walked up behind him and put one in the back of his head." He reached over and pointed his index finger at his friend's head like a gun, "Pop. It's that simple."

"It wasn't the right time. Wendy would have been more upset if he was killed. She would have been pining away for him, and I couldn't let that happen. And I definitely don't want to take the chance of having the cops trace it back to us."

"Why are you worried about the cops? Those stupid bastards couldn't find their asses with both hands. How are they going to find out who popped some loser? You need to stop being such a pussy."

Jamison looked over to meet the eyes of his friend Adrian Hirsch. Adrian's steel-gray eyes met his. Jamison suppressed a shudder before he turned away to see the car that they had been watching for the last hour and a half pull out of the restaurant parking lot.

"Show time," he said as he started the car and put it into drive.

• • •

Leaning across the counter, Debra pulled back the curtains on the kitchen window to watch as Simone and Alan talked. *He will be good for her,* she thought to herself. *I know he will. This young man is going places. He has ambition, I can see him one day taking over my position at the institution, and Simone will be right by his side.*

Debra Porter was the sort of woman who liked order. Her office was organized, her kitchen was immaculate, even her closet was arranged in order by color and season. She was in control of every aspect of her life. When she first met Joseph Porter, she knew that he was going to be her husband. And she was sure that when his butterscotch complexion and green eyes combined with her rich mahogany skin tone they would produce beautiful babies. Their children would have their father's looks and her intelligence.

She had met Joe at college. She had seen him walking briskly from the campus parking lot toward the library and followed him. After striking up a conversation, Debra had been able to arrange a date with him while letting him believe it was his own idea. She later learned that Joe's father was African American and his mother was German and white. This had not fit in with Debra's idea of having a husband with strong African American roots at all, but she later decided that she could learn to live with it.

When she had found out that Joe was in school on a scholarship and had to work to pay his living expenses, she nearly broke things off. She couldn't very well date a janitor. But after careful consideration she decided the end justified the means. A year after they started dating Debra convinced Joe that his idea of being a public-school teacher just wasn't for him. They, as a couple, had aspirations, and they couldn't reach their goals on the salary of a school teacher. So Joe aimed higher and became a professor at the local university. Debra maintained a position as the head of a prestigious mental-health facility.

Controlling her children was another story. When they were young she had told them where they could go, what clothes to wear, and who they could have as friends. As they got older, her three children started to go their separate ways. Her oldest, René, had chosen what Debra accepted as an adequate career, but she married a man whose ideas Debra thought were obtuse, with his anti-government ideas.

Her middle child, Charles, made the right career move and had married well, but at 32, Charles tended to be a little headstrong and immature. Then there was her baby, Simone. Simone looked more like her father with her fair skin and long, wavy hair. She also had his idealistic view on the world, but Debra had been able to control Simone longer than her other children.

When Simone and Alan started walking toward the house, Debra dropped the curtain and walked to the sink, pretending to fill the dishwasher.

"It's really gotten cold out there," Alan said as they stepped into the warm kitchen.

"Sure has," Simone agreed, briskly rubbing her gloved hands together.

Alan stepped in front of Simone, took her hands and removed her gloves. He set the gloves on the table and rubbed her hands between his, warming them. Once Alan released Simone's hands, he pulled out one of the chairs at the table for her.

Debra watched the exchange, smiling proudly.

"Alan, why don't you go into the den with Joe and watch the game while Simone helps me with the dishes?" Debra said pleasantly.

He nodded, then went through the dining room toward the den.

Simone picked up her gloves, putting them in her coat pocket. After taking off her coat and scarf, she hung them on the back of the chair that Alan had pulled out.

Debra glanced down at the coat hanging on the chair, preparing to say something about it, then decided against it.

"Is René still here?" Simone asked her mother.

"No, they wanted to visit Max's parents before it got too late. She said that she would call you one evening during the week."

Simone nodded. "What do you need me to do?"

"Nothing, I just wanted to spend some time with you. So, what do you think of Alan? He's great, isn't he?" Debra asked Simone. "I told you he was very nice and he's extremely intelligent, too. He went to Brown University, you know?"

"Yes, Mother, you already told me, on quite a few occasions," Simone said as she slowly sat down.

"And he's handsome, too. The two of you make a lovely couple. Don't you think?" Debra waited for a response.

Simone bit her lip before speaking. "Yes ma'am, he's very handsome."

"And when you start working together, you two will grow closer, and maybe even get married. Did you call personnel about that counseling position on Friday?" Debra asked as she wrapped the leftover food.

"No," Simone said, watching her mother's back stiffen. Quickly, she added, "I haven't gotten around to it."

"How do you not get around to making a phone call?" Debra asked, glaring at Simone.

"I just haven't," Simone said softly. She instantly averted her eyes.

"Well, if you don't do it soon, the job will be taken, and you'll be stuck working with those delinquents for goodness knows how long. Who knows when another opportunity like this will come along again?" she said, turning back to the counter.

Simone looked at her mother's back, "Mother, they're not delinquents, and I don't mind working at the youth center."

"Nonsense, your major in college was psychology, and we didn't pay all that money for your education to have you waste your time doing something like that," Debra said, waving her hand.

"I have to go, Mother," Simone said as she rose from the chair. She pulled her coat off the table and put it on.

"What? You can't leave," Debra practically yelled at her.

"Mother, one of the kids from the center has to go to court

tomorrow, and I promised his mother I would accompany them. I want to call her before it gets too late, and I left the number at home." Simone turned and left the kitchen.

Debra grunted her disapproval and then followed her daughter through the house.

Alan looked up when he heard Simone approach. "Would you like to watch the game with us?" he asked, quickly moving over to make room for her.

"No thanks, I need to be getting home. Goodnight, Daddy," Simone said as she moved to kiss her father's cheek.

"I'll walk you out," Alan said, standing.

"No, you don't have to."

"Let him walk you out," Debra insisted, eyeing Simone.

" 'Night mother." Simone walked past her mother with Alan following her.

"I'm really glad we got a chance to meet. Your mother has been trying to get us together for weeks," he said as they descended the steps. Even though he stood a full seven inches taller than Simone, Alan had to walk in double-time to match her pace.

"It was nice to finally meet you, too," she said, suppressing a sigh.

"Maybe we could get together later?" he asked as they approached her car.

"No," she said, biting her lip as she realized she'd answered a little quicker than she had intended. "I really have to get home. I have a ton of things that I have to take care of tonight."

"Okay." He nodded, looking disappointed, and leaned close as she turned her head slightly to allow him to kiss her cheek. He pulled back, leaving a quarter-size wet spot on her cheek, and smiled as their eyes met.

She smiled back, praying it didn't show as a grimace and fighting the urge to wipe her cheek with her sleeve.

"Can I get your number from your mother and call you in a few days?"

"Sure — that will be fine," she nodded. Getting into her car, she started it, and watched Alan's tall, graceful form taking slow,

steady strides as he walked along the walkway leading to the porch. Her mother met him at the door, giving him one of her rare, but impressive, award-winning smiles.

Simone shook her head, not because she was disappointed or angry at the way her mother tried to push Alan on her, but because she knew her mother's thoughts all too well. Debra thought that with enough hard work on her behalf she could mold Simone into the sort of woman that she could be proud to call her daughter. Simone sadly put the car in reverse to back out of the driveway and head to the only place she knew she could find sanctuary from Debra Porter. Her own home.

Chapter 2

Simone slowed down as she made a right onto Route 214, following a white 1968 Chevrolet Camero about a quarter-mile ahead. She looked in her rear-view mirror and saw a car coming up quickly behind her. As it approached, it swerved around her, beating her to the light.

"Hey, slow down there buddy," she grumbled aloud to herself.

The shiny finish of the black Porsche glistened in the moonlight while the driver raced his engine, impatiently waiting for the light to change. After another 30 seconds, the light changed and the two cars in front of her took off. The Porsche driver pulled close to the Camero, beeping his horn and flashing his headlights. The Camero slowed down, keeping within the speed limit.

Simone saw the person in the Camero stick his arm out of the window, flagging for the Porsche to go around him. The Porsche slowed almost to a stop. She slowed to a creep behind him.

"Oh, come on, now," she said, "this is ridiculous."

The Porsche picked up speed, reaching about 50 by the time it caught up to the Camero. Then the driver of the Porsche sped around the Camero and swerved toward it, causing the other driver to make a sharp right and sending the Camero toward the embankment.

Simone's mind froze for a moment as she watched the Porsche pick up speed. She heard its engine as the taillights quickly disappeared. She watched in horror as the Camero rolled down the hill, flipping three times on its way down.

"Oh my God," she whispered, in shock. She stopped her car, put it in park, and just sat for a moment, her mind not quite processing what she had seen. Then she quickly grabbed her cell phone and called 9-1-1. She shouted for an ambulance, gave the address,

dropped her phone on the seat, and jumped out of the car. She ran to the embankment, looking down at the mangled car.

From where she stood the way down looked steep. She didn't know if she could make it but she knew she had to try. Sitting down and easing her way to the edge, she slid down as slowly as possible. She slipped for five feet before she stopped, banging her right elbow on a rock formation and ripping her coat.

She paused, holding her elbow as a sharp pain ran from her shoulder to her fingertips. She took a deep breath and continued to make her way down to the rocky ground below. Once she reached the bottom, she stood quickly, her adrenalin pumping so fast that she ignored the sharp pain in her arm as she headed for the car. The front of the car was crushed beyond belief, as was part of the roof. The windshield was smashed and she could hear the engine still running.

"Oh man," she whispered, covering her mouth and thinking whoever was in there could not have survived.

Oh shit, am I dead? Matt wondered. He took a deep breath as unbelievable pain shot through his body. *No — being dead would not hurt this bad.*

Drifting in and out of consciousness, Matt thought only of Wendy. He didn't want to leave her. He didn't want to die without seeing her one last time to tell her that he forgave her and that he still loved her.

Suppressing a shiver, Simone took a deep breath and squinted her eyes, preparing for what she might see. Slowly, she walked to the car and leaned closer. She looked in the window to see the driver slumped over the steering wheel. With shaky hands, she timidly reached inside, moving him back. He moaned, and she screamed. Her hand flew to her chest as she jumped back.

"Help," he whispered.

"I've called for help. They're on the way," Simone told him, trying to control her voice as she moved closer.

Sitting as straight as he could, Matt leaned his head against the headrest.

In the light from the dashboard, Simone could see blood

rushing from a gash on his forehead. She pulled the wool scarf from around her neck, gently applying pressure to the cut.

"Hey, don't go to sleep," she said. "Help will be here soon."

He nodded, then lurched in pain.

"I'm going to see if I can open the door," she said, and pulled the handle with her free hand. It didn't budge.

"Hey," she said, remembering TV shows that always tried to keep people awake with head injuries, "What's your name?"

"Matt."

"Hey, Matt. Is that short for Mathew?"

He nodded, instantly regretting the movement as pain burst behind his eyes. "Do you have a last name, Mathew?"

"Turner."

"Mathew Turner, my name is Simone Porter."

"Simone," he whispered her name.

"Yes," she nodded.

He inhaled deeply, struggling to breathe.

"Simone, please don't leave."

She reached inside the car, taking his hand and squeezing it gently. "I won't. I promise." She heard the distant sound of sirens. "Help is almost here, so let's not go to sleep just yet. Okay?"

He nodded, licking his dry lips. "I really could use some water."

"If you don't fall asleep until they get you out of there, I'll make sure you get all the water you want," Simone promised.

The firefighters carefully removed him from the wreckage and laid him on the gurney. Matt had heard someone say it took only an hour to free him, but to him it seemed more like years.

The woman who called for help was still there. Matt could hear her soft voice calming him. She had a nice voice, it sounded almost as if she were singing. He tried to listen to everything that was going on around him. He thought he heard someone mention his parents. *Ma's going to be so upset.* He heard the squawking of radios, roaring of vehicles and the crunching of shoes on the gravel.

He listened intently, trying to make sense out of everything that was going on around him.

Matt licked his dry lips, and felt a warm hand on his. "Everything is going to be okay now," she said.

He opened his eyes, seeing her silhouette for the first time. He tried to see the face of the person who saved his life, but was unable to make her out in the darkness.

"Miss, are you all right," a male asked her. "Your arm, it's bleeding."

"I'm fine, it's just a scratch. Can you give him some water?"

"No, ma'am, we can't give him anything until he gets to the hospital."

"I promised him that if he held on and did not go to sleep that he could have a drink of water," she said.

"Sorry, ma'am."

"He's been through a lot and all he wants is a drink of water. Now give the man a drink of water." Her soft voice squeaked as she yelled.

Then Matt felt a bottle being pressed against his lips. He parted them, feeling the water slide across his tongue and down his throat. He opened his eyes, trying to see her again.

"Thank you," he whispered.

"I always keep my promises," Simone whispered back.

• • •

Rushing into the emergency room lobby, Simone walked to the receptionist.

"Excuse me, Miss, the ambulance brought someone in by the name of Turner. Can you tell me how he's doing?"

"Are you family?"

"No, ma'am, I called for the ambulance. I just wanted to make sure he was ..."

"Miss ... " She felt someone place a hand on her shoulder.

Turning, she looked into the face of an older woman with salt-and-pepper hair. Her cobalt-blue eyes were tired and red from cry-

ing, exaggerating the contrast against her fair skin. Simone guessed her to be in her late fifties. She was a very attractive woman.

"The person you're asking about was in an accident on Route 214?"

"Yes."

"You must be the woman who saved my son's life?"

Simone remained quiet.

"Thank you," the woman whispered, reaching out and squeezing Simone's hand.

"No, that's not necessary," Simone shook her head.

"Yes it is. I don't know what would have happened to him if you hadn't been there."

"How is he?" Simone asked.

"We don't know anything yet." Rebecca Turner looked around nervously. "They just took him into surgery. My husband and I are in the waiting room." She said with her voice pleading slightly.

"Mrs. Turner, if it's all right with you, I'd like to wait?" Simone said, her eyes questioning.

"Yes," Rebecca answered, relieved. "I'd like that very much."

She looked down at Simone's tattered light-blue pea coat. Seeing a long tear, she glanced farther down to see droplets of blood trickle next to Simone's feet.

"Oh, God, you're bleeding!" Rebecca said, calling for one of the nurses.

"I'm fine," Simone insisted as the triage nurse took her into a room to look at her arm. Rebecca followed them.

After having her arm bandaged, Simone walked into the waiting room.

Rebecca sat in one of the padded chairs lining one side wall. Next to her, a man looked up when she entered the room, his dark eyes showing a combination of sorrow and fear while his mouth expressed barely controlled anger.

Rebecca stood quickly, smiling at Simone.

"Marty this is the woman who saved Matt. Miss ... ?" She looked at Simone.

"Porter."

"Miss Porter, this is my husband, Martin Turner."

"Thanks," he said, giving her a quick nod, then turning his attention back to the green carpet.

"Please sit with me, Miss Porter," Rebecca said.

"Simone," she corrected. Rebecca smiled at her.

"Simone, please sit with me." She said, gesturing to a row of chairs opposite her husband.

Looking through the glass door Simone spotted one of the doctors walking to the nurse's station. After he spoke briefly with her, the nurse pointed him in the direction of the waiting room.

Simone turned to Rebecca, touched her hand lightly and told her, "I'll be back." Then, picking up her coat, she walked past the doctor, offering him a faint smile. She sighed deeply, feeling tired, upset and helpless. She wished that she could have done more for the Turners. She had apologized to Rebecca for not being able to offer much in the way of information to the police. Rebecca said that she had been there to call for help and had stayed with her son until help arrived, but Simone could not help but think that she could have done more.

Leaning against the wall, she flinched from the pressure she put on her bandaged arm. She glanced to her right at the doctor talking to Marty and Rebecca Turner. She witnessed the distraught look on Rebecca's face as she turned and buried her face in her husband's chest and Simone felt tears welling up in her own eyes. She drew in a heavy breath and turned away, biting her lip and blinking back the tears. Hearing the door open, she stood as the doctor walked from the waiting room, followed by Rebecca and Marty.

Rebecca slowed her pace and stopped in front of Simone. Simone took her hand, squeezing it gently.

"My baby may never wake up," Rebecca whispered.

"I'm sorry," Simone said, taking the older woman in her arms, wishing that what little strength she had, she could give to Rebecca.

Rebecca drew back.

"Thank you for waiting with me. You will never know how grateful I am for all that you've done."

"No gratitude is necessary, but if it's okay with you, I'd like to stop by tomorrow?"

Rebecca smiled as she nodded. "Thank you," she whispered.

"I'll see you tomorrow," Simone said before walking down the corridor and out the sliding doors.

Chapter 3

Simone instinctively reached for the phone, bringing it to her ear. "Hello ... hello," she said, half awake. Then, realizing she had the receiver upside down, she flipped it over. "Hello."

"Simone?" Hearing her brother's voice, Simone turned over to look at the clock on the nightstand. It read 2:35 a.m. She instantly became alarmed.

"What, what's wrong, what's the matter? Is it Mother or Daddy?" She rambled, leaning on one elbow and rubbing her eyes.

"No, they're fine."

"Then what's happened? Are you okay? Is it Tamara? You guys haven't been in an accident ... ?" Simone rushed on.

"Oh no, it's nothing like that," her brother assured her. Then, taking a long pause and a deep breath, he asked, "So, how have you been? I didn't wake you did I?"

"I know you're not calling me at 2 in the morning to ask me how I'm doing," Simone said angrily, lying back down.

"Can't I just call and see how my baby sister is doing?"

"Charles, it's too late for this." She groaned and brushed her hair from her face.

"I know it's late, but I just wanted to talk to you." He paused again. "So, how are things?"

"Good night, Charles." She turned over, preparing to hang up the phone.

"Okay, okay," he said quickly, "I need a favor." She sat back, looking at the swirls of blue and white clouds she had one of the teens at the center paint on the ceiling. The girl had wanted a dress for a dance and couldn't find a job in time. Simone knew that she was an artist and she had asked the girl if she could do some artwork on one of her walls and her bedroom ceiling for a few hundred dol-

lars. Simone was so impressed with her talent that she helped her get a scholarship to one of the best art schools in Baltimore.

"Charles, I've had a rough day. I didn't get to bed until almost midnight. I have to go to work early. Can't this wait until some other time?"

"No, I swear, this is really important."

Simone sighed. "What's the favor, Charles?"

He was quiet for a few moments.

"Charles," Simone called impatiently.

He inhaled deeply. "Okay, I need you to tell Tamara that I was with you tonight."

"And you felt you had to call me at 2 a.m. to ask me this. You couldn't wait until say ... 9 a.m.?"

"No, I didn't want her to call before I had a chance to talk to you."

"Charles, I don't like this. I don't feel comfortable lying."

"Come on, Simone. This is important, and you've always been there for me. I wouldn't ask you to do this if it weren't necessary. Listen, Tamara and I had a fight. Afterward I went out for a few drinks with some friends. I don't want her to be upset — you know how she gets when she thinks I've been out drinking. Besides, she probably won't even call. But just in case she does — I just need you to do this for me. Please."

"Charles, are you sure that's all that's going on?"

He remained silent.

"I don't want to get involved in your mess. Whatever is going on, I think the best thing for you to do is to talk to your wife."

"I can't."

"Why not?"

"Because," he blew out a in a heavy breath. "I messed up. Real bad."

"Oh, Charles, what did you do?"

"I can't tell you, but this could cost me my marriage, and you're my last hope. I love Tamara and I don't want to lose her. I promise I'll make things right. I just need this one thing from you. Please, Simone."

Simone sighed. She really had a bad feeling about this. "Okay. But only this one time."

• • •

"Wendy, please don't do this — not again."

The scenes with her were often different but they always ended the same. They ended with him standing alone as he watched her walk away from their life together, shattering his heart. He hated when he went to the home they shared together. That's where it would always happen. Sometimes he would be in the kitchen. Sometimes in the bedroom. But it would always end the same. Then the setting would change, and he felt as though he was floating and he would be somewhere else. His eyes shifted quickly and he quivered from the coolness. The pounding of his heart was magnified by the intense darkness.

"I promise I won't leave you," the voice he had been searching for whispered. He turned toward the sound of her beautiful, soothing voice. A voice he thought he could listen to forever.

"Where are you?" he asked. "I can't find you."

"I'm here," she whispered. He looked around the dark space, not seeing anyone. To his left he saw a door. It opened slowly, allowing the majestic light behind it to enter the darkness. As the light touched his feet and moved up his body, he felt a wonderful sensation, warmer and more comforting than a mother's embrace. He felt himself slowly being pulled toward it.

"Mathew."

He glanced back.

"Don't go. It's not time," her voice whispered.

"But it's so warm; it's magnificent," he said, looking back toward the light.

"I know. It is wonderful, isn't it? But it's not time for you to go yet. You have to wake up. When you do, I'll be waiting for you."

He stopped moving.

"Do you promise?" he asked, his eyes scanning the area looking for her, trying to find his beautiful angel.

"Yes, I promise."

• • •

"Marty, it's been more than four months," Rebecca said, watching her younger son's face.

To her, he looked as if he were sleeping. Sighing to herself, she thought if only that were the case, she could wake him and everything would be fine.

"It's been so long, what if he never wakes up?" she continued.

Marty sat staring at the television screen. He only wanted one thing right now. It was for his wife to stop talking. He pretended not to hear her.

"Marty?" she called, turning to look at her husband's profile, his set jaw telling her that he wanted to be left alone.

She sighed heavily and looked back in the direction of the bed. Rising from the chair, she walked to her son's side. His eyes fluttered.

"Marty, I think he's waking up!"

Marty jumped to his feet, rushed to the bed and stood next to his wife. They both leaned forward, watching every movement as Matt seemed to struggle to open his eyes.

"Well, it's about damn time," Marty bellowed, causing Rebecca to flinch. "How are you feeling son?"

Matt heard his father's raspy voice through the fog and focused on it, using it as an anchor to consciousness.

"I'm good, Pop," he whispered, his mouth as dry as cotton. He tried opening his eyes, but the light caused instant irritation.

"Boy, you sure scared the hell out of your mama," Marty huffed. "Gave me a little fright, too. But I knew you'd be all right."

Matt felt a soft hand touch his.

"Hi, Ma," he said.

She laughed and cried at the same time. "How did you know who I was?"

He swallowed hard before speaking.

"I can always tell your touch."

"Are you in any pain?" she asked, tenderly squeezing his hand.

"No pain," he whispered.

•••

"Ma, how long have I been here?" Matt asked his mother.

Rebecca glanced at Marty, then nervously back to her son.

"A little over four months."

Matt looked at her, thinking that he hadn't heard her correctly.

She nodded. "Four months and a week."

Matt suddenly felt tired. He couldn't believe it had been that long. It seemed like only yesterday. He didn't remember anything. All he could remember was his car flipping down the hill and that incredible voice keeping him awake. The same voice that led him back to consciousness.

Matt said, licking his lips, "Ma, do you think you could get me a drink of water?"

"Sure," she said, patting his hand, "I'll be right back."

She left the room as Marty began to talk about the baseball game he had been watching on television. She walked down the long hall past the nurse's station to the ice machine. The table next to it held several empty pitchers. She filled one with ice, then added water. A moment latter she walked back down the hall to Matt's room. When she walked into the room, Marty was still on the same subject he had been talking about when she had left. She shook her head as she poured water into a glass and held the straw toward Matt's lips.

He took several sips.

"Oh," Rebecca said, remembering. "Simone has been a real help."

Matt looked confused.

"Simone, the lady that was there at the scene of the accident."

Matt remembered his dream.

"She comes by every week to check on you," Rebecca added. "I'm sure she'll be here today or tomorrow."

"Every week?" Matt questioned. "She comes every week?"

"Yes," Rebecca said. "For the first two weeks she would come every day, then she started coming once a week. Usually the first half of the week. She'd sit with you for a few hours and sometimes she would read to you. She said that it was supposed to stimulate your thinking or something like that. I'm not quite sure. Sometimes when your father wasn't here the two of us would go down to the cafeteria and have dinner together. She's very smart."

"She probably wants something," Marty growled, returning to his seat.

"No she doesn't," Rebecca said, glaring at her husband.

"I bet she does," Marty grumbled and folded his arms across his chest. "You know how those people are."

Matt didn't have to wonder who those people were. Knowing his father, she could be African American, Spanish or Asian. To Martin Turner, anyone who wasn't Caucasian was one of "those" people, and he usually had a problem with them. Rebecca looked at her husband in disgust.

"Matt, she's a really nice person. She's very sweet and she was really concerned about you. Don't listen to your father."

"Bullshit," Marty yelled, unfolding his arms and quickly picking up the television remote. "They always want something, those people."

• • •

"Simone Porter," Simone announced when she answered the phone.

"Well, hello, stranger," the familiar voice on the other end of the phone line said.

"Hey, Alan, how have you been?"

"I've been well. How about yourself?"

"I'm good," Simone said. "So what's going on?"

"Not a whole lot. I just wanted to see if you were free for dinner?" he asked.

"Alan, I'm sorry, but this evening isn't good."

"Are you working late?" he asked, surprised.

"Oh no, it's nothing like that. I'm going to the hospital to visit with the Turner's."

Alan was quiet for a moment.

"You know, I told you about an accident I witnessed some months back?"

He still didn't respond.

"I told you that there was a terrible accident on 214. I called for help and waited until they arrived."

There was a long pause before he said, "Yes."

"Well, the victim of the accident is in a coma. I go to the hospital once a week and sit with him and his family. You know, offer moral support."

Alan was thoughtful for a moment and then asked, "So you just go to the hospital and sit with this total stranger for a few hours a week?"

"Sometimes his mother is there, and I keep her company."

"How long have you been doing this?"

"Since January."

"That's very commendable of you. I hope she appreciates what you're doing for her child."

"It's not like that, Alan. They're good people."

"I should hope so. I don't know anyone who would do as much," he said.

Simone heard him sigh heavily.

"Well, my schedule is booked for the remainder of the week. What about getting together next week for lunch."

"I don't know," Simone said. "Sometimes I work through lunch to catch up on paperwork, and next Tuesday we're taking Travis out to lunch for his birthday."

"Hey, maybe I can join you?"

"No, I don't think you would like ... "

"I think it's a perfect opportunity. I want to meet some of the people that you work with and this will fit my schedule perfectly."

"Are you sure about this? I don't think that ... "

"I think it's perfect. We can discuss the meeting place and time this Sunday."

"Sunday?"

"Yes, your mother invited me to dinner."

Simone closed her eyes and massaged her brow. There was a silence between them.

"Simone, are you still there?"

"Yes."

"Is everything all right? My coming to dinner isn't going to be a problem, is it?" he prompted, his voice holding a slight edge.

"Oh no, it's no problem. It's just that mother didn't mention it to me," Simone answered. "I'm sure it slipped her mind. Alan, I have an appointment in 10 minutes. I'll let you go now."

"You have a good week. I'll see you Sunday," Alan said, beaming into the phone.

"See you Sunday," Simone said before hanging up.

She leaned forward, resting her face in her hands. Her mother was driving her crazy with her attempts to push her and Alan together. Things were progressing at a slow pace and it seemed to be working for both of them. She pondered the thought of not going to her parents for Sunday dinner. Then she pictured her mother having a conniption, and calling her every 10 minutes until Simone finally gave in. She would get dressed, and get to her parents' house an hour late only to have her mother tell her how she'd slaved over a hot stove to make them an outstanding dinner. Not tasty or delicious, but outstanding. All she ever asked for from her family in return was that they have the courtesy of being on time. Simone sighed heavily.

"Miss Porter?"

Simone jumped, not realizing that someone had entered her office. She looked at the young girl standing in the doorway.

"Yes, Mira?"

"Do you have a minute?"

Simone smiled at the young Hispanic girl, waving her into the office. "Sure, come on in."

The girl walked in and sat in the chair on the opposite side of the desk. Simone watched the girl fidget in her seat and pick imaginary lint from her pants.

"Is everything okay?" Simone asked.

"I need to talk to you about something personal," the girl whispered.

Simone stood and walked to the door, closing it gently. She went back to her desk and sat on the edge and waited, giving the girl time to gather her thoughts.

"Miss Porter, I think I'm pregnant," she said as tears welled in her eyes.

Simone reached for a box of tissues and pulled a chair from the corner to sit next to the girl.

"It'll be okay, sweetie. We'll figure this out." Simone let the girl cry. When she had dried her eyes, Simone asked, "What makes you think you're pregnant?"

"I missed my period."

"How late are you?"

"One month."

"Have you been to see a doctor?"

She shook her head.

"Well, there are other reasons for a woman to miss her period. Like stress and exhaustion, to name a few."

"But my breasts hurt," she said holding back a sob. "And I get sick all the time. Ramona says that's a sure sign. She said that's what happened to her sister."

"Well, the first thing we need to do is get you to a doctor. Have you talked to your parents?"

"No, I can't," she cried.

Simone reached for the girl's hand and held it.

"I really think you should. If it will make it any easier for you, I'll come with you?"

"Oh no, Miss Porter," she said, almost in tears again. "I can't tell Mami and Papà. They will never forgive me."

"But, Mira ... "

"Please, Miss Porter," she cried.

Simone sighed, nodding. She reached across her desk to pull the phone toward her. After looking in her rolodex, she dialed a number. "Hello, may I speak to Stephanie Reed, please?" she asked, after waiting a few moments.

"Hi, Stephanie, this is Simone Porter, from the youth center. How are you? Yes, I'm fine, thanks.

"Stephanie, I was wondering if you could do me a favor. I have a young lady who thinks she might be pregnant. She needs to come in and see you." Simone paused listening to the woman on the other end. "She's here with me now ... let me find out?"

She looked at the girl sitting next to her. "Do you have time to go there now?" The girl nodded.

"Yes, we'll be right over," Simone said into the phone. "Thanks Stephanie, I really appreciate you seeing her on such short notice. I owe you one. Um, hmm. Okay, I'll see you soon."

Hanging up the phone, she turned to Mira. "Let me grab my things," Simone said as she stood up.

"You don't have to go with me. I can walk."

"It's more than 15 blocks."

The girl hunched her shoulders, looking down.

"No," Simone said, "I'm taking you."

• • •

Alan pressed the button on the telephone while holding the receiver in his right hand. Resting his chin on the receiver he debated if he wanted to spend the evening out or just stay in. Running his tongue over his bottom lip, he punched in the familiar sequence of numbers.

"Hello, how are you? Do you have plans for tonight?"

• • •

Pulling into the parking garage of Anne Arundel General Hospital, Simone had to drive up to the fourth level before she found a parking spot. She turned off her car, put the parking-lot ticket in

the sun visor, and then rested her forehead on the steering wheel, allowing the events of the day to catch up with her.

She had learned that over the next three months funding could be cut at the center. She found out that one of the kids from the center was arrested for armed robbery. And then there was the situation with Mira.

On the way to the clinic, Mira had told Simone that she and her boyfriend, Juan, were planning to get married as soon as she turned 18.

At least it had turned out that she was not pregnant. If she had been pregnant, Simone did not know if she wanted to keep something so significant from the Mira's parents. Simone was more concerned with Mira's state of mind and the fact that she had seemed more distraught when she learned that the pregnancy test had come back negative.

She got the feeling that the girl was hoping that she was pregnant so her parents would allow her to marry early.

Sitting back, she took a deep breath. Maybe she could make arrangements to take Mira out in the following weeks and see what was going on in her head. She sighed, leaned forward and checked her image in the mirror before she stepped out of the car and headed to the third floor for her weekly visit.

• • •

Using every ounce of strength, Matt surfed the television channels until he found one showing something of interest. He let the remote drop on the bed with a soft thud. Closing his eyes, he took a deep breath, trying to regain the strength he had used doing such a small task.

On the overbed table sat his dinner tray of turkey with mashed potatoes and gravy. The aroma drifted toward him, taunting and daring him to eat it. He opened his eyes and stared at the tray in front of him as if he were trying to use telekinesis to move the food from the plate to his mouth.

Simone stopped in the doorway when she saw that Matt was awake. She watched him as he dropped the television remote on the

bed in frustration and rested his head on the pillow propped behind him. She took a step back, not knowing if she should enter the room. She didn't want to intrude or make him feel uncomfortable. She turned away, watching the staff rush to and fro as she pondered what she should do. She looked back in the room and watched him. His ruggedly handsome face was thin. His dark eyebrows slanted in a frown and the muscle along his jaw was tight, betraying his frustration. He stared hungrily at the tray of food in front of him.

Simone nervously moistened her lips. She nodded slightly to give herself encouragement and walked into the room.

"Hello."

Matt glanced in the direction of the greeting.

"Am I disturbing you?" Simone asked. He smiled, instantly recognizing her voice.

"No, not at all. Come in," he said.

He watched her as she walked farther into the room. Studying her closely, he tried to memorize everything about her. She laid her bright yellow spring jacket on the chair next to the bed.

He opened his mouth to speak, his brow creasing, trying to remember her name.

"Hi, I'm Simone Porter," she said.

"Yes, Simone," he repeated her name, letting his tongue play with each syllable.

Simone was momentarily mesmerized. She looked into the darkest dark brown eyes with the longest lashes she had ever seen. *Man, it should be against the law to have eyes like that.*

She realized she was staring, then quickly asked, "How are you feeling?"

"Not too bad, considering," he said, glancing at the tray.

"Looks like you haven't eaten very much," she said, gesturing toward what held his attention and not wanting to look at him for fear she might stare again.

"I'm having a small problem moving my arms."

When he spoke again she heard magic in a voice so deep and sensual it sent a ripple through her. She suppressed the urge to close her eyes.

"Could you use a hand?" she offered, still watching the tray.

"Oh, yes, please," he said, close to begging.

She smiled at his eagerness, finally looking at him. Then, stepping close to the bed, she picked up the fork and knife to cut the turkey.

He glanced up at her honey-kissed complexion and smiled as he examined her features. Her gray eyes had explosions of green flecks and were ringed by long, dark brown lashes. Her auburn hair looked as soft as silk and had natural waves. She wore it in a thick plait that hung loosely down her back. The faint smell of her perfume drifted toward him, and he closed his eyes, trying to store the exotic smell of jasmine combined with something he couldn't quite identify in his memory.

"Ready?" she asked.

His chocolate eyes popped open, meeting hers.

She smiled at him, her full lips rounded over perfect teeth.

His pulse quickened and he had to force himself to breathe evenly, hoping she didn't notice. Slowly he opened his mouth, allowing her to slide the fork across his lips, his dark eyes never leaving hers.

"How is it?" she asked, her eyes focused on his sensual lips.

"Wonderful," he whispered. "Thank you," he said, still watching her.

"No problem," she said, scooping up a forkful of mashed potatoes.

"No," he said, shaking his head slightly "I mean for helping me during the accident."

"No," Simone said, "You don't have to ..."

"Yes, I do," Matt spoke, cutting off her words. "If it weren't for you, I might not be here. And my mother told me how you'd stop by to check on me."

She nodded nervously.

"That means a lot to me. I just wanted to say thank you."

She smiled weakly, nodding again, then, biting her lip, she looked away.

• • •

"Hi, Simone!"

Simone looked up and smiled at the couple coming through the door.

"Hello, Mrs. Turner, Mr. Turner."

"I told Matt that you would probably be here today," Rebecca said. She seemed happy to see Simone.

Marty, however, glared angrily at his wife, then at Simone.

"One of the nurses should be doing that for him," he said, jerking his head toward the bed. "That's what they get paid for." Marty looked at Rebecca. "Becca go over there and do that."

Rebecca glared at him. "Marty," she said in a tight voice.

"No," Simone said quickly. Then, more slowly she said, "I can do it, I don't mind."

Marty glared at her angrily and fumed as he sat down in the chair by the television.

After helping Matt with his dinner, Simone left, saying that she would come back in a couple days to see how he was doing.

On the drive home she thought back to that cold January evening when she had first met the Turner's. The forlorn look on Rebecca's face had made her want to help and be there for her in any way she could. The next day, when Simone had gone to the hospital, Rebecca had seemed lonely and afraid even though her husband was right next to her. Simone felt Rebecca's "woman pain" of feeling lonely and alone even when the person you needed most was close by. That's how she sometimes felt with her mother, and she thought that Rebecca struggled to deal with the feeling of being alone on top of the possibility of losing her son. Simone had had no choice — she had continued to go to the hospital to offer comfort and support as often as she could.

Now that Matt Turner was awake there was no longer any

need to go to the hospital. She would stop her weekly visits and that would be that!

Now all she needed to do was forget the way she had felt when Matt had looked at her. How her heart had skipped a beat, then started racing when she looked around and found him watching her. If only she could think about anything other than Mathew Turner's gorgeous brown eyes and sexy voice.

Chapter 4

"It's been weeks since he woke from that coma. He should be up and about by now, shouldn't he?" Marty grumbled, looking at his son, his total disappointment shading his dark eyes.

"Mr. Turner, it takes time," the physical therapist informed Marty. "He has to build up the muscles that deteriorated. Four months is a long time to be immobile."

"Well, if it was me, I would have recuperated by now, and be well on my way back to work," Marty snapped.

"Marty, hush," Rebecca whispered, embarrassed for her son.

Matt made his way back to the bed as his father told the therapist how he had dislocated his shoulder as a teen and how he had a friend help him put it back.

"That was a very dangerous thing to do," the therapist said. "You were extremely lucky."

"I wasn't lucky," Marty boasted, poking his thumb in his chest. "I was tough." He grunted and cut his eyes in Matt's direction. "Ya hear that boy? I was tough. I didn't go running to the doctor for every little bump or scratch I got, and I damn sight didn't need some woman that was half my size to help me get around," he said, referring to the physical therapist. "I just sucked it up and went on with my business. Back in my day, we were real men," he announced proudly as he watched Matt's jaw clench. "Matt? Matt? Are you listening to me boy?"

"No," Matt barked, becoming more and more frustrated with each word his father said.

"Why the hell not?"

"Why do you think?" Matt said, giving his father an icy glare. "Because, you're getting on my damn nerves."

Marty and Rebecca, both stared at their son, surprised at his outburst.

Martin Turner was sometimes harsh. He thought he needed to be that way. He believed that if he didn't make his family strong,

~ 37 ~

they would never survive in the world. Rebecca thought he some-times pushed a little too hard. Their oldest son Martin Jr. would push back just as hard as his father would push him, and their daughter, Sarah, decided the best course of action was to move away. But Matt would never say a word. He would just take with a grain of salt whatever his father dished out.

It took Marty a minute to get over his sudden shock. He chuckled. "You're just upset because you know it's true."

"I don't want to hear it," Matt declared. "Either shut the hell up — or leave," he said, meeting his father's gaze. The two men locked eyes momentarily.

"Humph," Marty grunted, raising his head high. He walked to the table next to the bed, snatched the remote control and sat in his usual spot in front of the television.

"Good thing my show is coming on," he said, turning on the TV.

• • •

Simone closed the folders she had spread out on her desk, stacking them on the left side. Her fingers brushed the Chinese paper yo-yo that Alan had given her when he went with her work group to lunch. She picked it up, rolling it between her thumb and index finger as she thought back to that afternoon.

The look on Alan's face could only be described as sheer horror when he had walked around the corner and spotted Simone and her co-worker, Robin, waiting for him with six teenagers. He wasn't rude, but he barely said 10 words to Robin or the kids.

Later that evening Alan had called Simone and apologized for his behavior. He said that he assumed the people she was having lunch with were all adults, and he didn't have much experience with teenagers. He added that since he didn't associate much with teens that he didn't say a lot to them because he didn't want them to feel uncomfortable, as if he were analyzing them.

Simone wanted to ask him about the way he had avoided Robin, but he wouldn't let her speak as he repeatedly asked for her forgiveness. When she finally told him that she understood his

behavior, he quickly changed the subject, and it was never brought up again.

That had been close to two months ago. Surprisingly, since then, she and Alan had been spending more time together; they usually went out to dinner once or twice a week.

"I guess that's long enough to hold onto this thing," she said, dropping the restaurant souvenir into the wastebasket. Picking up her purse and a box that she had sitting next to the door, she turned off the lights, locked up the building and headed to her car.

"Do you need help with that, Miss Porter?" A young Latino male asked as Simone carried a box from her office. She looked to her left to see Juan Rodriguez.

"Yes, Juan, I would really appreciate that."

As they crossed the parking lot Simone asked him how his family was and how his job was going. Juan put the box on the back seat of Simone's pepper-white Mini Cooper.

"Thank you," She said, closing the door.

"No problem." He turned to walk away.

"Juan, do you mind if we talk for a moment."

"Sure."

"I wanted to talk to you about Mira."

Juan shoved his hands into his pockets and looked around anxiously.

"I'm not going to give you a hard time. I just want to talk."

He nodded, and Simone leaned back on the car.

"How are things going with you and Mira?"

He hesitated, "Uh, Mira and I broke up."

"I'm sorry to hear that."

"That's okay." Juan shifted his weight from one foot to the other. "She told me that you took her to the clinic to get that test. Thanks."

Simone nodded.

"Juan, I'm sure things will work out for the two of you. Mira believing that she was pregnant, then finding that she wasn't had to cause a huge strain on you two. Give it time."

Juan's head wagged vigorously as he spoke.

"Mira and I broke up a few weeks before she told me she thought she was pregnant."

Simone was surprised, believing that Mira and Juan were planning to be married.

"When she told me that she was having a baby, and I told her that I would take care of it, but that I still didn't want to be with her. She completely freaked. She started hitting me and stuff. I just got away from her. I can't be getting in any trouble like that, Miss Porter. Now she's really tripping. She shows up at my job and keeps coming to my house."

"It sounds to me as though she hasn't accepted the fact that you two are no longer together. Sometimes when you're in love, some of the things you do don't always make a lot of sense."

"I can't get through to her."

"Maybe I can talk to her."

"Do you think you could?"

"I'll try."

"Thanks, Miss Porter."

• • •

Matt checked the time on the large wall clock above the television again. Five minutes had passed since the last time he had checked. It was Tuesday, and Matt was anxiously awaiting Simone's arrival for her weekly visit. Since the day Matt woke from the coma, she had come every Tuesday evening around 6. That was the bright spot of his week. When she left, he could not stop thinking of her. She intrigued him in a way that no other woman had. Not even Wendy.

"Hey guy," Matt's best friend Josh Peterson said with his usual loud and zealous flair.

"Hey man," Matt smiled at his friend. "How's it going?"

"Good, good," Josh said, pulling up a chair. He proceeded to tell Matt some of the events that had taken place in the last few months. Ten minutes into the visit, Josh asked Matt, "Why are you in such a bad mood today? Are you in pain or something?"

"Na, I'm all right," Matt said as he absent-mindedly checked the time again.

Josh looked over his shoulder at the clock, then back at Matt. "Are you expecting someone?"

"No," Matt said, meeting Josh's gaze. "How are things on the home front?"

"We started the Hanson job a few weeks back and we had a little problem."

"Oh yeah?" Matt said, only half paying attention to Josh.

"Yeah, Mrs. Hanson was upset because Albert put the wrong colored tile in her bathroom," Josh said.

Matt sighed and asked, "How did you handle it?"

"I gave her an upgrade on her countertop, and it seemed to smooth things over."

"Good," Matt nodded and checked the time once more.

"What the hell is going on?" Josh said, laughing. "That makes the tenth time you checked that clock in the last half-hour. If I weren't so secure about myself, I would think that you didn't want me here."

"Man, shut up," Matt said.

"And you're grumpy as hell," Josh kidded.

"Kiss my grumpy ass," Matt shot back.

Josh burst out laughing.

"Man I've never seen you like this. You're nervous and jumpy. What's going on?"

A voice came from the doorway, "Hello."

Josh looked over his shoulder toward the greeting in time to see Simone entering the room.

"Hi," Matt said, smiling broadly. Josh stared at Simone as she approached the bed.

"Hello," Simone smiled at Josh. "I'm Simone, Simone Porter," she said, extending her hand.

A smile slowly spread across Josh's face, as realization hit him. He rose to accept her hand.

"Ooh, Simone," Josh said, glancing sideways at his best friend. "I'm very happy to meet you. Josh Peterson."

"Nice to meet you, Josh," Simone said, still smiling. He sat back in his chair, watching her. Simone looked at Matt.

"How are you feeling today?"

"I'm good — just visiting with Josh."

"Yeah, he's visiting with me, but he had someone else on his mind," Josh teased. Matt looked at his friend, wanting to tell him to wipe the goofy grin from his face.

"I brought you something," Simone said, drawing Matt's attention back to her.

Matt smiled, saying, "You didn't have to do that."

"I know. I'll be right back."

She walked out of the room, Josh's eyes following her every move. He turned to Matt quickly.

"Whoa, she's hot," he whispered. "Now I see what you were waiting for."

"Man, shut up," Matt said, as he watched the door.

Simone returned with a large cardboard box. She set it on one of the chairs in the corner of the room. "I remembered how much you like sports, so I was able to get a copy of Sports Illustrated and a few other sports magazines for the last five months. I borrowed several video tapes of some football games and a VCR. Now you can catch up on what's been happening in the sports world. My father likes sports and he would be lost if he missed a day."

Matt looked at the box of magazines, then at her. "Thanks, I really appreciate this."

"Oh, it's nothing," she said, waving her hand at the small gesture. "So Josh, have you guys been friends long?"

"My family moved here from Toronto when I was 15. The first day at my new high school I didn't know anyone, and Matt took me under his wing. Now I'm the foreman at Matt's construction company."

"You know what," Matt added quickly, "Josh was just about to leave before you arrived."

Josh looked at his friend mischievously and faked a surprised look.

"I was?" Matt eyed him, causing Josh to chuckle. "Oh yeah, I was."

"I don't want to intrude. I can come back later," Simone said, preparing to leave.

"No, really I'm just kidding," Josh said, "I really was leaving." He looked at Matt, wiggling his brows. "See you later buddy," he said, patting his shoulder.

"See ya," Matt said.

Josh's gaze met Simone's. "It was really nice to meet you Simone. I hope to see you again," Josh said.

"You too, Josh." Then Simone walked around the bed to sit in the seat that Josh had just vacated. "So how much longer do you have to be here?"

"Another week, then I'm sprung."

"That's wonderful," Simone said, feeling a little sad that she would not be visiting him any longer.

"When I get out of here, don't be a stranger," Matt said quickly. "We can exchange phone numbers and maybe hang out sometimes."

"Sure," Simone said, "that sounds good."

• • •

Simone pulled her car into Alan's driveway and turned off the engine. Gathering the food bag and her purse she got out and walked to the house. She shifted the bag in her arms, rang the doorbell and waited.

"Simone," Alan said, out of breath, "what are you doing here?"

"I thought I'd surprise you. I picked up some Chinese. I thought we could watch a movie."

He looked around anxiously and then looked at the bag she held. "You know you're not supposed to be eating that stuff."

"I know. I don't do it often. I just thought it would be fun."

"Simone, you know that I really don't like you stopping by unannounced," he said, stepping outside and closing the door behind.

"I wanted to surprise you. I thought it would be nice to just stay home and ... "

"Look, why don't we go out to dinner and then afterwards we can do something."

She frowned at him. "Alan that doesn't make any sense. I already have the food here. We can go inside and eat and then we can go out later if you like."

He shook his head, took the bag from her arms and led her back to her car.

"Alan, is something wrong?"

He stopped next to the car, looked at her intently and then he smiled. "No, nothing's wrong."

"It seems as though there is."

He leaned close, kissing her on her cheek. "I'm sorry. It's just that the house is a mess and you know it bothers me when things aren't in order. I just don't want you to see it like that."

She watched him for a moment, then nodded.

Opening the car door for her, he waited until she got inside. "Let me take this inside, grab my keys, and then we can leave." He turned and walked away. Stunned, Simone watched his retreating back as he headed for the house.

• • •

Simone had left the beautiful July day and the open space and festivities in the Porter family's back yard. Instead, she chose to hide in the stuffy, blistering kitchen to escape her mother's constant badgering. She sat at the table, sipping a glass of lemonade, biding her time until her mother found another pet peeve that disturbed her more then her daughter's life. Simone's attention was drawn to the squeaking of the screen door. Her brother Charles stepped into the kitchen, smiling when he saw the look of dread on her face.

"Hey, it's just me," he said to his younger sister.

"Hey," Simone replied dryly, then took another sip of her lemonade.

"Why are you in here?" he questioned.

She rolled her eyes toward the ceiling. "Do you have to ask?"

He chuckled. "Well, I'd say it should be safe to go back out in another ten or fifteen minutes. I just saw Warren parking his car and I'm guessing that's how long it will take before mother pounces on him."

Simone shook her head, feeling sorry for her cousin. He had gotten 60 days in jail for a DWI and lost his job because of it. "Poor Warren," Simone said. "Mother's going to have a field day with him."

"Better him than us."

"Yeah, right. She never treats you the way she treats every-one else," Simone said, frowning at him.

"She's always prying and asking unnecessary questions. And she's forever minding my business," Charles said, leaning on the counter.

"Humph," Simone grunted, watching her glass as she swirled the ice cubes around. Then she whispered, "I should be so lucky."

Charles glanced at Simone. He did not want to get into a debate about which of them their mother aggravated more. Rubbing his hand across his chin, he asked, "Have you talked to Tamara?"

"Not since last Sunday."

"I mean, did she call you asking about me?"

"No," Simone said, not looking at him.

"I mean, has she ever asked you about that night?"

"Charles, that was months ago."

"Yeah. I was just checking," he said, letting out a sigh of relief.

Simone sucked her teeth, setting down her glass.

"Everything is working out okay," he said, more to himself than to her.

Simone glared at him angrily. "Can you tell me what you were doing that was so important that you wanted me to lie to your wife?"

He looked at her, trying to decide if he wanted to tell her the truth or not. He sighed.

"Simone, I'm in trouble. I've made a terrible mistake and I'm afraid I'm going to lose everything because of it."

"Whatever it is, it can't possibly be that bad."

"Yes, it can," he said too quickly.

"What is it? I'm sure you're just exaggerating," she added with a wave of her hand.

"Simone, I've been having an affair," he blurted out.

Simone stared at him, her mouth wide open.

He shook his head as he continued, "And the woman I've been seeing told me that she's pregnant."

Simone looked at him as if he were speaking a foreign language.

"Simone, I don't know what I'm going to do."

"I don't think that's a very funny joke," she said seriously, her eyes still on him.

"This is no joke," he said, sliding his hands in his pockets. "I wish it were."

"Oh, my God, Charles," she said, looking at her brother in disbelief. "I can't believe you."

He closed his eyes as he spoke. "She called me that evening and asked me to meet her. She told me then."

"Oh, my gosh!" Simone said, shaking her head. "I can't believe you would do something so stupid."

"I am not stupid!" he yelled defensively, looking at her.

"What do you call this? You have a wife!" Simone shouted.

"It was a mistake," he responded.

"Breaking a glass is a mistake. Stubbing your toe is a mistake. Getting someone other than your wife pregnant is not a mistake." Simone said, still shaking her head in disbelief. "Geez, I can't believe we come from the same gene pool."

"You act like you don't make mistakes," he said sarcastically.

"I do, and quite often, but I try not to make ones that could ruin other people's lives."

"Come on, Simone, give me a break." He looked anxiously

at the door and lowered his voice. He hoped that no one would hear them and come inside to investigate.

Simone took a deep breath.

He looked at her, speaking quietly. "I need your help."

"What now?" Simone groaned, glaring at him.

"Come on, don't be like that," he said evenly. Simone took a calming breath and shook her head again.

"Charles, I'm not going to do this. I'm not going to help you hurt Tamara."

"I don't want you to help me hurt Tamara. I want you to help me save my marriage."

"And how am I supposed to do that?" she asked, not believing anything about this whole conversation.

"I was hoping you could convince this woman to get an abortion. The last time I spoke to her she was close to the end of her third month, and ... "

"Oh no, I don't think so." Simone held up her hand, shaking her head vigorously.

"Why not?" Charles asked, unable to believe that his sister wouldn't do this for him.

"Because it's wrong. That's why not."

"But I'm certain she'd listen to you," he said, trying to reason with her.

"And why would some total stranger listen?" She paused, and then asked, "Who is she?"

"No, that's all I'm telling you unless you agree to help me."

"You know what, Charles? At this moment, I'm ashamed to call you my brother." She looked at him as if it were the first time she had ever laid eyes on him.

"To hell with you, Simone," he said, storming out the screen door, letting it slam behind him.

Simone sat at the table and stared at the screen door. Then, sighing deeply, she put her face in her hands.

She didn't know what had happened to Charles. When he first met Tamara, he adored her. A few months ago, he told Simone that Tamara wanted a child and that he didn't know if he was ready

to share his wife with anyone yet, not even a baby. It was in November that he confessed his undying love for Tamara. She couldn't fathom the idea of Charles cheating. But not only had he admitted cheating on Tamara, his mistress was now pregnant.

She picked up her glass and looked at the ice floating in the lemonade. The ringing of her cell phone brought her mind back to the hot kitchen. Simone unclipped her cell phone from her belt to answer it.

"Hello."

"Simone?"

"Yes."

"This is Matt — Matt Turner."

She sat up straight and ran her hand through her hair as if he could see her. "Hi, how are you?"

"I'm fine. I hope it's all right — calling your cell? I only had your home number. When I called that I got your machine, so I got your cell number from my mother. I hope that's okay?" He cringed, then mentally cursed himself for babbling.

"That's perfectly all right."

"Um, I was wondering if you would like dinner. I mean, I wanted to fix dinner for you. I mean ... ," he paused feeling anxious. "Uh, I mean, I don't want to disturb you or anything, and I'm sure you're probably busy ... "

"Sure," she said, laughing, "I'd love to." She reached for a piece of paper and a pen her mother kept on the counter for jotting down notes. "Give me your address."

After scratching down the address and directions, she walked out the back door and across the yard to where her parents were standing. Joe was turning chicken and burgers on the grill. Debra was instructing him on which way to turn the burgers so that the charred marks on them were going in the same direction on both sides.

Simone stopped, seeing the look of anguish on her father's face. She offered him a sympathetic smile. "Hey guys, I'm leaving now."

"No, you are not," Debra said. "The food is almost ready and I made my coleslaw."

"Sorry, Mother, I have plans for dinner."

"Ah, why don't you have Alan meet you here instead of going to some restaurant? That way he and your brother can ... "

"Mother, I'm not going out with Alan," Simone said, before kissing her father and walking toward the gate.

"If you're not going out with Alan, just who are you having dinner with?" Debra demanded, getting to her feet and following Simone across the yard.

"Just a friend."

"Simone!" Debra called as Simone quickened her steps. "Simone, I know you hear me!" Simone got into her car and started it.

"I'm running late. Gotta go, Mother. Love you," she waved, pulling out of the driveway before her Mother could make it around the car.

Chapter 5

Matt hung up the phone and looked around the kitchen. He opened the refrigerator, looking for something to cook for dinner. He took out a steak, examined it, shook his head and placed it back in the refrigerator, deciding on chicken breast instead.

Looking down at his clothes, he surveyed the blue t-shirt and tattered gray sweatpants that he liked to wear bumming around the house. Rushing upstairs, he showered and changed into a light green polo shirt, his favorite bluejeans and comfortable dark blue deck shoes.

He hurried back to the kitchen and busied himself marinating the chicken as his mind drifted to all the things he had to do to catch up on the last five months. After the accident, Josh had taken care of the business, and everything was running smoothly. His mother had made sure all of his finances were in order. It was mostly the personal things that needed his attention. He sighed.

He needed to go to his old condominium and move the rest of his things out. There was nothing keeping him there now. The house was done and he was settled. He kept telling everyone that he wanted to keep the condo until his house was finished, but that was not the real reason. The truth was he did not want to let go of the past. A part of him thought that as long as he held on to the home that he and Wendy had shared he could also hold on to the hope that they could find their way back to each other.

Then there was that part of him that had moved on, that had let go of the past and was looking forward to the future. A future where he didn't feel that his best wasn't good enough — where there was happiness and laughter — and Simone. She made him feel things that he hadn't felt before. His heart skipped a beat, then soared through the universe just being around her.

The buzzing of the doorbell jarred Matt from his thoughts.

His pulse raced as he put the bowl with the chicken in the refrigerator and walked briskly to the front door. Wiping his hands on the dishtowel he had thrown over his shoulder, he opened the door. He froze as he stared at the woman standing on his stoop.

• • •

Jamison Cartwright made a left turn off of the main road, careful to stay far away from Wendy's vehicle, so she wouldn't notice him in her rearview mirror. He still couldn't believe that he had stooped to such measures. In the last few months, he'd gone from hiring someone to follow her to checking her cell phone calls to searching through her purse and, finally, following her himself.

The rational part of his mind told him that he was being paranoid, because Wendy truly loved him and she would never leave him. But there was the irrational part, that little voice that whispered to him, that she had cheated on her ex-husband and she would do it to him.

Jamison pulled his car to the side of the private road and watched Wendy as she parked her car in front of a house. He saw her sit for a few minutes looking at the house. Jamison leaned forward trying to figure out what she was doing. A short while later, she got out of the car and slowly walked to the house. When she reached the door, she paused for a moment and then rang the bell.

Jamison's stomach lurched as Matt Turner answered the door and stepped aside to allow Wendy entrance into the house. Even with the air conditioner on high in the car, Jamison became hot. His eyes burned from the sweat trickling from his brow. With both hands he swiped at his face and brushed his hair back. Then he reached behind his seat and grabbed a rag that he used to wipe his windshield. He used it to dry his hands and mop his brow.

He put the car in reverse and quickly backed down the road in the direction that he had come. When he reached the end of the road, he backed across the intersection in front of a dark blue Honda with a man and woman in it. The Honda driver blew the horn, and Jamison turned to glare at him with a look of utter hate and contempt. The Honda's driver quickly pulled around Jamison's car and

drove away. Jamison shifted the car into drive and sped away. He needed to put as much distance as possible between himself and Wendy and Matt. He bit his lip angrily until he tasted blood. Using his right hand he wiped his mouth and looked at the blood. After wiping the blood on his pant leg, he took a deep breath.

He didn't know why he loved Wendy. It wasn't like she was on his level, but he still idolized her. She was the closest thing to perfection that any woman could be in his eyes. Her naturally blond hair and milky skin made her flawless. She was sexy, sensuous and greedy — just like him. Hell, he sometimes felt like he was dating himself.

The difference between them was that she had a weakness. She gave in to her feminine emotions too easily, which is why she was drawn to Matt. Matt Turner was pathetic, and Wendy felt the need to protect him. All women felt the need to protect the weak and pathetic. Or at least that's what he wanted to believe.

Look at his mother. She was weak. Always out to help this charity or that organization. His father gave her the world and she could have spent her days doing any number of things, but she wasted her time on uncountable worthless causes. Always worrying about some supposed family in need. His father had once told him that the reason some people were needy was because they were lazy.

His mother spent so much time with those people that she became attracted to one particular man. Jamison still didn't know what his name was or what he did for a living — nor did he care. All he knew was that his mother thought another man's compassion and love was far greater than anything her husband and child could give her.

One sunny spring day, Jamison came home from school and his mother told him that they were leaving. Leaving the only home he'd ever known and leaving his father. She had told him that she had it all worked out. She instructed the housekeeper to pack a small bag for him and that he just needed to gather whatever personal items he needed until they were able to pick up the rest of his things. She said that she had purchased a small house and that it was differ-ent from what he was used to but that he would adjust easily.

The 14-year-old Jamison couldn't believe his mother could be so stupid and he told her so. He would not go.

It hurt him that she would leave his father, leave their home. But it hurt him more when she left him.

A year later his father killed himself, but not before making sure that his only child was to be well provided for. After his father's death Jamison, devastated, and was sent to live with his fraternal grandparents.

Tears blinded him as he drove and Jamison turned into the first parking lot he found. He swiped at his eyes, rubbing away tears of bitterness and anger, along with the image of his mother's face as she appeared at his grandparents' home shortly after his father's death.

His mother informed his grandparents that she had come to collect him, and he had told her that she was no longer his mother. He told her that his mother had died the day that she had left him and his father. But that before she died, she had set the process in motion of killing his father slowly. Twenty years later, Jamison had not seen his mother since that day.

To Jamison there were only three classes of people: the haves, the have not's, and him. Anyone who fell in the other two categories was beneath him. Except Wendy. Wendy was different. When he first saw her, he knew he had to have her. Wendy was everything to him. And like his father with his mother, Wendy would probably be the death of him.

• • •

"Hey," Matt said, staring at the woman standing on his porch.

"Aren't you going to invite me in?"

"Yeah, sure." Matt stepped to the side allowing her access to his home.

Wendy smiled up at her ex-husband. Her buttercup yellow hair was parted down the middle, framing her oval face. It hung loosely around her slender shoulders.

It had been months since he'd seen Wendy. The last time

was at the courthouse during their divorce proceedings. Now, looking at her standing in the doorway, Matt had to admit that she was a beautiful woman.

"You look good," she said for a lack of anything better to say.

"Thanks, so do you."

They watched each other awkwardly, her waiting for him to say something and him not knowing what to say.

"I came to the hospital to see you."

"I know. My father told me."

"I would have come more often, but I could tell that your mother didn't want me there."

He couldn't believe his ears. This was the first time he had seen her since the divorce or the accident and her topic of conversation was one that was sure to lead to an argument.

"Wendy, I'm sure that's not the case," he said as he turned and walked into the kitchen.

Wendy followed closely behind him.

"Yes, it is, I can tell. You know how she looks at people with that judgmental stare. My God, that woman!"

Matt went to the refrigerator, took out the ingredients for a salad and carried them to the counter, slamming the items down.

"Well, what do you expect? I would think that most mothers wouldn't take too kindly to their daughter-in-law having an affair and leaving their son for another man."

"Come on, Matt, give me a break."

"No," he yelled, "you give me a damn break."

She blinked, seeing the piercing anger in his eyes. He had never raised his voice to her.

"What do you want, Wendy?" he demanded, his voice rising even higher.

"I came by to see how you were doing," her tone softened, "and to see if you needed anything."

"I'm fine, thanks," he said sarcastically.

He went to the sink and opened one of the overhead cabinets

to remove a large bowl. He rinsed the bowl and washed his hands before walking back to the counter.

"And I don't need anything. Make sure you close the door on your way out."

She watched him closely.

"What's wrong with you, Matt? You've changed. You used to be more forgiving of me," she said, wanting him to hear the pain in her voice.

"No, I was your doormat. Is there a reason for this visit?" He stared at her blankly, the dark soulful eyes she once gazed into were now cold and unresponsive.

"No, not really. I just wanted to see you." She looked away, scanning the modern kitchen. "I like what you've done to the place."

"Wendy I'm expecting someone for dinner. They should be arriving any moment."

"Is it anyone I know?" she asked, leaning casually on the counter searching his face again.

"No, it isn't. It was nice seeing you. Like I said, close the door on your way out."

"Matt?" she said, watching as he turned his back to her and continued preparing the salad.

She let out a slow breath, searching her mind for something, anything that would make him let her in. She debated if she wanted to tell him how she felt. That she thought that her leaving him was the worst mistake she had ever made and that she wished with all her heart that she could go back to change things. After a few minutes of silence, she turned and left the kitchen.

Matt listened for the sound of the front door closing. Walking to the refrigerator, he put the bowl of salad inside and took out a bag with several ears of corn on the cob. Then he walked to the table and pulled out a chair. He sat down and began shucking two of the ears.

He looked at the spot where the woman he had loved with all his heart had stood moments ago and wondered what happened to the feelings that he'd had for her. His feelings for her had changed

or at least he thought they had. There was a time when he would melt at the mere sight of her, and the nearness of her would make his heart flutter.

His mind drifted back to the condo he had shared with Wendy. Back to the day that he had come home and learned his world had changed. That day Matt had walked down the hall toward the bedroom. He had paused to watch Wendy move around the room and to admire the way her blond hair swayed gently as she moved. As he had gone farther into the room, he noticed the two suitcases lying on the bed.

"Hey," he had said as he entered the room. "What's all this?"

"Matt — we need to talk."

Walking to her side Matt had leaned in for a kiss, but she quickly turned away, walking to the other side of the room.

He frowned. "Wendy, what's wrong? Did I do something?"

"Matt, I'm moving in with Gail," she blurted out.

"What?"

"It's for the best."

"I don't understand." He shook his head.

As she spoke, she turned away from him, not wanting to look at him. "Matt I need time — time to figure out what I want."

"What do you mean? What do you need to figure out?" Matt asked, confused.

"It's complicated."

"Wendy, please talk to me. Tell me what's going on," he spread his hands as he spoke. "Whatever it is — I know we can work it out. Just talk to me."

"I'm in love with someone else," she blurted out the words.

Matt watched her, momentarily stunned. Taking a slow breath, he asked calmly, "Is it the guy you had the affair with?"

"Matt, don't."

"Tell me," he whispered.

She looked around the room, not wanting to meet his pained gaze.

"It's a lot of things. You can't give me what I want, and he

can. And — I realize that I'm in love with him, too, and I need time to figure out what I'm going to do."

Matt sat heavily on the bed and watched her for any sign that this was some sick, twisted joke that she would soon end.

"Figure what out? I am your husband! There is nothing to figure out. We've built a life together."

She suppressed a moan as her lip trembled slightly.

"That's just it Matt. I don't know if I want that anymore. I don't know if I want us anymore. I just need some time. Please understand."

"Wendy, it shouldn't be about what he can give you," he pleaded. "How can you just throw away all that we have? How can you just leave me?"

"Matt, you don't understand. I have to do this. It's not fair to anyone for me to stay with you when I'm in love with another man." She reached around him closing the smaller of the two suitcases.

"I'm sorry Matt. You'll never know how sorry I am." She looked at the other suitcase sitting on the bed. "I'll come for the rest of my things while you're at work."

She walked out of the room and out of his life, leaving Matt sitting on the bed, with a look of despair on his face.

Matt was so wrapped up in his thoughts that the ringing of the doorbell startled him.

"Thanks for the invitation," Simone said, stepping into the foyer and looking around the living room.

The walls were cream, as was the carpet. There was a brown leather sofa and loveseat. All the accessories in the room were brown, tan, leather, or wood. Everything about the room said that a man lived there.

Matt's eyes quickly scanned Simone from head to toe. She wore a vibrant floral-patterned tank top with a white short-sleeved button-down top over it, white capris, white sandals, and her hair in its usual plait hanging down her back. The bright colors made her honey skin more bronze.

"Thanks for coming," he said, closing the door behind her.

"If you like we can go into the kitchen? That's where I spend most of my time when I'm at home."

"Sure, that's fine," she said, following him through a high, arched doorway into the spacious modern kitchen. The cherry wood cabinets matched the hardwood floor. The Corian countertops and chrome appliances added a touch of sophistication to the room. It surprised Simone how different the style of the kitchen and living room were.

"Have a seat," he gestured toward the round, modern table and chairs. "Can I get you something to drink?"

"No, thanks," she said, pulling the chair from the small table and sitting down.

Matt stood next to the sink, leaning against the counter. He tried to think of something to say, anything, but his mind went blank.

Simone cleared her throat. "Looks like you made a full recovery."

"Oh, yeah," he said, fidgeting. "Almost as good as new. I didn't take you away from anything important, did I?"

"No, in a way you rescued me," Simone said.

"Is everything all right?" he asked.

"Sure," she said waving her hand. "It's a long story"

"Well, we have a while before dinner will be ready, would you like to take a walk out to the lake?" Matt asked.

"Sure, that sounds good."

Matt led Simone through the house, across the parking pad and private road to the lake.

"This is beautiful," she said as they stopped on the edge of the water. "Is it a natural lake?"

Matt shook his head, "Man made. It's been here for about twenty years or so."

"How long have you lived here?" Simone leaned forward to get a better look at the floating white and yellow water lilies.

"I bought the house two years ago. It needed a lot of work, and I wanted to take my time doing everything. I just moved in when I got out of the hospital."

"Where did you live before?"

"Just outside Bowie. I still have a condo there. I haven't had time to move everything out yet."

Simone studied his profile as he talked. It had been almost a month since she had last seen him and he had gained weight. His face was strong and handsome with a bit of his mother's gentleness and even more of his father's stubbornness. His thick dark hair hung in loose ringlets just above his shoulders, tempting her to run her fingers through it. He turned to her, his dark eyes meeting hers. In them she saw the independent spirit of a man who had so many emotions he could barely handle them. She glanced away nervously, admiring the lake.

"What about you?" Matt asked her. "Have you lived in the area all your life?"

"Yes, my immediate family is still in the area."

"Do you have a large family?"

"My parents and two siblings. One brother and one sister."

"Tell me about them."

"Well, my sister René is a retail buyer and she has been married for six years to a wonderful man. My brother Charles is an architect. He's also married to a kind and caring woman."

Simone thought about what Charles had told her about his affair and how it would devastate Tamara. She sighed, "You have a sister and a brother, also, right?"

"Yeah, my brother Marty Jr., MJ, died a few years ago, in a car accident. My sister's name is Sarah. She's four years older then I am. She's married and has two little girls. Sadie's four and Amanda's three. Vincent, her husband, is a good guy."

They stood in silence, looking out on the lake for few moments. Matt pointed out a house on the other side that he had done some work on. He explained that before the accident the construction company had a lot of jobs lined up for months in advance and that if not for Josh's help, the business might be in trouble.

Simone talked about the youth center and told Matt about a vacant home next to it that she and Robin were collecting donations to purchase. They wanted to turn it into a home for runaways.

Matt told her that he didn't know much about fund-raising but offered to help in any way he could.

"We probably should be heading back to the house," Matt said. He waited for Simone to start up the path and followed her.

Matt moved about the kitchen as if it were his natural habitat. He removed the chicken from the oven, then whistled as he basted. He checked the fresh herbs and orange peels he'd tucked under the chicken skin, then he covered the chicken to put it back into the oven. He reached into the cabinet to grab two plates and scooped Greek salad onto both. Then he sprinkled crumbled feta cheese on top. He strolled to the table to place one plate in front of her and the other at the setting he had for himself. He walked back to the counter to get the drinks he had poured, then went to the table and sat down across from her. He watched as she picked at her salad.

"You don't like it? I can make you something else."

"Oh no, everything is fine. In fact, it's very good." She felt awkward with him watching her eat. She had to suppress that tiny voice inside her head telling her to remember her diet and that she needed to watch what she ate.

"Have you gone back to work yet?" Simone asked, hoping it would shift his mind from watching her to something more interesting.

"Yeah, there wasn't much to catch up on. Josh did a great job keeping things running smoothly," Matt said.

Simone could tell that he loved what he did and that he took pride in it.

He picked up his plate and reached for hers to take them to the sink.

"Do you need me to do anything?"

"No, just relax. Can I get you another drink?"

"Just water please."

He filled a glass full of ice and filtered water, then served the main course.

"You're a very good cook," she said.

"I learned a lot from my mom. She always said that if my

brother and I grew up to be anything like pop, we would be cooking a lot of our own meals. We should know how."

Simone smiled.

"So what about you, do you cook?" he asked.

"Yeah, but I'm not home often enough during the week to cook for myself, so I usually have dinner out. Sometimes at my parents or with friends. Sometimes at the soup kitchen."

"What?"

"The soup kitchen," she said, seeing the shocked look on his face. "Oh no," she laughed. "I serve food there. Sometimes I stay and have dinner with some of the regulars."

"Ah," Matt smiled. He could see her serving hot food and a warm smile to strangers. "What days do you go?"

"Usually Wednesday and Friday."

"Maybe I could help out sometimes."

"That would be great. They can always use a helping hand. As a matter of fact, Cheryl, she's the director at the shelter, was looking for someone to do minor repairs inside the building. Funding is sort of tight, so they may not be able to pay a whole lot, but I'm sure you guys could work something out."

"Yeah, I'm sure we can," Matt said. "Maybe I could meet you there on Friday and you could introduce me to Cheryl."

"Wonderful," Simone said, beaming at him as she told him about some of the characters at the center.

Matt smiled at her enthusiasm and laughed at her descriptions of one person after another. Folding his arms, he leaned on the table, listening to every word. He couldn't remember the last time someone had made him laugh out loud.

Chapter 6

Two hours after arriving at the mission, Matt installed the last of the light fixtures in one of the small offices. Climbing down from the ladder, he closed it and picked it up, carrying it with him toward the storage room. He met Cheryl on his way down the hall.

"Hey, I was just coming to look for you," he said. "Is there anything else you need me to do?"

"Oh, no, you've done so much already," she said, gently placing a hand on his arm. "Why don't you go on into the dining room and have something to eat."

"Thanks." Matt placed his hand over hers, squeezing lightly. Proceeding to the storage room, he put the ladder and his tool belt inside, then went down the hall to the dining area.

Simone was standing behind a row of tables, next to several other people who were serving the masses in line. As Matt walked closer to the table, he heard the man standing across from Simone raise his voice.

"I don't want this shit. You got gravy on my bread."

"I am sorry, Mr. Manchaze," Simone apologized.

"I can't eat it now. You done went and ruined it. All you people have to do is scoop up some damn food and put it on a plate. You can't even do that right."

Matt stepped next to Simone, looked intently at the man standing on the opposite side of the table, and said, "Excuse me, is there a problem?"

He looked down at Simone, asking her, "Are you all right?"

"Sure, I'm fine," she smiled apologetically at the man across from her. "Just a minute."

She walked to the beginning of the line to get a new tray and filled it with everything that Mr. Manchaze had on his first tray. She then put gravy in a separate bowl and passed it to him.

"Better?" she asked.

"Yeah, you're such a sweet girl. You're the only one here that looks out for me."

He reached in his pocket, took out a quarter and pressed it into the palm of Simone's hand, closing her hand into a fist. He patted her hand saying, "This is for you." Then, turning, he searched for the people he usually sat with during dinner before he walked away.

Simone smiled at Matt.

"Mr. Manchaze is a Vietnam vet and sometimes he becomes easily agitated. But he is a very sweet man."

She looked at the quarter in her hand, smiled and then dropped it in her pocket.

Meeting Matt's intense gaze she asked, "So how are you feeling. You're not doing too much are you?" She studied him closely, looking for any sign of fatigue, worried that he might be overexerting himself.

"No, I'm good," he answered, nodding.

Simone smiled again and then, turning back to the table, she placed a hand on the shoulder of the woman next to her, who was serving for her in order to allow Simone time to talk to Matt.

"Thanks, Tina," she said.

The woman smiled at Simone and moved back to her original spot.

Matt stepped next to Simone, taking one of the serving spoons from her.

"Do you mind if I help?"

"No, not at all." Simone leaned close to him, sliding her arm around his waist, giving him a quick, warm hug. Turning, she moved away and went back to the task at hand.

Matt momentarily held his breath, his heart raced, and he felt as if he were struggling to breathe. He took a slow, steady breath. As he served the potatoes and gravy, he glanced at Simone.

• • •

Matt walked back to the dining area, carrying his tool belt in

his left hand and his step ladder in the other. As he crossed the room, he watched Simone talking to one of the volunteers.

Simone had finished her conversation with Tina when she turned to see Matt walking toward them. She smiled broadly at him.

"Hey, how would you like to go down to Romano's to grab something to eat?" Matt asked.

"That sounds fun," Simone said, "but I'm meeting some friends."

He nodded. "Well, maybe some other time."

"What are you doing tomorrow evening?"

"I didn't have anything planned," Matt said, his heart skipping a beat and his pulse beginning to race at the thought of Simone suggesting that they go out.

• • •

Walking briskly back to his truck, Matt put the ladder and tool belt in the back before getting inside.

"What the hell are you doing?" he scolded himself.

He sat in the truck, his mind going a million miles a minute. There was no way he wanted to spend an evening with Simone and her boyfriend. When she asked what he was doing tomorrow, he thought it would be just the two of them. It never occurred to him that she would suggest a double date. He looked back at the building he'd just exited and sighed heavily, thinking about the sort of man that Simone would find attractive. *He's probably some tall, dark and handsome guy that makes women swoon at the sight of him.*

His imagination wandered to the restaurant with him sitting across the table watching Simone gaze into Mr. Tall, Dark and Handsome's eyes, and her hanging on to his every word like he was Don Juan and Superman all rolled into one. Then he imagined himself sitting there like Jimmy Olson wishing he was Super Don Juan.

"Shit, way to go, dumb ass," he cursed himself. "What the hell are you going to do now?"

Tapping on the steering wheel as he devised a plan, he reached into his back pocket and pulled out his wallet. Searching for

the phone number he had tucked in there so many months ago. He unfolded the paper and looked at the two numbers: one her cell and one her home.

"Please be free, please be free," he whispered, pushing the buttons on his cell phone. After the second ring a rich voice with a slight southern accent answered.

"May I speak to Cassie?" he asked.

"This is she."

"Hi, Cassie, I don't know if you remember me. This is Matt. Matt Turner."

"Oh, hello, Matt! Josh told me about your accident, how are you?"

"I'm well, thanks. How have you been?"

"Wonderful."

"Good. The reason I'm calling is I wanted to see if you were free for dinner tomorrow?"

"Dinner, huh? I think I might be able to rearrange my schedule."

"Great."

"What time?"

"I can pick you up between 6:30 and 7."

"Sounds good. I'll be ready." She gave him her address.

"Great. See you tomorrow."

• • •

Simone sat on the sofa that doubled as a bed in her friend Tanya Manson's tiny apartment. To Simone, it was more like a living room/bedroom/bathroom all in one. The bathroom only had a shower, sink and toilet. If you sat down, your knees were either pressed against the base of the sink or the shower door. The kitchenette was so small that if you stood in the center, you could reach out your arms and touch opposite walls with the tips of your fingers.

Karen Edwards, Simone's childhood friend, sat on the floor next to her. Her highlighted shoulder-length hair was pulled back with a hair clip. Karen was five-foot-eight and as slim as a profes-

sional model. Simone envied her style and flawless mocha complexion as well as her ability to take control of any situation.

Tanya was the complete opposite of Karen. She was five-foot-three and a few shades darker than Simone's honey complexion. Simone and Karen had met Tanya in college. Tanya was sometimes so absorbed with her own strong desire to be the center of attention that it drove Karen crazy. In spite of this, the three women quickly became best friends.

"Well," Tanya said, throwing her waist-length, micro-mini braids over her shoulder, "I think Don Cheadle is hot."

"He's all right, but not as hot as Colin Farrell," Karen said.

"What? He's white."

"So? He's still hot."

Tanya took the bowl of chips from the middle of the table, placed them on her lap and began pulling the dip closer.

Karen reached across the table, taking the bowl and setting it back on the table.

"Take it easy with that stuff. Your ass is getting as wide as the Mississippi!"

Then Karen realized what she had said. The subject of weight had always been a sensitive subject for Simone. Karen glanced up at Simone saying, "Sorry."

Tanya rolled her eyes at Karen. "Well, I guess Colin is hot, but not as hot as Dave Pearson."

"Oh my gosh! Dave from work?" Karen looked at her for a moment and then burst out laughing. "You're joking right?"

"No, I think he's hot."

"Hotter then Colin Farrell? Girl you're crazy."

"Simone," Tanya asked, "who do you think is finer?"

"I don't know. They're both good looking."

"But which one is finer?" Karen prompted.

"Well, if I have to say so myself, I'd say Alan."

Karen and Tanya looked at Simone, stunned for a moment.

Karen spoke to Simone as if she were a little girl who was afraid to say something that would get her in to trouble. "Simone, Debra's not here. She can't hear you. You can tell the truth."

"Alan is hot," Simone lifted her chin in defense.

"No, Alan is handsome. He's not hot," Karen corrected.

"Not hot," Tanya agreed, shaking her head.

"You're not obligated to say someone is hot just because you're dating them. And we promise we won't tell," Karen raised her hand as if to take an oath.

Tanya grinned, crossing her heart and quickly raised her hand.

Simone chewed on her bottom lip.

"Well," Simone said.

Karen and Tanya watched her with what seemed like baited breath.

"Okay." She smiled at them sheepishly. "My friend Matt. I think he's hot."

"Oooh," Karen said, rising on her knees and giving Simone her full attention.

"Who's Matt?" Tanya asked.

"What makes him hot?" Karen asked.

"Who's Matt?" Tanya yelled.

Simone told them about the accident.

"Why is this the first time I'm hearing about this?" Tanya asked.

"Cause you only want to talk about yourself when we're together and you never ask about anything that's going on with us," Karen said quickly.

"Whatever," Tanya retorted.

Karen turned her attention back to Simone. "So what makes Matt so hot?"

"Well, for one thing, he's good looking."

Tanya leaned forward, "Good looking like boy next door good looking?"

"Or," Karen asked, "super jock good looking?"

Simone paused shaking her head. "Have you ever seen a guy and your breath literally catches in your throat? He's that good looking."

"Oh shit," Karen said, taking her wine glass and swallowing a gulp.

"And not only is he good looking, but he's a great guy."

"Is he gay?" Tanya asked quickly.

"No," Simone answered. "He was married."

Karen quickly shook her head. "That doesn't matter. Take it from me. Nothing is what it seems."

Tanya and Simone looked at each other and then back at Karen.

Karen had been married and a year later she caught her husband in bed with a 20-year-old woman. When she kicked him out of the house, he went to the bank and withdrew $15,000 from their joint account. Karen had told Simone that the savings was insurance money she had gotten from her grandmother and that they were going to use it as the down payment for a house. That was two years ago and Karen said that she had gotten over it, but Simone wasn't quite so sure.

"So," Tanya asked, taking a sip from her wine glass and drawing all attention to herself. "Hey, how long have the three of us been friends?"

"What?" Karen asked, eyeing her suspiciously. "Why the hell would you ask something like that?"

"I was just thinking out loud."

"Yeah, I bet." Karen said, her expression saying that she didn't believe a thing her friend had said.

"Seriously."

"Uh-huh."

Sighing, Tanya set her glass down. "All right, I need you guys to do me a favor."

"No," Karen said quickly.

"See," Tanya said, sucking her teeth, "you don't even know what it is."

"Don't care."

Simone laughed, asking, "What is it?"

"Don't fall for it Simone. She's just setting you up," Karen

said, shaking her head, knowing all the while that she was agitating Tanya.

"No, that's all right. Forget it," Tanya said, folding her arms across her chest.

"Karen, stop it." Simone nudged Karen with her knee, then, sitting forward she asked, "Come on Tanya, what's the favor?"

"Well, I'm seeing this guy and I'm trying to figure out how he feels about me?"

Karen grunted and giggled at the same time.

Simone glanced down at her, then, turning back to Tanya she asked, "Why not just come right out and ask him?"

"Girl, since when do you ask a man how he feels about you and get a straight answer?" Tanya asked, surprised that her friend would even suggest such a thing.

"You'd do better adopting a monkey and teaching it to talk," Karen added matter-of-factly. "At least that way you can have intelligent conversations during the Super Bowl."

Simone laughed, gently shoving Karen's shoulder.

"Yup, that's true," Tanya agreed, her head nodding vigorously. "So that only leaves when he's getting some. That's when he thinks by being honest with you he's going to be getting some more. And when he thinks you are so pissed at him that you might damage something that he adores like his car, laptop or stereo."

Simone and Karen looked at Tanya, and she smiled at them sheepishly.

Tanya said, "I haven't done anything like that. It just came to mind once or twice. You know, during those times when you are daydreaming and crazy things just pop into your head."

"You have way too much free time on your hands," Karen said, shaking her head.

Simone chuckled, saying, "Isn't that the truth?"

"Okay, back to the problem at hand," Tanya said, trying to keep her friends on the right track.

"How long have you been seeing this guy?" Karen asked.

"It's been a couple months now."

"And you haven't brought him around for the seal of

approval," Simone said, faking a surprised look. "What's his name?

Tanya looked at the two women and didn't answer.

"Well?" Karen said.

Tanya sighed. "Jay."

"Damn, you act like we want him or some shit." Karen eyed Tanya, and a slow grin spread across her face. "Oh, I see — he must be a dog."

"No, girl, he's fine. With beautiful brown skin and good hair. Nice ass, too."

"Yeah right, I know you. If he were all that, you'd be flaunting him all around and talking him up. Jay did this, Jay said that. There has to be something wrong with him."

"She's right Tanya," Simone said. "Why haven't you let us meet him?"

" 'Cause she's trying to hide him, I bet he doesn't have a job," Karen said.

"Girl you are crazy," Tanya injected, rolling her eyes.

"Tanya, he does at least have a job?" Simone asked.

"Of course he does."

"Yeah right, I bet he's a bum and not your regular 'don't have a job' bum. I mean the whole digging in the garbage-bin, shaking-a-can-on-the-corner bum. And he probably wouldn't even stand on the highway, washing windows if you supplied him with a bucket and a squeegee. He would rather beg," Karen said.

"Girl please, my man has a damn good job," Tanya said rolling her eyes. "I would never think about being with someone without a job. I don't care if he flips burgers. If he can't at least buy me a happy meal, then he can keep on walking," she said, getting to her feet and strutting in front of Karen and Simone.

"Amen to that," Simone said raising her glass.

"Ladies, your standards are way too low," Karen said, reaching for the bottle of wine and refilling her glass. Then she held the bottle up and waited for her friends to signal if they wanted a refill.

She filled Tanya's glass as she spoke. "Happy meal my ass! If he can't afford to take me out to a real restaurant, and I mean a

classy one, not one with paper napkins and cheap-ass china — I'm talking about linen tablecloths and napkins — he might as well not even look my way."

"Girl, that isn't right. You act like it's all about the money," Tanya said. "Everybody doesn't have it like that."

"Yeah, that's true, but my man has to at least make more money then I do," Karen said, taking a sip from her glass. "If he makes less than I do, then I may have to share my wealth with him and that definitely isn't happening." Karen snorted her laugh.

Simone laughed at her saying, "You would share your wealth with the right man."

"Yeah?" Karen said with a smirk, "you just keep right on believing that."

Simone shook her head. "Girl, you are crazy."

"Yeah, I might be crazy, but I'll be a crazy bitch that still has her money," Karen said, laughing and leaning against Simone's leg.

"C'mon guys, you know, I'm serious about needing you to do something for me," Tanya said, becoming slightly frustrated. "I need you guys to help me come up with a plan."

"What sort of plan?" Simone asked, reaching for a chip and dipping it in the salsa.

"A plan to see how true Jay is to me. I don't know, maybe get some girl to approach him and see if he tries to hit on her."

"Girl, that's crazy. We haven't done that sort of shit since high school," Karen said, pursing her lips in disgust and waving her hand.

"I know, but this is important."

"Nope," Karen said, shaking her head. "I am not doing that. I'm not getting caught up in that shit."

"Come on, please."

"Hell no. If I wanted drama in my life, I would have stayed with Travis," Karen said, folding her arms, signaling that the subject was closed to her.

"Simone?" Tanya whined.

"No, I can't do that. I'm not good at that kind of thing," Simone said as she shook her head.

"You won't have to do it yourself. Just see if one of your co-workers will do it."

"I wouldn't feel comfortable asking someone else to do something like that, either."

"Geez, some friends you guys are," Tanya said, pouting and folding her arms like a child.

"If you're so concerned about your so-called man cheating on you, maybe he isn't your man," Karen sang before taking a sip from her glass.

"You have no idea what you're talking about," Tanya said defensively. "He loves me. I know he does."

• • •

Turning from the bay window, Jamison glanced around the lavish bedroom he shared with Wendy. He walked toward the bed and fingered Wendy's sheer, pale blue nightgown that Sunee, his housekeeper of eight years, had laid out.

He was losing her. He could tell. She wasn't as attentive as she once was. When they first met, she couldn't wait to see him and she was thrilled when he bought her this house. Now it seemed as though she didn't even want to be near him. He got the impression that she never wanted to return to the home they shared.

Although he never said anything to her, Jamison knew what was going on. He always had. It was that loser Turner. It was always him. He tried to convince himself it was just his imagination, but now it all seemed to add up.

He'd done some checking and found out that the son of a bitch had been out of the hospital for over a month. That's when she had started to change, always being evasive about her whereabouts. Never wanting him to accompany her when she went out and never telling him where she was going.

Yeah, it added up all right. Sitting on the side of the bed and reaching toward the nightstand he picked up the phone and dialed the familiar ten digits of her cell. He looked at the clock. It was 8:46

p.m., and there was no answer. He slammed the phone back on the cradle abruptly, stood and walked over to the window.

The white Lexus SUV drove down the narrow drive, stopping in front of the house. He watched as Wendy emerged from the vehicle. Reaching in the back seat, she removed a garment bag, draping it over her left arm, then she reached for her handbag, closed the door, and walked to the main entrance of the house.

Jamison left the bedroom, stopping at the top of the landing as Wendy entered the house. He moved back in the shadows, watching her.

Wendy crossed the massive foyer slowly on her way to the stairs.

Jamison stepped out quietly as she reached the top, causing Wendy to shriek and drop the garment bag. She swayed slightly, losing her balance, and Jamison gripped her arm, pulling her toward him and stopping her fall.

"You scared me," she said, breathing fast.

He smiled at the fear he saw in her eyes and at the rush of adrenaline he got from it.

"I'm sorry," he said as he moved closer, allowing his lips to brush her temples. "How was your day?"

"It was good. How about yours?"

"Good."

He bent to pick up the garment bag and placed his hand on the small of her back. Then Jamison guided her into the bedroom. He dropped the bag on the bed, crossed the room, and sat on the lounge chair watching Wendy as she approached the dresser.

"Are you ready for dinner?" he asked. "If you like we could…"

"No, I've had dinner already," she said, looking back at him. "I'm sorry, I thought that since it was so late you would have probably eaten already. I was going to have a bath and relax, maybe read a little."

"I'll draw your bath."

"You don't have to do that."

"I know. I want to." He stood, removed his blazer and laid

it over the chair. Then he walked toward the bathroom. When he reached the door, he stopped, turning back to her. "Where were you this evening?"

"Lindsay's new exhibit at the museum opened this evening, and I stayed a little longer than I intended."

"I didn't know she had a new exhibit. You should have told me. If you had, I could have accompanied you."

"I did tell you."

"No, I don't believe you did."

"Hmm, it must have slipped your mind."

"Wendy, you know better than anyone that I never forget anything," he said, his eyes seeming as if they never once blinked.

She bit her lip nervously and ran her fingers through her hair.

"I'm sorry. I thought I told you."

Jamison nodded, walking into the bathroom.

Wendy listened, hearing him turn on the tub. She slowly removed her dress. She didn't want to tell Jamison that she'd had coffee with Marty Turner. There was really no reason not to tell him. Marty was a kind old man. Surely Jamison wouldn't have a problem with her meeting him. She watched him come from the bathroom, and, seeing the look on his face, thought that it was in her best interest to say nothing at all.

• • •

Heading south on Central Avenue, Alan stopped at the traffic light and waited for it to change. He was amazed at his luck at finding Dana, someone he was so compatible with, who wanted to take their relationship one day at a time. He smiled, thinking of Dana's sexy smile and compact body. Feeling himself becoming instantly aroused, he adjusted himself slightly, shifting in his seat.

The car behind him beeped, signaling the change of the traffic light. He drove two blocks before turning into the apartment complex parking lot. After grabbing the bag from the passenger seat, he went into the building and headed to the second floor.

"Hi baby," Alan greeted as the door opened. Walking into

the apartment he held up the bottle of wine. "I brought red. I hope its okay?"

"Ah, perfect." Dana's long, slender fingers grasped the bottle. "We're having baked ziti. I hope you don't mind."

"No, not as long as I can have you afterward."

Dana smiled up at Alan, stroking his strong jaw, then giving him a long, lingering kiss. "Most definitely love...most definitely."

• • •

Alan was furious that Simone had made a date with Matt for dinner. He said he didn't feel up to spending an evening with people that he didn't know and he wasn't all that eager to become involved with one of her charity cases.

She finally convinced him how important it was for him to get to know her friends. During the course of the day Simone had picked up the phone three times with the intention of calling Matt and canceling. She didn't really know why, but she didn't want to see Matt with whomever he was dating. She felt silly for thinking that way, but it was true.

A small part of her was curious about the sort of woman Matt was attracted to. Now, standing outside of the restaurant she wished she had called and canceled. The sight of him caused her heart to pound, and her breath caught when she saw the beautiful redhead that was on his arm. She bit her lower lip, looking away, telling herself to take deep, slow breaths.

When Matt walked around the corner, he took one look at Alan and immediately decided that he didn't like him. Alan looked like an arrogant asshole. He was also confused by the sudden anger he felt at Alan's hand resting on the small of Simone's back.

"Hey," Simone said as Matt and his date approached them.

"Hi," Matt said, forcing a smile. "I hope you guys didn't have to wait long?"

"It was entirely my fault," Matt's date apologized. "I wanted to look my best for Matt." She said, looking up at him with her bright eyes sparkling. He smiled at her, taking her hand in his.

Clearing her throat Simone said, "Alan Whitaker, I'd like you to meet Matthew Turner."

"Good evening," Alan said to the other couple.

"How's it going, Alan?" Matt said, as the two men shook hands. "Do you mind if I call you Al?"

"It's Alan," Alan corrected.

Matt nodded slowly. *Yeah I'm gonna love spending the evening with this asshole.* "Alan. Right." Then Matt turned to introduce Cassie to Alan and Simone.

Simone took in the other woman's appearance. Her red hair was cut stylishly, complimenting her small face and perfect makeup.

Simone brushed her hair from her face, casually looking down at her own sleeveless floral dress and lightweight, white summer blouse. The chiffon moved slightly with the summer breeze, giving her a romantic look, but she instantly wished she had opted for a sexier, sleeker look. She crossed her arms instinctively. Looking up, her gaze met Matt's and she glanced away, awkwardly shifting her weight from one foot to the other.

"Shall we?" Alan said, gesturing toward the restaurant. The couples entered, stopping at the hostess station.

Matt gave her his name, telling her that he had made reservations for four.

As Simone walked past him, he leaned close, whispering in her ear, "Has anyone told you that you look wonderful this evening?"

She smiled up at him. "Thank you."

The waiter described the specials of the day, with recommendations on what meal was the very best, and took their orders.

"Cassie," Simone asked, "what do you do?"

"I'm a registered nurse. I work out of North Arundel General. I'm in maternity."

Simone smiled at the other woman, admiring the work she did.

"And what do you do?"

Simone told Cassie about her work at the center.

"That's a wonderful position," Cassie said sincerely. "I've been waiting over a year for a position in the children's ward to open up. That's what I initially went to school for. I love working with the little ones best."

Simone smiled openly at her as they talked about their love for their careers.

Matt sat forward in his chair. "So, Alan, Simone tells me you're a psychologist?"

"Yes," Alan said, his tone flat.

"What sort of other things do you do? Do you like to fish?

"No."

Matt nodded. "So, what do you do during your spare time?"

"Work," Alan said, his eyes boring into Matt's.

Okay, Matt thought as he sat back and focused on Simone and Cassie's conversation.

When the waiter finally brought their meals, Alan slid his chair close to Simone's, resting his arm on the back of her chair. He spoke to Simone quietly as he casually ate from her plate.

Matt watched the intimate interaction between Simone and Alan with a sudden twinge of jealously. He bit the inside of his mouth, reminding himself that he didn't have a right to be jealous because Simone was Alan's woman and that he was just a friend. As much as he told himself that, he couldn't help but fantasize about Simone with him. Alone.

After dinner, Matt and Cassie decided to share a dessert and ordered Black Forest cake. Taking her fork, Cassie cut a off a small piece and fed it to Matt. His sexy lips wrapped around the fork, and Simone watched as Cassie slowly removed the fork.

Suddenly Simone's mouth felt dry and she reached for her glass to take a gulp of water. She watched Matt smile at Cassie, their eyes locked, and Matt leaned forward gently kissing Cassie's cheek. Simone wanted to scream. She glanced to her right at Alan and back at Cassie. Simone liked Cassie — she really did — but at that moment, she wished that she could make both Cassie and Alan disappear. She wanted Matt, that pie and his sexy lips.

Chapter 7

"Simone, I'd like for you to strive to be best at everything in life. I know you could be so successful. Why you settle for being just a social worker is beyond my comprehension," Debra said, not looking up from the coupons she had scattered on the kitchen table.

"Youth counselor, Mother," Simone quickly corrected, quietly wondering why in the world she hadn't ignored the request her mother had left on her answering machine, asking her to breakfast. She should have gone straight to work.

"Whatever," Debra said, finally looking up at her daughter. She tilted her head as she spoke. "I had such high expectations for you. Charles and René are successful, but I thought you would be the one who would make your father and me the proudest. You were always so smart."

"Mother," Simone sighed, "I like what I do. Besides, I've always felt as though I was meant to help people."

"Well, you certainly can't save every sad and confused teenager you come across." Debra eyed her daughter and continued, "And there are people that need help who can actually afford to pay for it."

Simone rose from the table, and went to the counter where Debra had a serving tray with coffee cups, saucers, cream, and sugar. On one side was a chrome coffee maker, on the other, a stack of dessert plates to match the cups and saucers, and napkins. Simone picked up a coffee cup, glancing in Debra's direction when she heard her mother clear her throat.

Debra looked from Simone to the coffee cup to the saucers.

Picking up one of the saucers, Simone moved to the coffee pot, filling her cup and adding cream and sugar substitute. Taking her cup, a dessert plate, and a napkin, she went back to the table and

selected one of the apple-cinnamon muffins from the plate in the center of the table.

Debra looked at the muffin in Simone's hand, frowning. "Put that down. You don't need to be eating that stuff."

Simone looked at the muffin she held.

"Those aren't for you," Debra said, returning her attention to her coupons. "I made multi-grain muffins for you."

Simone groaned, "Mother, I don't want multi-grain muffins. I'd prefer to have an apple-cinnamon muffin."

"Think of your diet."

Nibbling her lip, Simone hesitated, then said, "I'm no longer dieting."

Debra looked up, shock clearly evident by her features. "And why is that? You are overweight."

"But daddy says..."

"It doesn't matter what your father says. He's a man and he doesn't know what it takes for us women to look our best. And you know we really must do something with that hair. You have such nice hair," Debra tilted her head slightly, examining Simone.

Simone self-consciously brushed her hair back.

"I was thinking a cut and maybe some highlights would look great on you," her mother said.

"Mother, I don't want to change my hair, and everyone can't be a size two."

"René is," Debra said, offering Simone a sly smile.

Simone's eye twitched. She slowly put the muffin back on the plate as she looked around the kitchen, searching for another topic of conversation.

"René is a good size," Debra continued. "She has a great career and a wonderful husband."

"Mother, please," Simone whispered.

"And that," her mother said, looking at Simone with determination, "is what I want for you. That's all I've ever wanted for you."

"Mother, when I meet the right man, I'll marry him. I'm in no major hurry." Simone didn't want to have the same conversation

again. Her mother waved her hand, dismissing what Simone had said.

"You have the right man. All you need to do is work on your relationship." Debra studied her daughter. "When was the last time you and Alan went out?"

Simone met her mother's gaze, not wanting to answer her question, because Debra already knew the answer. Debra's brows rose as she waited.

Sighing, Simone finally said, "We haven't gone out in more than a week."

"Why not?"

Simone looked down her index finger as she traced the rim of the coffee cup. She didn't want to tell her mother that lately she had been spending a lot of time with Matt, and she was happier spending one hour with Matt than spending one whole day with Alan.

"You'd better not let him get away. He's a good catch. And he's interested in you."

"Mother, he's a great guy. He's just not the man for me."

"And what in the world would make you think that?"

"There's no chemistry."

"Your father and I didn't have chemistry when we started dating, but I knew he had potential."

Simone closed her eyes. *Here we go again*, she thought.

"Mother, I'm sorry I'm such a big disappointment to you."

Debra's mouth dropped open.

"I'm sorry I'm not a successful architect like Charles or a svelte, beautiful retail buyer like René. I'm just plain old Simone Porter, the youth counselor wasting her life because she won't take the wonderful man offered to her.

"Mother, why can't you just accept that I like what I do? Why can't you at least respect me for who I am?"

Debra watched her daughter, stunned. Then she slowly shook her head, clasping her hands and resting them on the table.

"Simone, you are 28 years old, and I understand you want to make your own way. But sometimes, when someone is as emotional as you are, you don't always make the right choices. I'm only trying

to help you, and all you can see is me attacking you," Debra sighed in defeat.

"Mother, I know you're only trying to help, and I appreciate it," Simone said, guilt-ridden.

"And I love you," she said as she rose from her chair and kissed her mother's cheek. "I have to go now or I'll be late for work."

• • •

Walking into Nikko Japanese Steak and Sushi, Matt told the hostess that he was expecting a friend to join him and asked for a booth. After following her to the booth, he ordered a coke for himself and an iced tea for Simone.

Ten minutes later, she walked in wearing a turquoise sleeveless top with camel slacks and her usual button-down matching blouse.

"Hey," Matt said, standing when she neared the booth. He remained standing until she slid her handbag in the seat and sat down.

"Sorry I'm late. Traffic was murder."

"Don't worry about it; I haven't been waiting long. I ordered an iced tea for you."

"Thanks," Simone adjusted in her seat, getting comfortable. "How are you doing today?"

"Good. You?"

Simone thought about it for a moment. "Actually I'm having a great day."

Matt smiled as the waiter came and took their orders. They ordered the standard selection of sushi and a pan of fried, crumbed pork to share.

Simone watched Matt for a moment and said, "Can I ask you something?"

"Sure."

"I'm just curious. Why have you never mentioned your brother?"

Matt looked down momentarily, then back at her. "If it both-

ers you that I ask, just say so. I didn't mean to pry. It's just that when you were in the hospital, your mother spoke of him a few times."

"No, you're not prying. MJ passed away more than five years ago. He was 10 years older than me. We were close even though he was older. He would play ball with me. Let me hang out in the basement with him and his friends while they listened to music. He and Sarah even taught me how to dance."

"You dance?"

"Yeah, a little. When I was about 16 I saw how uncomfortable a lot of guys felt about dancing. I also realized that it was a good way to get girls," he nodded, with a huge grin on his face.

Simone laughed. "Did he ever marry?"

"MJ was always a ladies man. He said that he couldn't see himself settling down with one woman.

"Really?"

"Yeah. One day MJ told the family that he'd met someone special and that he was really in love. It was the week before Thanksgiving. We were so happy for him. Ma asked him to bring his friend, Alex, to Thanksgiving dinner. And of course pop freaked."

Simone frowned, knowing what little she knew of Marty. She could only imagine what MJ must have gone through. She instantly felt sorry for the man she had never met.

"So what was the problem with Alex?" she asked.

"Nothing, Alex was great. I never saw MJ any happier than when they were dating."

"Well, if she made your brother happy, I don't understand why your father had a problem with her?"

"Because Alex was Alexander."

Simone's mouth dropped open.

"Ooooh," she said as she realized what that meant.

"Yeah," Matt said dryly. "You could not possibly imagine the look on pop's face when they walked through the door."

"I think I can."

"No, it was brutal," Matt said, shaking his head.

"When MJ walked into the house with Alex, everyone was looking for his girlfriend. As he introduced Alex, we were all

stunned, but Ma, being the person she is, gave Alex a hug and welcomed him into our home.

"Pop just stood there looking at him, his mouth hanging open and his face as white as a sheet. He said some things that I'm ashamed to repeat and told MJ that he was embarrassed to call him his son, picked up his coat, and walked out of the house. He did not say another word. He just left. As far as I know, he's never mentioned it to anyone.

"That's so sad."

"To this day, I don't know why MJ decided that was the best way to come out."

"Maybe he thought that if he showed you what a great person Alex was and how happy they were together, it would be all right."

"Maybe. MJ and I started Turner Construction together. Not long after he came out, he told me that he wanted me to buy him out, and he went to work at M&T Machine Tool as a press operator.

"He told me he thought that if he worked with Pop, maybe he would start to respect him more and learn to accept his relationship with Alex.

"About four months afterward is when they had the car accident. He and Alex were killed instantly."

Simone reached for Matt's hand, squeezing it slightly as he turned and looked around the restaurant. After a minute Matt looked down at their hands and at her. She released his hand and self-consciously adjusted her blouse.

"Now, do you mind if I ask you something?" Matt asked, watching Simone closely.

"Sure."

"Why do you always wear two shirts?"

Simone didn't answer. She just met his steady gaze.

"I mean, I've seen you several times now and every time you're wearing something that's like a cover-up.

"I... Well..." Simone's eyes shifted nervously.

"Simone, you're a beautiful woman. You should be proud of..."

Matt was interrupted by a familiar voice.

"Hey, guy."

"Hey," Matt said as Josh approached the table.

"Hi," Simone smiled brightly. "How have you been?"

"Great, just stopped by to get some lunch and take it back to the job site."

"Why don't you join us?" Simone asked, looking toward Matt for confirmation.

"Ah, sure. Join us." Matt moved over to make room for Josh. Josh quickly slid in on the seat next to Simone.

"Thanks." Josh grinned across the table at Matt.

Once Josh sat down, the waiter approached the table. Josh told him that he had ordered a curry chicken and he would be eating lunch with his friends. The waiter returned bringing their food.

They ate in silence for a few minutes until Simone offered Josh some sushi.

"I'm not too keen on eating uncooked meat," Josh said, frowning at the food in the middle of the table. "I'll eat it medium or even medium rare. But for the most part if it's not at least seared, I'm gonna have a problem with it."

"Come on, Josh." Simone gave him a friendly nudge on his shoulder and pushed the plate of sushi toward him. Josh picked up his fork and speared a piece of fish, dipped it into the soy sauce, and chewed enough to swallow.

"How is it?" Simone asked.

"Fishy," he said, taking a sip of his cola.

"How about the salmon?"

"Okay, I'll try it, but I'm warning you. I'm not adventurous when it comes to food. I'm gonna need something a little stronger than cola."

He flagged down the waiter and ordered a Miller Lite. After the waiter returned to the table with his beer, Josh made a production of grabbing a piece of fish from the center plate and quickly putting it into his mouth. Grimacing, he chewed, swallowed, and chased it down with a gulp of beer.

"I don't like that," Josh said, leaning close to Simone, his shoulder brushing hers.

Matt glared at him, feeling a sudden pang of jealousy.

"Maybe you need to try one that's a little milder. They all have a slightly different taste," Matt said.

Josh pointed to everything, asking which was what before he agreed to try another bite.

"What's that?" he asked, leaning closer to the plate.

"Why don't you try it. It's squid?"

He frowned. "No way."

"Come on. It's good. Give it a try."

Josh groaned, took it from the plate and gave it a quick sniff.

"Don't do that. Just eat it," said Simone.

He gingerly put it in his mouth and chewed. Simone chuckled at the look on his face.

"See, now that's downright nasty," he said, grabbing his beer and washing the squid down.

Then he stuck out his tongue and asked, "Do I have any suckers on my tongue?"

Simone laughed. "No, silly."

"Are you sure? Cause I think my tongue is sticking to the roof of my mouth."

Simone laughed as he made a production of opening and closing his mouth causing a suction sound.

"Okay," Simone said. "How about trying the tuna? It has a much milder flavor."

"No more," Josh said, shaking his head and fanning his hands.

Standing outside of the restaurant Matt and Josh said goodbye to Simone before walking across the street to the parking lot. Matt glared at Josh again, punching him in the arm.

"Ouch! Man, what the hell was that for?" Josh said, grabbing his arm and moving away from Matt.

" 'I'm not that adventurous with my food,' " Matt mocked Josh once they reached the parking lot.

Josh grinned at him as Matt said, "Man, what the hell was that shit. You know you'll eat anything that's not nailed down."

••••

Simone looked up from her desk and greeted her friend with a smile.

"Hey, come on in."

Karen walked farther into the office to sit opposite Simone.

"You look great," Simone complimented her, admiring her crisp, white designer outfit.

"Thanks," Karen said, dropping her handbag on the floor next to her chair. "So, what's up?"

"Nothing much. Same old thing," Simone sighed.

Karen nodded her understanding.

"I stopped by to see what you were doing tonight."

"Nothing. What do you have in mind?"

"I was going to take Beverly to Club Hollywood tonight. She broke up with Tony, and I thought it might be fun to hang out. Wanna come?"

"I don't know," Simone said, shaking her head slightly. "You know I'm not into the club scene."

"I know, but it'll be fun. Bev's all bummed out and walking around like a zombie. We can cheer her up and have a good time in the process."

"I don't know," Simone said as she glanced at the ringing phone. "Let me get that," she said as she held up her hand and reached for the receiver.

"Simone Porter."

"Good afternoon." Alan's rich tone flowed through the phone line.

"Hi, Alan," Simone said, looking at Karen. Karen smiled, making a funny face, and grinned when Simone waved a hand at her.

"How're you doing?" he asked.

"I'm doing well. How about you?"

"I've had a hectic morning, but things are already looking up now that I hear your voice."

Simone fidgeted in her seat.

"So, what's up?" she asked, wanting to get to the point of his call.

"I was hoping that you didn't have plans for dinner. I was thinking maybe a candlelight dinner at Sam's Waterfront and a moonlight walk?"

"Oh, Alan that sounds wonderful, but I've already made plans with Karen. She's having a family crisis, and I promised her that I would be there for her."

"Karen's a big girl," he said sarcastically. I'm sure she can handle whatever problems she has without you."

"I've already made arrangements to meet at her apartment at 6 and I can't back out at the last minute. I'm sure you understand." Simone could picture him sitting, his brow puckered in anger, as he contemplated what she was saying. Knowing Alan, he was definitely angry.

"Yes, of course. Maybe when you wrap things up with her, we can have a late dinner."

"I don't know, it sounds big. It might take most of the evening."

"I understand. I must say that I'm a little disappointed. When I talked to your mother earlier, she didn't mention anything about you having plans," he said.

Simone paused before speaking. "I spoke to Karen just five minutes before you called. When did you speak to my mother?"

"Earlier this morning, she invited me over for breakfast and she said that I just missed you. She also mentioned how you confided in her that you missed seeing me. You were on my mind all morning. Once the staff meeting was over, I rushed to my office to call you."

"That's sweet, Alan, and I'm really sorry about this evening. We'll get together soon, I promise. I have to go now. I have someone in my office."

After saying their good-byes, Simone hung up the phone. She looked at Karen's smiling face, beaming at her from across the desk.

"I thought you didn't want to go out tonight?" Karen teased.

"Looks like there's been a change of plans," Simone said.

Karen leaned forward, her elbows propped on Simone's desk. "Sounds like Debra's been up to her old tricks."

Simone met her gaze and sighed. "You know how she is, unfortunately."

Karen said, "So, what's going on with you and the prick?"

Simone started to say something about Karen's comment but instead let it go. "We went out with Matt and his date a few nights ago. Alan was so rude to them. He barely said two words to Cassie and he wouldn't even talk to Matt.

"And that surprised you how?"

"It's like he doesn't want to be a part of my life. He doesn't like my friends or the things that I like to do. Whenever we go out, we go where he wants to go and we do what he wants to do. Most of the time I feel like what I want isn't important to him."

"When you first met him you did have reservations," Karen added.

"Yeah, I did. I thought he was going to be a jerk. But as I got to know him, he seemed sweet and considerate. Now things are different. It's like he's a totally different person. The change has been gradual, but noticeable."

"Have you ever thought that he was always like that and he just displayed his overbearing side slowly to break you in?"

"I think I would have seen it."

"No, sometimes you don't see things if they're happening to you. With Debra on your shoulder, whispering what a great guy he is, it's a wonder you see it now."

Simone shook her head. "He couldn't be that sort of person. He is a psychologist. He knows what that does to a person."

Karen chucked. "Debra's a psychologist, too, and she's probably the craziest person I know." Then she reached for her purse and rose from the chair, sliding the purse strap over her shoulder. "I'll pick you up at 7 p.m."

• • •

Matt parked his truck in front of Josh's gray ranch-style home. He strolled up the walkway and onto the small porch and reached for the doorbell. He paused, turned the doorknob, and pushed the door open. Stepping into the house, he walked quietly through the living room.

"Hey guy!" Josh greeted, as Matt entered the family room.

"Damn, man, don't you ever lock the door?"

"Nah, if someone wants something I have that bad, then they're more than welcome to it," Josh said, lying back in his easy chair with beer in hand.

Matt chuckled. He always got on his friend about not locking anything up. Not his house or his truck. Josh would say he didn't want to live in a place where you had to lock your doors.

"Pull up a seat and grab a brew!" Josh thrust his chin in the direction of a blue cooler full of ice-cold beers.

Matt grabbed one of the bottles, twisted off the top and chucked the cap into the wastebasket. He flopped down in the easy chair next to Josh asking, "What's the score?" as they watched a player run to second base while the crowd roared.

"Red Sox 10, Mariners 2 — the sorry bastards," Josh mumbled.

Matt laughed. "Bet on the game again?"

Josh glanced at him and grunted.

"Don't you ever get tired of losing?"

"Yeah, I do. I figure one day these guys are going to pull their heads out of their asses and earn their pay," Josh said, taking a gulp from his bottle.

"You need to pick a better team," Matt told him.

"Nah," Josh shook his head, "I like the underdogs."

They watched the game, and Josh suffered each time the other team scored. Matt rubbed it in with every painful groan Josh uttered.

"So?" Josh asked, sitting up straight, his voice light. "Have you talked to Simone since lunch? Did she ask about me?"

Matt grunted, instantly irritated. "No. Why would she?"

"Oh yeah?" Josh smiled at Matt. "I thought for sure she wouldn't be able to resist my charms."

Matt snorted. "Ooh no, she couldn't possibly resist your charms."

"Women love me," Josh said, taking a swig of his beer. "Simone sure is a fine looking woman."

"She's absolutely beautiful." The words left Matt's mouth before he thought about them. He frowned, keeping his eyes on the television.

"I wonder if she's seeing someone," Josh asked.

Matt looked at him.

"Yes, she is," he snapped quickly.

"Well if she wasn't, I would definitely ask her out."

"Aren't you seeing someone?" Matt asked, surprised at the sudden anger he felt.

"She's just a friend."

"A friend that you sleep with?"

"Hey," Josh laughed, "they're the best kind."

Matt shook his head. "Simone's not like that."

"Yeah, what's she like?" Josh asked, glancing at his friend.

"She sweet and sensitive. Nothing like the women you go out with."

"Ouch." Josh grabbed his chest. "Damn man, that hurt."

"Come on, you know what I mean. She's intelligent. She's innocent with a beautiful heart. Not like the women you go for. You like 'em with big breasts and small brains."

Josh laughed. "Not all the time. That girl, what was her name? You know, the dancer..."

"Sable?" Matt said.

"Yeah, Sable. Now, she was fine," Josh grinned, holding his hands in front of his chest as if he had large breasts aiming them at Matt. "She was pretty smart."

Matt shook his head and laughed. "Yeah, she sure was, especially when she wanted to bet me $50 that Canada was in North America."

Josh laughed, remembering the look of determination on the

woman's face as she challenged Matt. "Yeah, that was funny wasn't it?"

"Yeah, hilarious," Matt said, shaking his head. "Well anyway, Simone's not like that."

"If she wasn't seeing anyone, would you have a problem with me asking her out? I mean, I won't if you have a thing for her?" Josh asked, peeking at Matt.

Using his thumb and index finger, Matt pinched the bridge of his nose.

"Josh?"

"You want me to stop talking?" Josh teased.

"How can you tell?"

"Lucky guess." Josh was silent for a moment. He smiled to himself and said, "But you know, if you did have a thing for her..."

The ringing of Matt's cell phone gave him a reprieve from Josh's questioning about Simone. He quickly answered it.

"Hello," Matt said into the phone.

"Hey what'cha doing?"

"Ah... nothing?" he said, trying to recognize the voice of the caller.

"I just wanted to call and say thank you."

"Excuse me?"

"Thank you for being my friend."

"Simone?"

"What?" she shouted.

"Are you all right?"

"Yes, I'm fine. How are you?" she said, her voice slurred.

"Have you been drinking?"

"Yeah, how'd ya know dat?"

He sighed, laughing at her. "I don't know, um, lucky guess. Where are you?"

"Um?"

He heard rustling on the phone, and over the music he heard her say, "Hey, where am I?" He heard someone talking to her, then she spoke into the phone, "I'm at Club Hollywood."

"Who's with you?" he questioned.

"I'm with a whole lot of people."

He heard rustling again, and another voice talking to Simone, "I'm Kevin. What's your name, pretty lady?"

"I'm Simone. I'm talking to my friend Matt right now. He just wanted to know your name."

"Oh, geez," Matt whispered, covering his eyes with his left hand, then looking over at Josh. "I have to go, sorry," he said to Josh as he got up from the chair.

"What about the game?" Josh asked, waving his hand in the direction of the television and looking confused.

"Sorry, man, gotta go," Matt said to Josh as he walked toward the door.

Then, into the phone Matt said, "Simone, is there anyone with you that you don't have to ask their names?"

"Sure there is," she answered quickly.

"Can you tell me who?"

"Of course I can."

He waited a moment for her answer, and when it didn't come he asked, "Well?"

"Well what?" she said.

He walked down the sidewalk to his truck, getting in and starting it in record time. "I want you to do me a favor. Can you do something for me?" he spoke softly.

"I guess so," she said slowly, mocking him.

"I want you to find a chair and sit there and wait for me. And I don't want you to talk to anyone until I get there."

"Why?"

"I just want you to do that for me. Can you do that?"

"Okay," she said, so loud that he had to move the phone from his ear.

"I'll be there soon." Hanging up, he dropped the phone on the seat next to him.

Chapter 8

Adrian Hirsch brushed his blond, wavy hair from his face. His steel-gray eyes were cold and observant as he scanned the bar while talking to the the only person that he had ever called a friend. Adrian didn't have any friends. He didn't have any family. And he liked it that way. In his eyes families were leaches, always wanting something, sometimes physical or sometimes emotional, and he didn't want to be bothered.

Most people found him frightening, especially men. Women thought he was very attractive, but the ones who had the ounce of courage to come near him were usually the women who wanted bad boys — real bad boys.

Jamison and Adrian had met in this very bar more than four years ago. Although Adrian couldn't remember what they talked about, he found that he could tolerate the other man. Maybe it was that Jamison, like himself, seemed to be on the outside looking in. Or maybe it was that fact that Adrian didn't get the feeling that Jamison was going to shit himself when Adrian so much as looked at him.

Jamison sat at the bar next to Adrian, hunched over an Absolut on the rocks. He was fuming over Wendy's decision to go out with her friends. He had planned a romantic dinner for the two of them. He'd had his housekeeper set the dining room table elegantly and put candles around the room that he'd scattered with dozens of yellow roses, Wendy's favorite. He had arranged for the chef from her favorite restaurant to come to the house and cater a special dinner for two.

But then she had called and said that her friends had "surprised" her with tickets to 13 Rue de l'Amour and "would he mind terribly" if she stayed at Gail's house tonight? She would be home in the morning.

Jamison hadn't told her that he had had a special night

planned; he had been too pissed off. If he had told her, she would have come home. She would not have had to pretend that she was with her friends when she was really with that asshole Matt Turner. He would have known the truth and he would have ended up killing her. He took a large swallow from his glass and signaled to the bartender to get him another drink.

Jamison looked around the bar and watched as a gorgeous redhead walked past them. Leaning close to Adrian she whispered, "You have beautiful eyes."

Adrian's head turned slightly, glancing at her as she passed him. He reached out quickly, grabbed her arm and pulled her toward him as he stood up. Letting his nose brush her hair, he held her tighter asking, "Wanna fuck?"

She pushed away from his chest and stepped back with a look of total shock on her round face. "What?"

"Wanna fuck?" Adrian repeated, smiling wickedly at her. "We can go to my truck; it's parked out back."

In the cramped bar there wasn't much room for her to maneuver, but she stepped back a few inches from Adrian and looked him over from head to toe.

"Is that how you talk to women? You need a little help with your pickup line."

Adrian grabbed the back of her head and pulling her to him again kissed her hard. He drew back, leaving her slightly breathless. Then bringing his lips close to hers he said, "If you aren't gonna fuck me, you need to scurry your little ass back to where you came from." He pulled her close, allowing her thigh to brush against his engorged manhood.

She gasped then glanced down.

"Well?" he demanded, his voice drawing her eyes back to his. She bit her lip and looked back at her friends sitting a few tables away. She licked her lips again as Adrian shoved her away, turning back to the bar.

Jamison watched the entire exchange in amazement. This had not been the first time he had witnessed this sort of thing with

Adrian. In fact, it happened quite often, but it still amazed him nonetheless.

The woman stepped close to Adrian and whispered in his ear.

He nodded and spoke without looking at Jamison or the female standing next to him, "Hey man, I'll be back. Save my seat." He walked toward the door with the short redhead following him.

Jamison shook his head. How can a psycho like Adrian have women throwing their panties at him left and right, and he couldn't even get the one woman he loved to stop thinking about another man?

• • •

Twenty minutes later Matt pulled in front of the night club, double-parking his truck.

He got out of the truck and walked inside, looking through the crowd until he spotted Simone sitting at a corner table alone. Her chin was resting on her hands and her eyes were closed.

He wove his way through the crowd and sat in the seat next to her.

"Hey," she said, smiling at him.

"Hey yourself. What are you doing here?"

"Just hanging out," she said, spreading her arms wide.

"I think I need to take you home."

"I'm here with Karen," she said, her eyes glassy.

"Do you know where she is?" Matt asked.

"Nope," she said, shaking her head.

"Hello?" Matt turned in his seat to meet the gaze of a slim, brown-skinned woman standing with her hands placed firmly on her hips.

"Hi. Karen?" he asked, rising from his seat. She nodded. "I'm Matt, a friend of Simone's."

"Oooh, hi," she grinned as she reached for his extended hand. "Simone's told me about you." She looked at her friend shaking her head. "I think she had one Long Island Iced Tea too many."

Matt looked down at Simone. "Yes, I believe she has."

"I was just going to take her home. I've been trying to convince my sister that it was time to leave," Karen said, rolling her eyes.

"I can take Simone home if you like," Matt said, still watching Simone.

Karen looked at Simone and then at the dance floor where she saw her sister slow-dancing with some guy she had just met. She turned back to Simone.

"I don't know? It's a little hard for me to handle both of them. But..."

"I definitely understand your concern. You don't know me from Adam — but you said Simone has mentioned me, and it does look like you'll have your hands full with your sister."

They both looked at the dance floor and watched Beverly's dance moves go from R-rated to X-rated in no time at all.

Karen's mouth dropped open as she groaned.

"I promise I'll make sure she gets home safely," Matt said, gently brushing Simone's hair from her forehead.

The action didn't go unnoticed by Karen. She looked closely at him, then nodded.

"Okay, but tell Simone I'll call her in the morning."

"Will do," he said, leaning over and coaxing Simone to stand with him. "Come on, angel, time to go home," he said, his tone soothing.

Karen watched as Matt led Simone outside. "Angel?" she said, smiling to herself.

Chapter 9

"Angel, I need you to stand there," Matt said to Simone, propping her against the door of her home.

"You never called me that before. I like it. It makes me feel special," Simone said, her voice slurring slightly.

Matt looked down at her smiling face as she beamed up at him like a child.

"Do you have your keys?" Matt asked.

"Um-hm," she nodded, shaking her purse in front of her.

He chuckled as he took her purse and searched inside for the keys. Opening the door, he picked her up and carried her inside.

"You're so strong," she said, holding him tightly around the neck.

"Oh yeah?"

"Mm-hm," she smiled up at him, her eyes shining like green marbles. He set her on the sofa.

"I think we need to get you to bed."

"Nope, I can get myself to bed," Simone said, and then, standing abruptly she took a step forward and fell over the small coffee table.

"Whoa," she said, as she hit the floor with a thud. "Who put that there?" She scrambled to her knees as quickly as someone in her condition could scramble.

Matt laughed, bending over and helping her up.

"I have no idea. Come on," he said, walking her down the hall to her bedroom.

"Hey." She spun around to face him. "You've never seen my bedroom before, have you?" she slurred.

"No, I haven't," he said, turning her back toward the bedroom and holding her steady as she walked.

"Well," she said as she stepped through the doorway, "this is

my haven." She spread her arms. "My hideaway," she continued as she threw her head back, unbalancing the rest of her body. "Whoa," she said, as she fell back into Matt's arms.

"Easy," he said, picking her up. He took a few steps and sat her on the foot of the bed. Then, walking to the head of the bed, he pulled the quilt and sheets back.

"Life sucks," she said, staring into space.

"Now, what would make you say that?" He walked in front of her, squatted down and unfastened her sandals.

"You wouldn't understand," she moaned.

"I don't know," he said, looking up at her. "Try me,"

She heaved a sigh, brushing her hair from her face. "The runaway home needs a ton of work and even with all the donations that we were able to accumulate, it won't be enough. After telling Robin that he needed a three thousand dollar deposit for electrical work, the electrician only did two hours' work and won't answer any of my phone calls...one of my co-workers just decided she wanted to take her vacation this coming week without notice...we're supposed to be having a community fair at the center...I haven't even begun to plan things...I hate my boyfriend...and my mother hates me," Simone said, barely taking a breath.

Matt looked up at her.

"Mother's always disappointed in me," Simone continued, staring across the room. "She's always complaining about something — 'Simone why do you work with those delinquents'...'Simone you need to lose weight'...'Simone why don't you have a husband?' I don't have a husband because I don't want one, lady," she said, shaking her finger at whatever imaginary person she was talking to.

Matt stood and helped her walk to the head of the bed.

"The next time that lady gives me a hard time, I'm going to tell her I don't want...damn you're really cute," she said changing from one topic to the next.

Matt blinked and then smiled down at her.

"You really are. Did you know that?" she asked.

"Ah, no. I didn't. Thank you."

She sat up abruptly. "Sit down," she said, patting the bed next to her.

He did as she requested.

"You know what?"

"No. What?" he asked, shaking his head.

"I've always thought you were very handsome," she whispered, as if it was a secret for his ears only.

"Is that so?"

"Yep, I would never tell you that though because I'm sure it would go to your head."

"I don't think so," he said, keeping his voice low.

She puckered her lips as she looked at him. Then she leaned forward, pressing her lips against his. "Mmm," she whispered, once she drew back. "Your lips are so soft and warm. When Alan kisses me it's kind of wet and mushy like kissing a fish." She made a fish lip face as she spoke, and Matt laughed.

"You have nice lips," she said, bringing her right hand up and running her fingers across the outline of his lips.

"Oh my god," she groaned, covering her mouth quickly.

"What? Oh boy, here we go," Matt said, helping her get to her feet.

She rushed in to the bathroom, kneeled in front of the toilet and threw up.

He squatted next to her and gathered her hair in one hand.

Once she emptied the contents of her stomach, she slid down to rest her forehead against the cool marble floor.

Matt opened the linen closet and removed a wash cloth. Wetting it, he went to Simone to wipe her face and rest the towel on the back of her neck.

"C'mon, honey, let's get you back to bed," he whispered, trying to help her sit up.

"Nooo, I think I'll just stay here," she mumbled, bringing her knees to her chest, lying in the fetal position, and then she groaned. "Oh god, I think I'm dying,"

"No, you're just a little sick. Tomorrow morning is when you're really going to think you're dying." He slid his arms behind

her back and under her legs, gently lifting her and taking her back to bed. Laying her down, he pulled the sheets up to her neck.

He sat on the side of the bed until he heard her breathing pattern change. He watched her as she slept, admiring her long, thick lashes and perfectly shaped lips that he was sure most women would kill for. Even in a drunken stupor she was beautiful. He brushed away a tumble of hair from her face as he let his fingers trace her jaw.

"Things must be pretty tough if you have to drink to chase away your problems," he sighed heavily. "Good night, angel," he said, kissing her brow and then leaving the bedroom.

Taking off his shoes, Matt stretched out on the sofa. He thought about Simone in the next room. They had spent quite a bit of time together since he had left the hospital and he felt a building desire for her that he tried to ignore. The desire to taste deeply of what he knew to be the most perfect and probably the sweetest lips ever. The need hold her sexy body close to his. Then he would always remind himself that what he shared with Simone was friendship, nothing more, and that he felt a bond with her because she was there for him when he was in need. Besides, she was in a relationship with Alan. Even though he didn't like the man, he would never do to another man what had been done to him.

• • •

"Morning," Matt whispered, entering the bedroom.

Simone popped up into a sitting position, looking around, confused.

"How are you feeling?" Matt asked, keeping his voice as low as possible.

"Why are you shouting?" she asked, pulling a pillow over her face.

"I'm not shouting."

"And why is the sun so — bright?" she complained.

He laughed and she lifted the pillow, giving him a confused look.

"What are you doing here?"

"You don't remember?" he asked

"No," she said.

He smiled wickedly at her.

"I saw a side of you last night that I'm sure most people have never seen."

"Oh...my God," she said, looking under the covers at herself and seeing that she wore the same clothes she had on the night before.

He laughed again shaking his head.

"Don't worry, you were safe. I like my women coherent."

She glared angrily at him, repeating her question.

"What are you doing here?"

"You called me from the club last night. I came to pick you up and brought you home," he said, looking down at her as she racked her brain trying to remember the night before.

"How's your head?" he asked.

"It's good," she said, trying to sit up. "Ohh," she moaned in agony, flopping back on the bed and pulling the pillow over her face again. "Oh, my head," she cried. "What in the world happened to me? Was I in an accident?"

"No, you just had a little too much to drink," Matt said.

"No, this can't be from drinking. If I wasn't in an accident, I must have a tumor or something."

"No, angel, just a hangover."

She peeked out from under the pillow at him.

"Here, drink this," Matt said, holding a glass with something resembling blood in it.

"What is it?"

"Don't worry about what it is. Just drink up."

She sat up reaching for the glass and took a gulp.

"Yuck, tastes like horse urine."

"Now how would you know what horse urine tastes like?"

She smirked at him and drank the remainder of the concoction. A few minutes later she ran in the bathroom and threw up again.

He smiled, looking inside the glass. "That did the trick."

Simone stepped out of the shower. She reached for a towel, dried herself, and used her favorite jasmine-vanilla body cream. She walked into her bedroom where she selected a tangerine-colored tank top and dark blue sweatpants from her dresser. After dressing, she brushed her hair, leaving it to hang loose down her back. She reached for a button-down shirt, slipped it on, and stopped to examine at herself in the mirror.

When Simone had started going through puberty, her mother noticed that Simone was becoming very shapely. By the time she was 13, Simone was a 32C, and Debra insisted that her daughter wear a blouse over anything form-fitting. She had told Simone that she shouldn't draw attention to herself because boys would think that she desired their attention even when she didn't, and that in the long run it could cause all sorts of problems.

Tilting her head slightly she studied herself a little longer and removed the blouse, laying it on the bed before heading to the kitchen.

"How are you feeling?" Matt asked, glancing at Simone as she entered the kitchen.

"Much better, thanks." Simone walked up next to him and looked at the food in the frying pan. "I hope that's not for me," she said, shaking her head.

"Yep."

"I'm not very hungry," she said, grimacing at the food.

"You need something on your stomach," he said, putting the food on two plates. "Come on," he ordered, setting the plates on the table. She saw that he had the table set with orange juice, coffee and fruit salad.

She took a seat opposite him and picked up the fork. She looked at the plate, then at him.

"Spanish omelet," he said, nodding.

She tried a small piece, smiling.

"How is it?"

"It's good," she said, then dug in.

He watched her as she ate. Then, picking up his fork, he

started eating. Glancing at her, he said, "You look pretty with your hair down. You should wear it like that more often."

She instinctively ran her hand through her hair, trying to focus on her food.

"Are you okay?" he asked.

"Sure, I feel much better than I did earlier," she said, still concentrating on her food.

Matt set his fork down.

"Is there anything bothering you, maybe something going on at work that I can help you with?"

Simone looked at him.

"I'm a good listener if you just want to talk."

"No," she said hesitantly.

"You said a few things to the contrary last night," Matt said, looking earnestly at her.

Simone sat straight in her chair not meeting his gaze.

"What did I say?"

"You said that you were having a problem with an electrician that you hired."

"Yeah," she brushed her hair from her face, happy that she hadn't said anything embarrassing.

"Have you tried contacting the Electrical Board?"

She bit her lip as she shook her head.

"I didn't want to do that just yet. I wanted to give him a chance."

"How long has it been?"

"A few weeks."

Matt nodded. "Give me this guy's number. Let me call him and talk to him. If we don't get results, we'll go to the Electrical Board then."

Simone smiled at him, relieved. "Thanks," she said.

Matt rested his elbow on the table and with his chin on his fist said, "I've been doing some thinking about the house that the two of you purchased for runaways."

He glanced at Simone, and she nodded, her eyes on him.

"Well, I'm sure that a couple of my friends wouldn't mind lending a hand and helping out on a few Saturdays."

"Really?" Simone asked, her spirits lifting.

"They're really good guys. I'm sure they would help."

"You would do that," Simone asked, meeting his gaze.

"Sure."

"Thank you," she said, smiling at him with such candor and joy that his heart fluttered and danced in the delight of knowing that he had put that smile on her face.

Matt let out a quiet, slow breath, forcing his heart to slow down before he spoke.

"What about this person who is taking off next week. Is there any way I can help you?"

"We're stretched pretty thin as it is, but there's nothing anyone can do. I'll just have to cover for her until she gets back."

"That doesn't sound fair to you."

"I'll manage," she said casually.

"Aren't you guys supposed to give a notice or request time off in advance?"

"Yes, we usually have to, but she said it was some trip that her boyfriend had won and that he had to take it now or he'd lose it. And I didn't have the heart to tell her that she couldn't go."

"Sounds to me like she's taking advantage of you."

"I don't think so. Sometimes things just can't be avoided," Simone said, with some of the omelet still in her mouth.

"You know what? You're too nice," Matt said.

"What is that supposed to mean?" She dropped her fork and folded her arms across her chest.

"Just what it sounds like." Matt was amused to see her riled up; it seemed so out of character for her.

"You can never be too nice," she said, feeling the need to defend herself.

"I thought that at one time, too. Now I know better."

"You are totally wrong," Simone said, shaking her head in disagreement.

"Hear me out," he said, holding up a hand. "When my ex-

wife and I were married, I would do anything for her. I've always wanted children, and Wendy told me she wanted a family, too.

"After our first year of marriage, she decided that she didn't want children. I thought, okay, as long as we have each other that was enough. She was a medical secretary and after a few years she wanted to leave her job to be a housewife. That was fine with me. Then she said that all her friends had housekeepers and that she thought we needed one too."

Matt shook his head as he spoke. "I knew we didn't need a housekeeper, but whatever she wanted, I made sure she got it. Later in the marriage, she started hanging out with her friends a few nights a week. My mother heard through the grapevine that she was having an affair. I didn't want to believe it, so I swept it under the rug. The tension built between her and my mother and it caused them to argue all the time. Eventually she told me that she had been having an affair, that it was just a fling, and she was sorry."

Simone watched him as the pain of those memories washed over his face.

"Is that when you got a divorce?" she asked.

"No," he said quickly, "I loved her so much that I forgave her. A few months later, I came home from work and found her packing. She told me that she still loved me, but she was attracted to this other man and she was going to stay with one of her girlfriends until she could sort out her feelings.

"I did everything I could to win her back. I took her to dinner and sent her flowers. Whatever I thought would make her happy. I handled the situation as if we were just starting a new relationship. I thought it would rekindle the love she had once felt for me."

He stopped to take a breath.

"Then a couple of months after she moved out, and she moved in with this other guy. It really hurt. Sometimes, she would come to the condo to see me. She would tell me that she was in love with two men and how hard that was for her. I know it's sad, but a small part of me still hoped that she would come back to me. Shortly after she moved in with him, she filed for divorce.

"I would have given her the world, even during the divorce proceedings." He looked at Simone. "I was foolish."

"No," Simone said softly, "you were in love."

Matt picked up the napkin in his lap, wiped his mouth with it and droped it on his plate.

"I guess I was a nice guy."

"Yeah." She smiled sadly at him. "I guess you were."

"I was nothing like you. You're sweet, kind, and caring. But — you're also gullible and naive."

"I am neither gullible nor naive," she said, trying to give her voice a hard edge and not quite pulling it off.

Matt rubbed his eyes. "Simone in the past two months, I've seen you give every bum who asks you a dollar. Babysit what I'm sure are probably three of the most evil kids that ever walked the face of the earth while the she-devil who bore them deceived you saying that she had to work, but instead went to ladies' night at a local bar.

"Oh, and let's not forget you picking up the pregnant homeless woman with the intention of taking her to the women's home for help only to have her steal all of your cash from your purse."

"Matt, things like that happen."

"Not to the same person and not that often. Simone, you want to believe almost everything everyone says. Especially, if they need help and they have a sad enough story."

"There's nothing wrong with wanting to help people," Simone said. She looked away from him, not wanting him to see the pain in her eyes. She thought that he of all people could accept and appreciate her desire to help others.

He ran his hand through his hair and then he took her hand.

"All the things you do, working at the center, volunteering at the soup kitchen, taking this troubled kid Mira under your wing — every selfless thing you do is awesome. But the point I'm trying to make is that this woman taking off without notice and every bum that asks you for money may not be worthy of your concern."

He looked deep into her eyes. Butterflies danced in his stom-

ach. He wanted to take her in his arms and shelter his sweet angel forever. He took a deep breath, blowing it out slowly.

"You know what? The world would be a much better place if people had an ounce of the compassion that you have. And I hope you never change."

She swallowed hard, fighting the tears that were just under the surface.

"I'd better go," he said, sliding the chair back and standing up.

"Matt, can I ask you something?"

"Sure."

"When you said that you saw a side of me that not many people see, what did you mean?"

Matt grinned. "I had the pleasure of witnessing you barf."

"Oh my gosh," she covered her face, embarrassed. "I'm so sorry!"

"Don't worry about it. I've seen a lot worse."

She looked at him, smiling sadly. "Can I ask you something else?"

He leaned on the back of the chair looking down at her. "Anything."

She bit her lip, looking away before she asked the question. "Did I say anything else last night?"

Matt studied her for a moment and he shook his head. "No, you didn't say anything else."

She nodded, satisfied with his answer. "Thanks for everything," she said, looking up at him.

"It was my pleasure." He bent down and kissed the top of her head. "Have a good day, Angel."

Chapter 10

"Morning," Matt said as he walked into his parent's kitchen.

"Well, good morning to you, too," Rebecca said as she smiled. As always, she was happy to see her son.

He walked to the table, grabbing one of the chairs and flipping it backwards as he sat down.

Marty walked into the kitchen and flicked a ringlet of Matt's shoulder-length hair with his index finger.

"What's going on with this?" Marty said, as he sat at the table.

"What?" Matt asked, glancing at his father.

"The hair?"

"Nothing."

"Well, you've been out of the hospital for a while now. Don't you think it's time to get a hair cut?"

"I'm thinking of keeping it this length for a while."

"I like it," Rebecca commented, as she reached out, running her fingers through Matt's hair. "I think it's very attractive."

Marty scowled, asking, "What are you going to do with long, curly hair? Are you trying to follow in your brother's footsteps?

"What? No, Pop, I just want to keep my hair long for a while. That's all."

"See, Becca," Marty said, shaking his head. "I told you. If you coddle them boys too much, this was gonna happen. See what you did? The next thing we know he'll be wearing hair barrettes and carrying a pocketbook." He grunted in disgust. "It was only a matter of time."

Rebecca saw the look on Matt's face and glanced at Marty, understanding it was best to change the subject.

"Matt," she quickly asked, patting the back of his hand, "what brings you over this early on a Saturday morning?"

"I'm meeting Simone here. I'm helping her with a project at work."

"What?" Marty said, nearly choking on his coffee and burning his lip. He quickly wiped the coffee from his mouth with his sleeve. "And you have her coming here?"

"Yeah," Matt said, taking a slice of bacon from the plate in the center of the table and shoving it into his mouth. "What's the problem?"

"You can't have those people coming to my house, boy. What's wrong with you? She'll be checking out the place and memorizing all of our valuables. That way she can tell her friends — have them come back here and burglarize us!"

"Oh yeah," Rebecca chuckled, with a hint of sarcasm. "With all of our great riches, she's bound to be overwhelmed."

Matt laughed at his mother.

"Ma, do you want me to hide the Monet."

"I wish you would. While you're at it, stash the Picasso somewhere, too."

"Oh, to hell with the both of you," Marty grunted angrily. "We have a lot of good stuff and people who aren't used to seeing nice things are gonna want them. That's all I'm saying."

He looked at Rebecca and pointed a beefy finger at her. "And don't you come crying to me when you see some porch monkey running down the street with one of those there humble things you got in that cabinet," he said, gesturing toward the china hutch in the dining room.

"It's Hummel, Pop — not humble," Matt said, knowing it made his father angry whenever someone corrected him.

"Shut up, smart-ass. I'm talking to your Mother."

"Marty, that will be enough," Rebecca stood, taking her purse that hung on the back of her chair.

"Sons a' bitches," he continued.

"I said that's enough," Rebecca said in finality. "I don't want you talking like that when Simone gets here." She looked down at

her husband. "I'm leaving for the market. If you're rude to Simone when she gets here, you're gonna be fixing your own supper today and tomorrow."

"Ah, go to hell woman," he mumbled, waving his hand at her.

Smiling, she said, "I'm glad we understand each other."

• • •

"Good morning, Mrs. Turner. How are you today?"

"I'm good, Simone. Just a little neck pain."

"Ohh," Simone said, concerned. "I'm sorry to hear that."

"Don't be. When I pull out of the driveway, I'm sure it will ease up," she said, smiling.

"I'm supposed to meet Matt here," Simone said.

"He told me. Where are you guys off to?"

"He has a few of his friends from work meeting us at the center to do some repairs for us."

"Well, Matt's in the kitchen," Rebecca said, gesturing toward the house. "With my pain in the neck, go on and let yourself in."

Simone laughed.

"If I don't see you when I get back, take care," Rebecca said.

"Yes ma'am. You do the same."

Simone climbed the steps and went into the small house. She walked toward the voices she heard coming from the back, prepared to call out but paused, listening for a moment.

"Boy, I don't know why that gal keeps hanging around. She seems like a real pain in the ass. I don't see how anyone can stand being around that dumb cow," Marty said.

"Come on, Pop — give it a rest."

"Well, she's not much to look at," Marty continued, "but I guess if you like them big ol' titties, she might be acceptable."

Backing from the door, she put her hand to her mouth, trying to still her tongue. She turned away quietly and walked down the hall. She eased the screen door open and walked out onto the front

porch. She walked to the steps, mechanically stepping down, and turned to look back at the door.

"How could I be so foolish?" she asked herself.

She had to get away from there. She needed to be alone. Then she thought about the kids at the center; they needed this and she was not going to let that jerk take it from them. She walked slowly to her car and got inside. Closing her eyes she took several calming breaths. She would just wait outside for him. She wanted to get her thoughts together before she saw him.

Matt watched his father as he tore open a five-pound bag of sugar, wasting half of it on the floor. He laughed at the look of surprise and anger on his father's face.

"Pop, I think Simone is beautiful and she's perfect."

"What the hell do you mean by perfect?" his father yelled.

"There's nothing wrong with her. She's fine the way she is. And I don't like you saying things like that about her."

"Boy, you don't need that sort of trouble," Marty turned, pouring the remaining sugar into a canister that sat on the counter. Stepping over the mound of sugar on the floor and innocently looking at Matt, he said, "I'll clean that up."

Sitting at the table across from Matt, Marty continued, "Anyhow, she probably just hangs around 'cause she thinks you have something and she wants it."

"That's not true," Matt said, shaking his head.

"And," Marty added, "she probably don't make much working at the place with them criminal kids."

"They're not criminals, Pop. They're just kids that need someone who cares."

"Yeah, whatever you say. She probably wants someone who makes more money than she does to take care of her, and your dumb ass fits the bill."

"Pop, Simone doesn't need money from me or anyone else. She is a very smart woman. If all she thought about was money, she could have a job making twice as much as she does now. It's not about the money Pop. Life means more to Simone than just material

things. It's about helping people and making life better. It's about being happy."

"Well if she could make twice what she makes and she isn't, then she can't be as smart as you think she is, now can she?" Marty said smugly.

Matt shook his head at Marty, realizing that his father didn't get anything he had just said. Pushing his chair back, he rose from his seat.

"I'm leaving now, Pop. See you later."

He walked through the house to the front door, wondering what was keeping Simone. When he opened the screen door, he saw her car sitting at the curb. He walked down the steps as she got out of the car and walked toward him.

"Hey, how long have you been here?"

"Not very long," she said, her tone flat.

"Are you ready to go?" he asked. She looked up the street, not wanting to meet his gaze, and then nodded.

"Would you rather I drive?" Matt asked.

She shook her head as she turned and headed back to her car.

Matt followed her around to the driver's side, opening the door for her.

When Simone looked at him, her glance was full of bitterness, and he was surprised.

"What's going on?" he asked.

"Nothing," she said, getting into the vehicle. He closed the door, watching her profile. Her jaw was clenched and her eyes were watery.

"Are you all right?"

"I'm fine. Let's just go, please."

• • •

Dipping the paint brush in the pale yellow paint, Simone slapped the brush against the side of the house. She hated doing such a mundane job and hoped that Matt would have given her something that she would have to concentrate on. That way she wouldn't have

time to think about the conversation she had overheard between Matt and his father. She didn't want to believe that Matt thought of her in that way as some unattractive pest.

"You need to go from side to side with that," Matt whispered from behind her. He grasped her hand that held the paint brush.

Heat moved through her, and she quickly moved her hand, leaving the brush in his. She didn't want to be touched by him. She didn't want to be near him.

He stooped, laying the brush on top of the paint can, and stood facing her. "One of the guys is going to get lunch. What would you like?"

"Nothing, thank you." Simone looked past him as she spoke.

"What did you have for breakfast?" he asked.

She remained quiet, looking past him.

"Well?"

"Grapefruit and toast."

"That's not enough to last you till dinner," he stated. "How about a roast beef sandwich?"

"No. Thank you," she said, still not looking at him.

"What's wrong with you? Are you not feeling well? You haven't said 10 words to me all day."

"There's nothing wrong with me. Not one thing," she retorted coldly, folding her arms across her breasts, feeling self-conscious. "I'm not hungry, but I will have a drink if you don't mind — something fruity."

Matt watched her, confused. He let his mind race back to the last time he saw her and tried to pinpoint what had happened that made her so angry with him. Turning, he walked back to where the men were working. He sent one of the guys that worked for him and one of the teens from the center to pick up lunch. Angry, he walked to his truck and sat inside.

When they settled down to eat lunch, Simone went inside, seeking solace in the small back room off the kitchen, just wanting this day to be over so she could go home and be done with Matt Turner. She wanted to put him out of her mind and out of her life.

Josh walked around the building and stopped next to Matt. "Dave and Isaac re-hung the doors on the bedrooms."

Matt nodded in acknowledgment.

Josh slid his hands in his pockets as he gazed around, then looked back at Matt. "And I finished putting that bathtub surround in the second bathroom upstairs."

"All right," Matt said, still working.

"So, what's up with you and Simone? Why is she mad at you?"

"She's not."

"Sure seemed like it to me. It doesn't seem like she wants to have anything to do with you."

"No, she's all right."

"I don't claim to know everything about women, but I know when one is pissed off at me."

"Isn't there something you need to be doing?" Matt asked through clenched teeth.

"Geez, don't get mad at me. I was just asking," Josh said, grinning as he held up his hands, backing away.

" 'I was just asking'," Matt said, his tone mocking Josh's. "Shut up," he said before returning his attention back to the wood trim that he was replacing on the back door.

While sitting on an empty paint bucket, Simone attempted to clean the yellow paint from the brush.

"Simone."

Hearing her name, Simone looked up to see her brother cut across the lot from the center to the house.

"Hey, Charles, how did you know I would be here?"

"Mother told me you were working today."

"Are you here to help?" she asked, a huge smile covering her face.

"You have the nerve to smile at me after what you've done?"

"What? I don't understand?"

"It wasn't enough that you told Tamara that I had an affair,

but you had to tell her that I'm going to be a father? What kind of sister are you?"

Everyone in the front yard stopped to see what the commotion was about.

"Charles," Simone whispered, looking at everyone gathering around. "Let's go inside and talk." She stepped close to him, touching his arm.

"No," he yelled, snatching his arm from her. "You want these people to think that you're someone you're not. Saint Simone. The person who never lies, never hurts anyone, and who never does anything wrong. Well, I have news for them. You're no saint and you were damn wrong."

Simone listened to him rant, so shocked at the things he was saying that she was unable to move or speak.

He stepped closer to her, yelling and pointing a finger in her face. "You stay away from me and you stay away from my wife." Turning, he stormed across the yard in the direction of his car.

"But?" Simone whispered, stunned and devastated, as she watched her brother walk away. *What in the world is going on? Is he losing his mind?* she wondered as she looked around and saw everyone in the yard watching her. She turned away, walked into the house, and went into the back office, closing the door behind her.

• • •

Matt rounded the house in time to see a tall, slim man yelling at Simone. A moment later Simone turned and fled into the house.

Tapping on the office door, Matt placed his ear against it, listening. The only thing he heard was the sound of pacing.

"Simone?" he called.

She didn't answer.

He called once again and when she didn't answer the second time he opened the door. He paused, seeing her pace back and forth in front the desk.

"Can I come in?" he asked, his voice low.

"What do you want?" Simone yelled at him.

"Are you okay?" He walked inside the office, closing the door behind him.

"I can't believe he would do something like that!" she said, addressing no one in particular. "What the hell is wrong with him?" She continued her harsh breathing.

Matt stepped in front of her, grabbed her around the waist, and stopped her from pacing. He pulled her close, allowing her head to rest against his chest, and gently stroked her back.

"It's all right. Calm down and take a deep breath. Breathe," he said, continuing to stroke her back.

She pushed him and moved away.

"Don't tell me how to breathe. I know how to breathe. What, do you think, I'm stupid?"

He looked at her and smiled. "No, I don't think that. Are you all right?"

"Why the hell do you keep asking me that?"

Matt's brows shot up; he'd never seen her angry.

"Do I look all right to you?" she asked, angrily swiping tears from her cheeks. "Well, do I?"

He looked at her paint splattered overalls and tank top, which both looked like she ended up with more paint on them than on the house. He grinned, saying, "You look good to me."

She sucked her teeth, angrily looking at him. "God you are such a jerk. I'm having a crisis here."

"I'm sorry. I know you are. Tell me what's going on and maybe I can help."

She sat on the edge of her desk, crossing her arms. She shook her head. "I don't know." She looked at Matt. "I honestly don't know. Charles has been so angry with me recently. He's been making remarks about his wife. Now he's accusing me of trying to ruin his marriage."

"Have you tried talking to him?"

"Yes, he won't take any of my calls at work and he doesn't answer his cell when I call him."

"Maybe you could call his wife. She might be able to shed some light on the situation."

"I don't know. If he learns that I spoke to her, it could make matters worse."

"How much worse can it get? I mean, he's just humiliated you in front of a dozen people."

"Thanks, that makes me feel better."

"I'm trying to help; what do you want me to do? I'll kick his ass if you want me to."

She looked at him, wiping her tears.

"I swear I will. Just say the word," Matt said, shaking his head as he spoke.

Simone grinned, walked to him, threw her arms around his neck and kissed his cheek.

"Thanks," she whispered, "you always know how to make me feel better."

"You're welcome," Matt whispered back, "but, I'll still kick his ass if you want."

Simone released him, playfully jabbing him in the ribs "I just bet you would."

• • •

Simone slowed her car, parking at the curb in front of the Turner's home. "Matt, thanks for everything you've done. On such a tight budget, I know we wouldn't have been able to afford to get all the work done."

"I was glad to help, and it made everyone feel good to help such a worthy cause." He paused a moment. "Now, do you think you can tell me what was going on earlier? Why were you so angry with me?"

He watched as Simone stiffened and glanced to her left out the driver side window.

"It's nothing really."

"Why don't you come in for a while? I'm sure Ma would love that," Matt asked, still watching her.

"No, I'd rather not. I'm very tired. And I would like to go home," she said, her voice close to a whisper.

He frowned, then a devilish smiled crossed his face. "Come on inside," he said, taking her keys out of the ignition.

"What are you doing?" she yelled, as he got out of the car, walking toward the house, then he turned back toward the vehicle.

"If you want to go home, you have to come in and get your keys." He walked up the sidewalk to the house.

Simone sat watching his back as the screen door closed behind him.

"I'm not going to let him manipulate me like this," she whispered to herself. "Nope, I'm just going to sit right here. When he realizes that I'm not going to give in, he's going to bring my keys back to me and I'll go home."

After 10 minutes, she looked at the house.

"Ugh," she yelled, frustrated. "I-can't–believe-this!" Getting out of the car, she slammed the door and walked up the sidewalk to the house.

Chapter 11

"Damn," Marty said when he saw Matt walking in the front door. "You back again?"

"Yeah," Matt said, glancing at his father.

"You were just here this morning. Don't you ever go home?" the older man complained. "You spend more time here now than you did when you lived here."

Rebecca smiled at her son. "Marty, he wants to spend time with his family. Leave him alone."

Matt stepped to the window, peeking out the curtain and watching Simone in her car. Leaning against the window frame, he folded his arms and waited.

"What the hell are you looking for? Boy, did you do something you don't have any business doing?" Marty asked suspiciously.

Matt ignored him, asking his mother, "Ma, would you mind if we stay for dinner."

"Hell yeah, we mind," his father yelled. "Wait a minute, what do you mean by *we*?"

"Marty, be quiet," Rebecca said. "Of course not, you don't have to ask that. This is your home."

"No it's not and he's wearing out his damn welcome," Marty mumbled.

"Don't get your drawers in a bunch, old man. I'm not here to see you," Matt said, smiling as he watched Simone get out of the car with her anger visibly showing. Matt quickly turned from the window.

"Thanks, Ma," he said, before walking down the hall toward the kitchen.

Simone took the steps two at a time and stopped at the door. She took a deep breath to calm herself before knocking on the wood

of the screen door. After hearing Rebecca Turner invite her inside, she opened the door and walked into the house.

"Good evening, Mrs. Turner."

"Hi, Simone."

"Hello, Mr. Turner," she said looking at Marty.

She studied the man sitting in his easy chair, trying hard to pretend that she was not there.

"Are you this rude to everyone or is it just me?" she asked him.

He frowned then pursed his lips.

"It's just you," he answered, not looking up.

Rebecca rose from the sofa, embarrassed, and gently taking Simone's arm she led her in the direction of the kitchen saying, "Don't let him fool you. He's this rude to everyone. I just made a cherry pie. Would you like a slice?" she offered as they entered the kitchen.

"No, thank you," Simone answered.

"Go on and make yourself comfortable," Rebecca told her and looked at Matt.

"Matt, your father said that you wasted a half-bag of sugar in the middle of the floor and left it for me to clean it up."

"I didn't do that. Pop did," Matt said, walking to the counter. She nodded.

"I'll be back," she said, leaving the kitchen.

Matt took the plastic wrap off the pie and cut two very thin slices. He looked at Simone standing next to the table with her hands on her hips, glaring angrily at him.

"Have a seat," he commanded, gesturing toward the table.

She glared up at him and folded her arms tightly under her breasts.

Matt glanced down at her cleavage and grinned. She looked down, quickly dropping her arms.

"May I have my keys, please?"

"Not until you sit down," he said, turning back to the counter, busying himself with his task.

She frowned at him and snatched the chair away from the table to sit down.

He put the pie on the two plates and went to the table, placing one plate in front of her. He went to the refrigerator, took out the milk and poured them each a glass.

"Eat," he commanded, sitting across from her.

"Why do you have to be so mean to her?" Rebecca whispered, stepping in front of the television.

"Hey, I can't see. Get out of the way," Marty said, leaning around her.

"Marty, you heard me," she said, keeping her voice low. "Why do you treat Simone that way?"

" 'Cause I don't like the way things are starting to look."

"What's that supposed to mean?"

"It means, have you seen the way our boy looks at her? Like she's the second coming or something."

"So, what's wrong with that? She's a pretty girl. She's nice and he likes her?"

"Nice for her own kind. I'm gonna put a stop to this," Marty said, leaning in the other direction trying to see the television.

"Matt's a grown man and he won't like you in his business." Rebecca said.

"Ah," he swatted at her as if she were a fly bothering him, saying, "I know what I'm doing."

• • •

"I see you changed your mind about the pie," Rebecca said with a smile.

"Yes," Simone said, looking at Matt.

"How was it?" she asked proudly.

"It was very good. Thank you," Simone answered.

"If you like, I'll cut you a piece to take with you?"

"No, I don't want to impose," Simone said.

"It's no imposition. I like knowing people enjoy my cooking."

"Ma," Matt said, standing, "I'm going to take Simone out and show her your garden."

"That's a good idea," Rebecca said, stepping closer to the counter and reaching into one of the overhead cabinets.

"Here," she said, giving Matt a small vase and pruning shears. "Cut her some flowers to take home. The carnations are doing really well this year," she said proudly.

Matt took the vase and walked out the door. Simone sat in her seat for a moment before she followed him.

Matt walked across the yard, his long legs reaching the stone patio surrounded by flowerbeds before Simone could.

"Come on, Matt, this game is growing old now. I want my keys," she said sternly.

"Nope, I'm not giving them to you until you tell me why you were angry with me."

He cut a pink rose and turning to her, he put it in her hair. "A pretty flower for a pretty lady."

"You are such a hypocrite," she yelled, pushing him. He drew back, looking at her in disbelief. "You can't think I'm pretty. I'm repulsive," she said, moving away from him.

"What are you talking about?" he asked, confused.

"I heard you and your father talking about how much of a dumb cow I am. What was it he said? 'How can anyone stand being around that dumb cow, but I guess if you like big tits she might be okay,' " she said, trying to impersonate Marty.

"How can someone so smart think something so dumb?" Matt asked, stepping closer to her.

Her eyes grew large with the shock of his comment sending her into momentary silence.

She gritted her teeth, "How dare you speak to me like that?"

"Shut up," Matt said, his voice still calm.

"You pig."

"No," he said, holding up his hand and shaking his head quickly. "Listen to me, please, before we say things we don't mean." He watched her taking deep breaths trying to control herself and

giving him time to speak. "If you would have eavesdropped a little longer..."

"I wasn't eavesdropping," she said defensively.

He held up his hand again, silencing her.

"If you had listened a little longer, then you would have heard me say that I thought you were perfect the way you are."

She looked around nervously.

"Perfect?" she asked.

"Yes," he nodded.

"Not a dumb cow?"

"Not hardly." He stepped closer, stroking her cheek. "You're absolutely perfect the way you are. I wouldn't change a thing about you."

She closed her eyes, enjoying the gentle touch of his fingers and the rugged scent of his hand.

"I wasn't eavesdropping," she whispered.

"Yes, you were. But I forgive you."

She opened her eyes to find him watching her. He watched her intently, desire growing in his dark eyes. She swallowed hard, backing up and looking in the direction of the garden.

"The carnations are beautiful," she stuttered.

Matt stepped closer.

"Nothing is as beautiful as you are."

"Hey, what the hell are you doing out there?" Marty bellowed from the back door.

Matt looked at his father and turned back to Simone. "I want you to stay for dinner."

"No, your father doesn't want me here."

"He doesn't want me here either. You don't see me going anywhere do you?"

She shifted her weight from one foot to the other. "Matt, give me my keys."

"Are you going to stay for dinner?" he asked.

She looked up at him, not answering.

"Then I'm not going to give you the keys."

"Why do you always do this?" she asked.

"Do what?"

"You always do things that you know are going to make me angry."

He frowned thoughtfully and shook his head. "I don't know. But I'm still not giving you the keys."

She looked at the sky, her fists balled tight, she shook slightly. It took every ounce of strength she had not to strangle him.

"You are infuriating," she screamed. "I honestly don't see how you've made it this far in life without someone choking the hell out of you."

He grinned, licking his lips. "It's cute. Isn't it? Tell the truth — you think it's cute?"

She shook with anger and turned around, storming across the yard toward the house yelling, "Ass!" over her shoulder.

"Damn, I love it when you talk dirty to me," he grinned, following her across the yard.

• • •

"I'd rather eat in front of the TV."

"No, we're eating at the dining room table," Rebecca announced. "We have a guest."

"They're not guests, they're freeloaders. You need to put everything in a paper bag. To go," Marty huffed.

"Why don't you go upstairs and change your shirt? Maybe comb your hair?"

"No. There is nothing wrong with my shirt. This is my house and if I want to eat my supper in my skivvies, I'm going to. And if others don't like it, they can just go on home."

"Marty, stop! I like having a guest for dinner and you need to mind your manners."

"There isn't anything wrong with my manners either," he said, pulling a chair from the table, flopping down, and folding his arms across his wide chest.

When everyone settled around the dinning room table, Matt, Simone and Rebecca talked among themselves. Every so often Simone would ask Marty a question or make a comment to draw him

into the conversation. But Marty would only grumble his answer and focus harder on his dinner.

After dinner Matt went to the hall closet, took out the Scrabble game, and proceeded to set it up on the dining table. "We're playing Scrabble, Pop. Do you want to play?"

"No," Marty barked from in front of the television set.

Matt and Simone sat at the table, leaving a space for Rebecca.

Matt looked at his father and whispered to Simone, "He's going to play. He can't sit there, knowing we're playing Scrabble and not join in. It will eat him alive."

Rebecca walked into the dining room carrying a tray with cookies and hot tea. She set down the tray and took her seat looking at her tiles.

Marty got up from his seat, walked to the table, and took a sugar cookie.

"Why didn't you make oatmeal cookies, woman?" he grumbled.

"Marty, hush, I'm trying to think," she said, trying to ignore her husband.

He leaned over looking at her tiles.

"There's a word right there."

"I don't want to use that one. Not enough points."

"Well you have to start somewhere," he moaned.

"I thought you said you didn't want to play," she said, shooing him away.

"I'm trying to help you, but if you're going to play like that, I might as well join the game. It won't take long to whip you," Marty said, walking around the table to grab a rack and some tiles before sitting down.

Laying out all seven of his tiles, Marty rubbed his hands together and looked around the table proudly at the curious faces. "That's 11 points, a double word score, making 22 points for me,"

Matt looked at the board, then at his father.

"What in the world is a 'didgaeat'? That is not a real word."

"Yeah, it is," Marty challenged.

Rebecca started giggling, knowing what was to come.

"What does it mean?"

"Did ga eat? Didgaeat."

"Pop, that's not one word."

"Yes it is. If you say it real fast."

"No one talks like that," Matt shook his head, reaching for the tiles.

Marty grabbed Matt's wrist, stopping him.

"Yes they do. When me and your ma went to your Aunt Helen's in Pennsylvania, she made dinner and asked us, 'Didgaeat?' I didn't know what she said at first, but when she said it slow it made sense. Did ga eat? If you say it fast like she does it's didgaeat?"

"Oh no, that's not going to work," Matt shook his head. "You have to make another word."

"This is my house and I can make the rules if I want," Marty said smugly.

Matt looked at his mother, and she just hunched her shoulders, turning to Simone.

"Okay, Simone, it's your turn."

Simone put her letters down using Marty's "E" and spelling out the word "zoomies."

She looked at Matt, winking, and said, "Eighteen points with a double word score, that's 36 points."

"Wait a damn minute," Marty shouted. "What the hell is that?"

"My uncle is in the Air Force, and they call the pilots Zoomies."

"That's not true." Marty shook his head vigorously. "Is that even in the dictionary?"

"I'm sure it is," Matt added casually. "It's probably in the same one that has didgaeat in it."

"You're a real funny one, huh, chuckles?" Marty said, rising from his seat and heading for the kitchen, "but don't quit your day job."

Matt gathered the game pieces while Rebecca showed Simone her collection of Hummels. She explained the history saying

that Hummels were made by a German artist Sister Maria Innocentia Hummel and Master Artist Goebel Porzellanfanbrik. Of the three shelves, the top shelf held Hummels depicting different holidays and seasons. Rebecca pointed out different ones and informed Simone when she had received each one.

She told Simone that when she started collecting them they were reasonably priced and that she still loved to shop for them even though she couldn't afford to buy them anymore.

On the bottom shelf was a collection of Snowbabies. These were newer additions as they were less expensive. She said she purchased new Snowbabies from time to time.

The center shelf held items that her children had made over the years.

Simone spotted a roughly made cup painted red with a yellow handle and the letters M.A.T. painted in blue on the front.

"Did Matt make that?" Simone asked Rebecca.

"Yes, M.A.T, Mathew Archibald Turner," Rebecca exclaimed.

Matt flinched at hearing his mother call his middle name.

"Archibald?" Simone said, smiling as she looked at Matt.

"Don't ask," Matt said, glancing at her. He looked at his mother.

"Gee, Ma, why don't you just break out the photos of my naked butt?"

She looked at Simone, laughing. "Would you like to see them?"

"Great." He laughed, shaking his head and rising from the chair. As he headed for the kitchen he said, "I'm getting a drink. Can I bring you something?"

"Sure Archie," Simone said, smiling and wiggling her brows.

"Hey, lady, don't even try it," he said, laughing as he walked into the kitchen.

"Why is she still here? You asked her to stay for supper, and we're done. It's time for her to go."

"She's a guest, Pop."

"Not mine," Marty said. "I suggest she best be getting on her way because Wendy will be here soon," he said, looking at Matt.

"Why would Wendy be coming here?" Matt asked.

Marty turned away before speaking.

"Because I invited her."

"What the hell for?" Matt demanded.

"So you two could spend some time together. That's the only way you're ever going to settle things between you."

"Pop, I seem to remember you suggesting that it was best that Wendy and I not be together."

"Maybe I was wrong. Maybe I've had a change of heart."

"And would that change of heart have anything to do with Simone's race."

Marty glared at his son and grunted, "That gal should be on her way because Wendy will be here soon."

"Pop, I can't believe you would do this," Matt said, walking through the door into the living room. He stopped, seeing his ex-wife introducing herself to Simone. Matt walked farther into the living room.

"Wendy, how are you?" he asked cordially.

"I'm fine," Wendy said, smiling at Matt.

Simone shifted her feet, suddenly uncomfortable.

"Wendy, it was very nice meeting you. Thank you for dinner Mrs. Turner," Simone said, and turned to Matt. "Would you mind walking me out?"

"Sure." He followed Simone out the door. Once they reached her car, Simone turned to him.

"Keys, please," she said, stretching out her hand. He slid his hand in his front pocket and pulled out her keys.

"Are we still friends?" he asked.

"Of course. Sometimes you get on my nerves, but I still like you." She looked up at the house, then back at him.

"You should probably get back inside. Good night," she said before getting into the car.

"'Night," Matt said, watching her car pull from the curb. Shoving his hands deeper in his pockets, he turned, looking at the

house. He had half a notion to leave without saying a word, but he didn't want to leave and not say anything to Wendy. He believed that she didn't know what was happening. She was just a pawn in his father's game.

Chapter 12

Matt walked up the steps and entered the house.

Wendy stood alone in the living room.

"Your father tells me that Simone was the woman who called for help when you had your accident."

He met her gaze.

"He also says that he thought that the two of you were becoming very close."

"So?" he said, frowning at her.

She cringed at the unpleasantness of his tone.

"Don't be upset, baby. He's just concerned."

"I'm not your baby. You lost the right to call me that a long time ago."

"Your father thinks we can work things out. He said that he knew you wanted that, too."

"Really! So now Pop's speaking for me?" He couldn't help becoming instantly angry.

"No bab— Matt, he's just trying to help."

His facial expression showed no emotion, but anger burned in his eyes.

"I can tell you're still hurt and angry at what I did. Maybe we should talk another time," she said.

"Wendy, I'm no longer angry because of what happened. I'm over that. I'm angry because you now feel the need to interject your-self into my life when you're not wanted."

She flinched visibly.

She took a step closer to him as she spoke, "Matt."

He shook his head, not wanting to hear what she had to say.

"Wendy, you moved on a long time ago. Now I'm trying to move on. Leave me alone, okay?"

He took a calming breath before continuing, "Don't be a

pawn in my father's games. We have our own lives now. Let's live them. Apart."

She nodded, then started to speak and changed her mind. Sighing heavily, she walked to the door, then turned to him.

"You know, you really have changed," she said.

She gave him a small smile and left.

Marty walked into the living room the moment the door closed.

"What, were you listening?" Matt asked his father.

"Why did you let her leave?" Marty asked, gesturing toward the door.

"For the life of me, I will never understand why you invited her here."

"I told you, so you can spend time together. I know you still love her and want to be with her. With enough time, you two will work things out. You are just being a fool, letting your ego get in the way." He paused, then said, "Matt, don't make the same mistake your sister made."

"Damn it, Pop," Matt yelled.

The roar of his voice echoed in the quiet house, causing Rebecca to rush into the room to see what was the matter.

"I don't see why you have a problem with me doing that," the elder Turner said.

"What does this have to do with Sarah?"

"It has everything to do with her," Marty said, raising his voice.

"She messed around and married the wrong guy, and I'm trying to stop you from doing the same thing. I see it happening."

Matt brought up his hand and covered his eyes.

"Pop, what I do is none of your concern."

"Don't be such a dumb ass, of course it is. You are just like your sister and brother. I thought that at least you would have some common sense," Marty yelled.

"Marty, calm down," Rebecca said, walking to him and stroking his back.

Matt shook his head in disgust.

"Pop, I swear, sometimes you can be such an asshole."

He walked past his father and out the front door, letting it slam behind him.

• • •

"I'd bet my life that she's thinking about that son of a bitch," Jamison mumbled angrily to himself.

"I swear if I see that faraway look on her face one more time I'm going to kill the both of them." He sat behind his desk tapping his foot quickly on the Persian rug.

"She should be home by now. She'd better not have gone to see him."

He looked at the half-full sherry glass he gripped in his right hand and threw the glass across the room. It shattered against the wall. A moment later he heard footsteps running down the hall. He looked up as the door slowly opened.

"Everything okay, Sir?"

"Yes Sunee. Everything's fine."

His cold eyes met those of his housekeeper.

"Is she home yet?"

"No, sir," the housekeeper said, nervously dropping her eyes from his. He nodded slightly and she knew that was her cue to leave. She turned and quickly left the room, relieved to escape his presence. He picked up the phone, rapidly punching the familiar numbers.

• • •

"Hi, baby," Wendy said happily, walking into the study.

Jamison let his eyes travel down her body, surveying her slowly.

"Where were you?"

"I went to visit Susan and Gail," she said, placing her purse on his desk and giving him a quick peck on the cheek.

"Did you have a good visit?" he asked in a pleasant tone.

"Yes. How was your day?" she asked as she walked to the bar. She picked up the sherry decanter and a glass, filling it halfway. She turned to look back at him, motioning the glass in his direction.

"Yes, thank you," he said, rising from his chair.

He walked behind her as she filled a second glass and he slipped his arms around her waist.

"You know what's funny?" he whispered in her ear.

"No, tell me," she said, giggling from his breath tickling her.

"I called Susan an hour ago and she didn't say anything about seeing you today."

She turned to him and gave him one of the glasses.

"So now let's try this again. Where were you?"

She sighed, "It's nothing really."

"Tell me?" he said, his voice alarmingly low. Her heartbeat raced and her mouth suddenly became dry.

"Martin called me and asked me to come over. He said he wanted to see me."

"And why would he want to see you?"

She hesitated.

"He says I'm like a daughter to him. He likes me to visit him from time to time. That's all"

"Why didn't you tell me that at first?"

"I didn't want to upset you."

"Was *he* there?"

She hesitated, forcing herself not to look away.

"Is that the real reason you went there? To see him?" Jamison said, as he reached up to stroke her cheek.

Her eyes met his. The slate-blue eyes that she thought held an unquenchable thirst for her were as cold as the Arctic. A chill ran down her spine.

"No, I went to see Martin," she said, trying hard to keep the fear from creeping in her voice. She knew not to let him know she was afraid. It would only make things worse.

"And he was there? Was he not?"

"I didn't know he would be there," she lied.

"If that were true, you wouldn't have felt the need to lie to me," he said as his fingers enclosed her throat.

"No," she said, suddenly unable to hide her fear. "I didn't want you to overreact, I swear."

"I can't bare the thought of you with him. Of him touching you," he applied slight pressure.

"It's not like that," she said, grasping his wrist trying to loosen his grip.

"I'll die if I lose you. I love you," he said, tears coming to his eyes.

"I know," she whispered, trembling with fear.

"Jamison, you're hurting me," she whispered, barely able to breathe.

He loosened his grip, but held his hand on her neck.

"Why do you keep going to him? Is it just to torment me?"

"No, I didn't go to him. His father asked me to stop by. Really. I would never do that to you."

He pulled her to him, kissing her and bit her lower lip.

"Tell me you'll never leave me," he prompted, his lip still pressed against hers.

She took a fraction of a second too long to answer and he tightened his grip on her throat again, shaking her slightly. "Say it."

"I'll never leave you. I love you," she whispered, as tears rolled down her cheeks.

• • •

After blowing her nose, Wendy examined herself in the mirror. The marks on her neck were barely noticeable and the bite on her lip would only last a few days. She grabbed a washcloth from the towel rack, ran cold water on it and pressed it against her face.

Jamison had scared the hell out of her. He always had a bad temper and was very jealous. It started with little things like him jokingly telling her that he didn't like it when she said Matt's name. Then he started checking her cell phone records and going through her purse. In the beginning it had excited her and turned her on. Now it made her skin crawl.

At first, his wealth, generosity and power were irresistible.

On their first date, he flew her to New York for dinner and dancing. It was so romantic. She thought it was better than any fairy tale. That night, when she came home to Matt, she almost told him that she wanted to leave him right then and there.

On their second date, Jamison told her that he wanted her and he wanted to spend the rest of his life with her. He was everything she ever wanted and he gave her everything her heart desired. He took her to France and Spain where she shopped the best boutiques.

Lately he was different. He was brooding and easily agitated. He was quick to fly off the handle at every little thing. No, she thought to herself. Not every thing. It was when she mentioned anything that made him believe she was thinking of Matt.

Jamison was afraid she would leave him and go back to Matt. She didn't dare tell him that for the last month she was having second thoughts about their relationship. That she thought leaving Matt was a mistake. If she could just do it all over again, she would not have chosen him. She had convinced herself that. If she told him that, it would kill him.

Deep inside, she knew that if she told him how she really felt, he just might kill her instead.

• • •

"I told you that we should have gone to his house, torn the place up, and made it look like a robbery. It would have looked like he came home, caught the burglars, and they killed him. But of course, we had to do things your way."

"I told you I wanted to be careful."

"And you think this is careful? The guy gets out of a coma. Someone robs his house and wastes him? I think the cops are some dumb sons of bitches, but even they aren't dumb enough to believe that."

"I know my plan doesn't sound that great. I haven't thought it all the way through yet."

"I suggest you let me do the thinking from this point on," Adrian poked his thumb toward himself. "So, what am I going to get out of the deal?"

"You can take whatever you want out of the house, and I'll give you $50,000 and the Porsche."

"The Porsche, huh?"

"Yeah, man, the Porcshe is sweet."

"Yeah, it is sweet," Adrian chuckled. "I don't want that piece of shit. You don't know a decent set of wheels."

Becoming instantly angry, Jamison looked at the man sitting across from him.

"What? You don't like me calling you a dumb ass?" Adrian sat back stroking his chin as he watched the other man, then laughed at the mix of emotions that passed across Jamison's face.

Adrian always did what he could to push Jamison's buttons, but Jamison didn't let it bother him. That was just Adrian's way. But in recent months, Adrian had taken up the art of making vulgar comments about Wendy. If it were anyone else, Jamison would have been in their face and would not hesitate to put them in their place. If you asked anyone, there wasn't anything or anyone Jamison was afraid of. No one, except Adrian.

It was a respectful fear, Jamison would often tell himself. Each man knew the other wouldn't back down from anything — even each other.

Jamison knew something that his friend didn't. Jamison was generally afraid of Adrian. He had heard talk about how Adrian had killed his grandmother to get her inheritance.

Some said it was just talk. Someone had made it up and Adrian was just feeding on the fable.

Jamison knew that at the age of 15 Adrian was at home with his grandmother, that she complained of chest pains and asked Adrian to call for help. Adrian said that he went into the kitchen, took the phone off the hook and left the house. And he never looked back. As far as he was concerned, the old bitch had lived long enough and it was her time to go.

Jamison was the sort of person who did what he wanted, within reason. He knew that some things you couldn't get away with regardless of how well you planned or who you were. But Adrian didn't care about such trivial things. He thought the world was his

playground and he did what he dammed well pleased, whenever he pleased. He also knew that Adrian would not hesitate to kill anyone — including him.

"Wendy says he still doesn't remember anything from that night," Jamison informed Adrian.

"What about that witness?"

"As far as I know, she just saw a Porsche. She didn't get the tag number and probably couldn't even tell the cops the year of the car."

"I don't know, man." Adrian looked around the room. "Maybe we should take care of her," he said, more to himself than Jamison.

"I don't think we want to be leaving bodies lying all around town," Jamison whispered, as if he thought someone were listening at the door. "Let's give it some time. If she knew anything, we'd know by now. Let's just be cool."

"We'll see," Adrian said, scratching his chin. He shifted in his chair. "Shit man, your sorry ass didn't even offer me a drink."

Jamison rose slowly from his seat and walked to the bar.

"Sherry?" he asked, holding up the decanter.

"Man that's a pussy drink. Give me a rum, straight up. Maybe I could sell that Porsche and get me one of them Hummers. What'cha think?"

"Sure, whatever," Jamison said, still watching Adrian. "So when do you want to do this?"

"I don't know if I want to yet. If you throw in your bitch to sweeten the pot, I might be inclined to say yeah," Adrian said, looking up at Jamison, watching his reaction. He smiled as he watched the other man momentarily lose his composure.

Jamison's brow creased and his lips twitched, then he quickly recovered.

Adrian chuckled, shaking his head. "Such a pussy."

• • •

Examining herself in the mirror, Wendy dabbed more makeup on her neck. With a darker shade of lipstick, it was easier to conceal

the mark on her lip than those on her neck. She closed her eyes, chasing away the tears and took a deep, calming breath.

When Jamison had allowed her to escape, he had sent Sunee to inform Wendy that he had made dinner reservations and that she was expected to be ready within the hour.

Wendy didn't want to go to dinner. She didn't want to sit across the table from Jamison, but if she wasn't ready at the time he stated, then she didn't know what he might do.

She dressed in a lightweight, cream sweater and gray slacks. She rechecked her reflection to be sure there were no visible marks before leaving the bedroom.

She walked down the steps and crossed the foyer to Jamison's office. She entered without knocking and nearly ran into Adrian.

He looked down at her, and she took a quick step back. Then she attempted to skirt around him. He grabbed her forearm, pulling her close to him.

Jamison stood quickly, walking around the desk in Adrian and Wendy's direction and stopping a few feet away.

Wendy trembled. Her heart beat furiously from fear, she was almost afraid to breathe.

Adrian buried his nose in her hair and wrapped a lock of her hair around his finger. He smiled at Jamison.

"Tell you what. Let your bitch blow me right now and I'll do whatever you want."

Wendy flinched, trying to pull away from him.

Adrian let out a wicked laugh and pushed Wendy toward Jamison.

Chapter 13

"Afternoon, Miss Porter," Matt's smooth voice sang through the phone line.

"Hey, Matt, how are you?"

"Great. What are you doing for lunch?"

"I don't know," she said, "I'm sort of busy now. I don't think I can go out for lunch today."

"I know you can't resist having lunch with a really cool and utterly charming guy," he said, his voice full of humor.

"Matt, I really can't get away."

"Not even if he were offering you your all-time favorite of ham and cheese on rye? With mayo and extra pickles? I know you can just picture it as I speak."

She laughed.

"Sounds good. I don't know — maybe for a few minutes," she said, glancing up at the form that just appeared in her doorway.

Matt grinned at her.

"That's what I thought," he said, closing his phone and sliding it in his pocket.

"Hey." She smiled brightly at him. "What are you doing here?"

He held up a bag, wiggling his brows.

"Lunch is served."

"You're a lifesaver," she said.

He hunched his shoulders, faking a heavy sigh.

"I know, what can I say?"

He walked farther into the office, sitting in the chair across from her. Looking at the mound of papers on her desk, he asked, "What'cha doing?"

"Going over the semiannual reports," she said, reaching into

the bag and setting the sandwich on her lap. She opened it, took a small bite and then looked up, offering him some.

He shook his head as he waved his hand.

"Need some help?"

"No, I can manage, thanks. Hey what are you doing this evening?" Simone asked, taking another bite from her sandwich.

"Nothing."

"I was hoping that you and Cassie would go out with Alan and me. We could go to the new restaurant in Crofton. I hear they have good music."

"Uh... um, I..."

"Come on," Simone prompted, "it'll be fun."

Matt looked at her for a moment.

"Sure, why not? I'll need to call Cassie and see if she's busy."

• • •

As evening fell a slight wind picked up. Cassie closed her gray, lightweight coat, blocking the wind and commenting on how nice the weather had been for the last week of October. Walking into the restaurant, she gave the hostess Simone's name.

Once seated, Matt ordered a coke, and Cassie ordered a coffee.

"Hey guys," Simone said, as she and Alan were escorted to the table.

She gave Cassie a quick hug. Taking off her coat, Simone hung it on the back of her chair and slid into her seat. She wore a brown metallic mock-neck top with cream slacks. The sparkles made her skin seem to glow and, as Matt watched, he felt lightheaded.

"...weren't here long, maybe 10 or 15 minutes. Right Matt?" Cassie was saying. "Matt?"

"What?" Matt asked, looking at her as if he had forgotten she was there.

"I was telling Simone that we weren't waiting that long."

"Oh, yeah — I mean, no. We weren't waiting long," he picked up his drink, draining the glass.

When their waitress came to take the drink orders, Matt ordered a Disaronno with Coke. A double.

Cassie was telling Simone that she finally got transferred to pediatrics.

Matt and Cassie both ordered seafood platters. Alan ordered steak medium-rare and Simone ordered Imperial crab cakes.

Alan leaned close to Simone as he spoke, "Simone, I think that you should get the steamed flounder. It would be much better for you."

"That's not what I want," Simone said quickly. Then to the waitress she said, "And I'd like a baked potato with sour cream."

She closed the menu, handing it to the waitress.

Alan made a disapproving grunt and handed the waitress his menu.

Dinner was finished with only a few awkward silences.

"I really like this song," Cassie said, once their table was cleared and coffee was bought.

She took Matt's hand, asking, "Wanna dance?"

He stood as she led him to the dance floor. After dancing to two songs, they returned to the table.

"I'm sorry I ran out of energy so quickly, but today we were really busy," Cassie spoke, fanning herself. "I didn't realize how tired I was until we got on the dance floor. I hope you're not disappointed."

"No, I understand," Matt said. He stood, taking Simone's hand while looking at Alan saying, "Do you mind?"

Alan looked at Matt, his eyes shifted to Simone, and back toward Matt. Alan hesitated, his jaw clenched.

"I don't know?" Simone said before Alan answered. "You've heard that all black people can dance. Well I'm the one person who can prove that's a myth."

"Come on," Matt said, pulling her from her seat, "you'll do fine."

Several couples were on the small dance floor as Matt led Simone to the center.

Simone looked around, watching the other dancers on the floor.

Matt placed his finger under her chin, turning her face toward him. "Watch me."

After a few minutes, she followed his steps, and they were moving in sync with each other and to the music. The music faded from a fast song into a slow one.

Simone smiled up at Matt and turned to leave the dance floor when he caught her hand, pulling her into his arms. Unsure, she glanced up at him and looked around at the people around them. She slowly put her hands on his shoulders as Freddie Jackson's "Say Yeah" boomed from the speakers.

Matt looked down at her. Singing with the song, he told her how she had more than just sex appeal. He slid his hands from her back to her sides and down to her hips holding her as their hips moved and swayed with the beat of the tune.

Simone couldn't remember ever feeling so aroused.

Alan and Cassie watched as Simone and Matt stepped closer to each other. Cassie saw the look that Matt gave Simone and turned to look at Alan to see if he saw it, too. His eyes narrowed as he watched the scene. He turned and glanced quickly at her.

"So," Cassie said, trying to engage Alan in conversation in hopes of drawing his attention from the dance floor, "I have a cousin that works at Alpine. Do you know her?"

"I don't know," Alan said looking back to the dance floor.

"Her name is Fawn. Fawn Nicolas."

"No, I don't believe I know her."

"I'm sure you do. She has the sort of personality that attracts attention. That and she doesn't look anything like a Fawn. She's about three hundred pounds, blind with only a peg leg, and a hook for a hand."

"What?" he said looking at her, confused.

She giggled.

"I'm just kidding. She's not quite 300 pounds — probably more like 275."

He blinked trying to figure out if she was telling the truth or not. He glanced back at the dance floor.

Matt leaned forward, his lips lightly brushing Simone's ear. He continued singing with the song, telling her how nobody had ever done this to him before. He drew back, watching her, a slight smile on his lips, desire burning in his eyes.

When Simone looked into his eyes, her heart beat faster. She took slow, deep breaths not wanting him to see the effect he was having on her.

As the music faded from one song to the next, Matt stood holding Simone, looking down at her. His smile broadened as his eyes traveled down to her lips.

She removed her hands, taking a quick step backwards, and walked back to the table.

On the ride back to Cassie's apartment, Matt tried to concentrate on the road, but his mind kept drifting back to the restaurant. Once Simone and Matt had returned to the table, Alan had taken her hand, leaned close, and whispered in her ear. Then he had pulled her close and had kissed her sensually in a way that caused Matt's blood to boil.

Shortly after, Matt had made up an excuse for him and Cassie to leave. He gripped the steering wheel, still seething.

"The restaurant was nice," Cassie said, trying to strike up a conversation.

"Yeah."

"And the music was great."

"Yeah."

"I hear that they have live music there on Thursdays."

"Yeah."

"My toad stew was a little salty. What about yours?" She asked.

"Yeah, mine was, too."

She giggled and he looked over at her.

"What? Oh, sorry."

"Don't worry about it. You seem to have a lot on your mind."

He turned his attention back to the road.

"So," she said, looking out the window. "Do you think it worked?"

"Did what work?"

"The plan. You know, the plan to make Simone jealous?"

"I wasn't trying to do that. What would make you say that?"

"Give me a little credit. I'm a little more observant than you might think."

"Really, that's not what I was doing," he said truthfully.

"Not intentionally. But that is what you were trying to do."

Matt looked over at her and sighed.

"I guess I owe you an apology."

"No, you don't," she sighed. "You know, I noticed that you had a thing for Simone the first time we went out. And I really like her. She's great."

She looked out the window as they drove along for a few minutes.

"I have to admit that I've done my share of dumb things to get someone to pay attention to me, too. You just don't seem like the type to resort to such tactics."

"I'm not. Well, usually I'm not," Matt said, drumming lightly on the steering wheel. "And I really don't know why I did it this time. All I know is that I find myself doing a lot of things out of the ordinary lately."

"That's because, we all do really dumb things for love."

She watched his reaction. When she did not see any, she continued, "I once went to this guy's house that I was in love with. I took two dozen balloons and tied them to his car. Then I put a bouquet of flowers on his stoop and called him, telling him I left a surprise outside for him.

"I sat in my car and waited for him to come out. I got real happy just thinking of seeing the blissful look on his face. But instead of things going like I had hoped, he opened the door and took the flowers. He quickly removed the card and put it in his pocket. He

gave the flowers to the woman who stepped out of the door behind him and pointed to the balloons on his car.

"She took the flowers, smelled them, and looked at his car as she screamed with happiness. After kissing him, they went back into the house.

"I assume that he told her that he had done all of that for her; I never called him. I guess I didn't want to know. All I know is that I thought that I was in love, and he really hurt me."

"Would you ever do something like that again?" Matt asked her.

"Oh, definitely," she said, laughing. "It's in my nature to go overboard with everything that I do. Even in a relationship. I just figure that one day I'll find the man who's right for me and we will live happily ever after."

Matt pulled into the parking lot of her apartment complex and put the car in park. He turned to her. "Cassie, I'm really sorry. I would never use you intentionally."

She watched him, smiling. "I know. That's why I went tonight. I didn't think you would, and I like Simone."

"Thanks for being so understanding," Matt said, leaning over and kissing her cheek.

"Thanks for dinner," she said.

"Thanks for coming."

"Call me sometime. You, me and Simone can hang out. And next time we can leave Alan at home."

Matt laughed. "That would be great."

• • •

The drive back to Simone's house was quiet. When they pulled up in front of the house, Alan got out of the car and walked to Simone's side, opening the door. He followed her to the house. When she opened the door, he walked in behind her.

"Alan it's late, and I'm very tired."

"There's something I'd like to talk to you about. It won't take long."

Simone looked up at him and took a deep breath. She followed him to the sofa and sat across from him.

"I want to talk to you about Turner."

"What about him?"

"What about him?" he asked incredulously. "I do not care for the way he acts toward you."

"I don't understand what you mean."

Alan sat back watching Simone. "I don't trust him. He's coming on to you constantly."

"No, he's not. That's just Matt. He doesn't mean anything by it."

"I really don't like you spending so much time with him. Things could get out of hand. I want you to end your friendship with him."

Simone looked at him in surprise, although she really wasn't surprised. She had to admit that the way they were dancing tonight was far more than friendly. She had hoped that Alan hadn't noticed, but clearly he had.

"Alan, I don't think it's appropriate for you to say who I can or can't spend time with," she sighed. "Matt's harmless and he's a good friend. I don't want to have to defend our friendship to you. It isn't fair."

"Simone, I want you to stop seeing him," Alan said, as he stood and headed toward the front door.

"Alan," Simone called to him.

He turned back to her, watching as she stood meeting his gaze.

"I think it's best that we take some time off from each other," she said.

"What?"

"I think we need to take a break."

"Where is this coming from?"

"I've been doing a lot of thinking lately. And I don't think our relationship is working out."

He watched her for a moment and Simone thought she saw fear and uncertainty cross his face.

He took a step toward her. "Simone, I'm sorry. I know I was out of line. I'm just worried about you," he said, taking her hand and kissing the back of it. "Forgive me."

"Alan this isn't about you thinking you can tell me who my friends can be. It's about us not being compatible, and we aren't. "

"Simone, you once told me that your parents weren't compatible, and they've been married for over 30 years."

"Alan, we're not my parents."

"Simone, please?" He stepped closer, taking her in his arms and holding her tight.

Simone could hear his heart racing as she rested her head against his chest.

"Please don't do this. Give us a chance. Please."

Simone raised her arms and, holding him lightly, and nodded.

"Okay," she said.

Chapter 14

"René, I've been thinking. Gabriella is a lovely name. What do you think?"

René looked at her mother and saw that all too familiar smirk.

"Huh," René uttered, looking first at her mother, then to Simone and back again.

The three women were sitting around a large brown wicker table on the patio at Simone's parents' home.

Suppressing a grin Simone mouthed *don't do it* as she shook her head slightly.

Debra looked up from her magazine to meet René's gaze.

"Uh," was the only thing René managed to utter.

"Don't you like the name Gabriella?" Debra asked innocently.

"It's a pretty name, Mother, but, um, well..."

"I think that Gabriella would be a wonderful name for your daughter and of course he will be a junior if you have a son."

"Mother," René said slowly, "Max and I have decided not to have children."

Debra looked at René as if she didn't fully comprehend what she had said. She closed the magazine and laid it on the table.

"Pardon?"

"Max and I have decided not to have any children."

"What in heavens name would make you come to that decision?"

"The state of the world, and it's only getting worse. With terrorists and the threat of nuclear weapons — we might destroy the world before our children have a chance to grow up."

"That's that husband of yours talking. I know you don't believe that," Debra said, waving her hand. "If your father and I had

thought that way, you wouldn't be here today. Everyone is here to reproduce. All of us. That includes you and Max."

"Mother, Max and I just want to enjoy each other."

"That's just plain selfish. Once your children grow up, you will have ample time to spend together. Besides, spending too much time alone with any man can drive a woman insane.

"Listen to me. I know what I'm talking about," Debra said, patting René's hand. "You wait. Once you are holding that adorable baby in your arms, you'll be glad you've had a change of heart."

"I haven't had a change of heart, Mother. We really aren't going to have children."

"Yes, you will. If you don't, who will give me a granddaughter?"

"What about Charles?"

"Charles and Tamara are so wrapped up in their own lives that they probably haven't thought about having children. You know how your brother is. The thought of him sharing Tamara's attention with anyone — even his own child — is unthinkable. And from the looks of things, Simone won't be having any children," Debra cut her eyes in Simone's direction. "That is unless she comes to her senses and makes an effort in her relationship with Alan."

"Or you can have a baby yourself?" Simone said, not looking at her mother.

"Don't be funny."

"I'm not trying to be funny. Plenty of women are having babies at your age."

Debra gave Simone a disapproving glare.

"You should be helping me talk some sense into your sister instead of entertaining such foolish thoughts."

Debra turned back to René.

"René you're such a warm, caring person with so much love to give. Tell me that as bad as you think things are in the world that you and Max would not make wonderful parents. Max is great. I don't know a man who's more kindhearted and loving."

Debra reached for René's hand. "Am I right?"

"Well, yeah. Max is really good with children and..."

Debra nodded in satisfaction.

"Good. Now that we have that settled, I wanted to show you something. I saw the most adorable bedroom set. It's white, which can be for either a boy or girl. I think I still have the catalog on my desk," Debra said, taking René's hand and giving it a gentle squeeze before standing and walking into the house.

René looked at Simone and frowned in confusion.

"What just happened?" René asked.

Simone hunched her shoulders.

"Did she just railroad me into saying that I was going to have a baby?"

Simone picked up the magazine her mother had set on the table.

"Yep, sure looked like it to me."

"That's not going to work. I'm going to talk to her."

"Good luck to you," Simone said to her sister as René rose and walked into the house.

• • •

Twenty minutes later Charles pulled into his parent's driveway and parked behind his father's car.

Simone watched as he got out of the car, taking a Graul's Market shopping bag from the back seat and walking toward the patio. He walked past the table not even glancing in Simone's direction.

"Hey, Charles," she said, once he reached the door.

Stopping, he waited, his hand on the doorknob, his jaw clenched in anger. Turning slowly, he glared at her.

"Charles, we're family and whatever differences we might have we should be able to talk them out. Now, I don't know what's going on, but…"

"Simone, don't play innocent with me, okay. I'm not buying it."

She sighed. "Okay, let's just pretend that I don't know what you are upset about. Why don't you enlighten me?"

"Tamara didn't know about me having an affair and she

didn't know about this so-called pregnancy until you and your little friend got together to decide that my wife needed to know."

"What?"

"Now I'm living in hell. In public everything seems perfect. Tamara acts like the dutiful wife, but at home she won't talk to me. She won't let me touch her. She won't even look at me."

"What friend are you talking about? I haven't talked to Tamara."

"Save it. I don't want to hear anything you have to say."

He pushed into the house and slammed the door behind him.

Okay, now he's really lost his mind. How could he possibly think that I would get together with my friends to ruin his marriage? She placed her face in her hands, and then ran her fingers through her hair.

This just doesn't make any sense. What would I or anyone that I know achieve from breaking up Charles and Tamara?

She remembered the day Charles told her that he had gotten someone pregnant and he wanted her to talk to the woman and try to convince her to get an abortion.

But how could she? She closed her eyes. *God no. It can't be.*

Getting up, she went through the house grabbing her purse and telling her mother that she would return before dinner.

• • •

Karen opened the door smiling at Simone.

"Hey girl, I was just about to call you. Tanya and I were planning to go to see that new horror movie later I was just about to call you and see if you wanted to come along," Simone stormed past her into the apartment.

"Karen, I can't believe you."

"Uh? I was going to call you," she said, confused.

Simone looked at her.

"What? No, not that," Simone shook her head. "I can't believe you would do something like this to Tamara. I know you

don't know her that well, but — for Pete's sake. You're the last person that I would think could do something like this."

"Do what to Tamara?" Karen asked, oblivious to what Simone was talking about.

"Sleep with her husband," Simone said, angry that Karen was denying it.

"Are you crazy? Where did you get a wacky idea like that?"

"Charles told me."

"He couldn't have told you that," Karen said, becoming angry herself.

"Well, he did," Simone yelled at her.

"Well, then, he told you a lie," Karen said, putting her hands on her hips.

"I would never demean myself like that! Girl, men come a dime a dozen. Why would I rent someone else's when I can buy my own."

Simone looked at her friend. She knew better than anyone how devastated Karen was when Warn had cheated. Karen did some crazy things. Simone just couldn't see her doing something that would ravage someone and put them through the same hell that she had gone through.

"I don't understand. Why would he tell me that?" Simone said, looking at Karen, confused.

"I don't know. Maybe he's crazy too?" Karen said, folding her arms. ,

"Karen, I'm sorry."

Karen took a calming breath. "Maybe you misunderstood Charles?"

"This is totally insane," she looked at her friend, biting her lip. "Okay, I'm going to tell you something, but you have to promise not to tell anyone at work."

"Okay, I promise."

"I'm serious, Karen."

"I know. I said I promise."

"'Cause if you do."

"Damn it, Simone. I said I won't say anything."

"Well," Simone said and proceeded to tell Karen everything from Charles calling a few months ago asking her to lie to Tamara about where he was to the conversation that they had prior to her arriving at Karen's apartment.

"So I just assumed that since he thinks that my friend and I were trying to ruin his marriage that it had to be someone I know. The only friends of mine that he knows are you and Tanya. Tanya can't stand him."

Karen rubbed her forehead with the fingertips of her right hand.

"How could she be so stupid?" she whispered.

"Who?" Simone asked.

"Tanya."

"Tanya? Are you sure?"

Karen heaved a heavy sigh. "Yeah."

A knock on the door drew both women's attention.

"Speak of the devil. Why don't you ask her yourself?"

Karen walked to the door and yanked it open before Tanya knocked a second time.

"Hey guys, sorry I'm late." She froze. "What?" she asked, as she slowly walked into the apartment.

Karen and Simone glanced at one another.

Simone said, "I need to ask you something. I'm not accusing you of anything…"

"Did you go and screw Charles?" Karen blurted out.

"Karen."

"Well shit, why beat around the bush?"

Tanya looked from Simone to Karen as they waited for an answer.

"Tanya, if I am wrong — I'm sorry for wrongfully accusing you," Simone apologized.

"I didn't plan it," Tanya blurted out, "it just happened. Honest," she said, shaking her head. "I made a dumb mistake and now he thinks I'm trying to trap him."

"Trap him into what?" Karen asked. Then after a moment she gasped, "Ooooh, Tanya."

"I don't know what to do?" Tanya cried, tears streaming down her face.

"We just worked together a few times and one thing led to another."

Simone took her in her arms.

"It'll be all right. We'll figure something out. Right, Karen?"

Simone looked at Karen, who still wore a stunned look. "Karen?" Simone called.

"Oh, yeah, right," Karen said dryly.

When Tanya was finally able to pull herself together, she excused herself, going into the bathroom.

"Hey, are you all right?" Simone said, sitting on the coffee table in front of Karen.

Closing her eyes, Karen gently massaged her brow.

"Sure, I'm fine," Karen blew out a heavy breath. "This explains the sudden weight gain."

Simone nodded, saying, "You've been pretty quiet for the last half-hour or so. I can tell that there's something on your mind."

Karen shook her head.

"Are you sure? Tanya should be in the bathroom for a few minutes."

"Okay," Karen said, folding her arms before continuing. "I know you're going to think I'm wrong, but if I don't say this it's going to drive me insane."

"Go ahead. Shoot."

"Whatever Tanya is getting, she deserves."

"Why would you say that?"

"Because. It's not like she didn't know that Charles was married. She knew it and did him anyway."

"She didn't mean for it to happen."

"Oh no. She may not have meant to get pregnant, but she definitely meant to have sex with him. How do you go from not

standing to be in the same room with someone to having sex with him?"

"You know what?" Tanya said, standing in the doorway with her lips pinched angrily, "I thought you were my friend."

"I am. I'm just speaking my peace."

"It sounds to me like you are talking about me behind my back."

"No, she wasn't," Simone said, "she would have never said that if I hadn't asked her."

"You didn't force her to say what she said." Tanya folded her arms.

"I understand that you're upset. You know I would have told you what I thought sooner or later, so don't start acting like you are hurt or surprised."

"It's easy to be all high and mighty when it's not you that all this is happening to," Tanya said.

"I've had my share of crap and you know it, but none of it involved someone else's husband," Karen said, raising her voice.

"Look, Karen," Simone said, "this is between Charles and Tanya."

"I know it is — I'm just saying — the situation is low."

Tanya glared at Karen, "I told you... It just happened!"

"How the hell did it just happen," Karen asked, frowning at Tanya "What, you were working together when you tripped and fell on his dick?"

"You're so ignorant. I can't talk to you," she grabbed her purse from the table.

"I'll call you later, Simone," she said walking toward the door.

"If you want to see ignorant, then you need to try looking in the mirror," Karen yelled as Tanya walked out the door, slamming it behind her. Simone looked at Karen, shaking her head.

"Karen, I know this brings up some painful memories for you, but Tanya is upset right now.

"Girl, I don't care, I meant what I said. She's wrong."

"Yes, she was. But she's not the only one at fault here."

"Yeah, well, she should respect herself. I heard some gossip about her at work. People were talking about her and Charles. I just chalked it up to rumors. You know how it is when you have too many women working in the same place. I just assumed that since they can't stand each other it couldn't be true."

"What am I going to tell Tamara?" Simone asked.

"Nothing. This is between her and her husband. You need to stay out of it."

Simone bit her lip anxiously.

"My mother is expecting me back at the house for dinner. What if Tamara shows up? I'll have to sit across from her knowing all of this."

"I'm telling you. Don't say anything. Too much drama," Karen said, shaking her head and fanning her hand dramatically. "Drama is like a soap opera. They are fun to watch, but you never want to be one of the characters."

Simone pursed her lips, "I have an idea. Why don't you come with me?"

"Ooh, hell no. I don't want to be breaking bread with Debra."

"Come on. She always makes plenty of food and…"

"Nope," Karen said, folding her arms and shaking her head briskly.

"Come on." Simone wrapped her arms around her friend, knowing how to make her have a change of heart. "Pleeease," she whined.

"I said, NO!"

• • •

"I'm back, Mother," Simone said, as she walked into the kitchen.

"Finally. Alan has been looking for you." Debra smiled as she looked up at her daughter. She quickly assessed Simone's outfit. Her smile faded as she said, "I assumed you were going home to change for dinner?"

"I didn't have time to change," Simone said.

"You thought this was acceptable attire when you left home this morning?"

Simone looked down at her dark bluejeans and long-sleeved, lime-green, scooped-neck t-shirt minus her usual button-down top.

"I'm sure they pay you more than minimum wage at the center. You can't afford anything better to wear than that?"

"Mother, there's nothing wrong with what I'm wearing."

"You could have at least gone home and slipped on a dress."

"It's my day off. I want to relax."

"Well, of course, it's your day off. I would hope you wouldn't walk around with your breasts hanging out at work?" Debra said, looking distastefully at Simone's outfit.

"No, most days I opt for a tube top and body shorts," Simone said, a hint of sarcasm in her voice.

Debra looked at her, surprised.

"Anyway," Simone said quickly before her mother had a chance to speak, "I hope you don't mind. Karen's with me."

"Whatever for?"

"We're going out to a movie later. I was thinking she could stay for dinner?" Simone said, meeting her mother's gaze.

"Why are you going to make arrangements to go out with her? Alan is here. You should be spending time with him."

Getting caught up with everything that was going on, Simone had totally forgotten that Alan was going to be at her parent's house. She just hoped she could get through the movie with him and Karen without them drawing their swords to fight in the middle of the theater.

"Okay, whatever," Debra sighed, waving her hand. "It's done now."

A moment later, Karen walked into the kitchen.

"Hi, Mrs. Porter."

"Karen," Debra greeted Karen giving her the once over. She wore a silk, floral peasant blouse and black slacks.

"I like your outfit," Debra said glancing at Simone.

"Thanks. I got it from Nordstrom's."

"Oh, you bought it yourself?" Debra asked casually, a hint of surprise in her voice. "Hmm, it's good to know you can hold onto a job."

She turned back to the oven and continued basting her ham.

Karen's lip twitched from anger and she looked at Simone silently mouthing *You owe me. Big time.*

Simone hunched her shoulders mouthing *Sorry* and holding up two fingers indicating that she owed Karen two free meals at her favorite Cajun restaurant.

They turned back to Debra as she continued speaking.

"I always thought you would end up with five or six children and a husband in prison by now."

"Mother, why would you say that to her? Karen has always had good work ethics and she's a lot smarter than you give her credit for."

Debra turned to look at Simone, who was frowning at her with her arms folded. Debra squinted, looking from Simone to Karen and back.

"We're going in the living room with everyone else," Simone said, grabbing Karen's arm. "Call me if you need any help."

"Add an extra place setting on the dinning room table on your way," Debra said, watching the two women leave the kitchen.

"Well, well?" she whispered to herself, turning back toward the counter thinking, *Simone seems to be getting a backbone. She is toughening up a little. It's about time.*

She nodded as she smiled to herself, but her smile slowly turned into a frown and she shook her head slightly. She had been noticing subtle little changes in Simone lately. She didn't come over as often and seemed to be growing more independent. On a few occasions, they had gotten into heated discussions when Debra demanded that Simone do something that she didn't want to do. Recently, Simone had disagreed with her a lot more than she would have liked. She sighed thinking that she was not sure she liked the changes in her daughter.

"Where's Tamara?" Debra asked Charles as the family gath-

ered around the dinner table. "I wanted all of the family together today."

"She couldn't make it, Mother. She had a few things she needed to take care of."

"On a Sunday?"

"Yes, Mother, on a Sunday."

"And this couldn't wait until Monday or any other day during the week?"

"No, Mother, evidently not," Charles said dryly.

"Is there something going on? Something that I should know about?" Debra asked her son.

"No, Mother, there isn't," he spoke staring down at his plate.

"Don't try to hide things from me, Charles. I can tell that there's something going on," Debra said, glaring boldly at her son.

Charles grunted, pushing green beans around on his plate.

"Why don't you ask your daughter?" he said, glaring across the table at Simone. "She can't seem to keep anything to herself."

Simone was in the middle of putting a forkful of candied yams in her mouth. She glanced up looking to her left at Karen, then to her right at Alan. She looked around the table and all eyes were on her.

"Shit," she whispered, under her breath.

René's husband, Max, started laughing.

"Simone," Alan quietly chastised her.

"Did I just hear you say 'shit'?" he asked Simone, a look of astonishment on his face.

"I absolutely will not have that language in my house," Debra said quickly, her eyes piercing Max's.

"I'm sorry, Mother Porter. It's just that I've never heard Simone say anything like that. It's — I don't know — funny," he said, trying to contain another laugh.

René started laughing, looking in her mother's direction. "Mother, you have to admit it is funny."

"I'll do no such thing," Debra said, glaring at Simone.

René looked at her sister. "Girl what have you been doing." she asked, still laughing.

"I'm sure it's the company she keeps," Debra said, glaring at Karen.

"Mother, get off her back. Geez," Simone said without realizing it. Max laughed harder.

"Simone," René said, looking at her sister, shocked.

"Like I said," Charles commented, "she can't keep her mouth shut."

Simone turned to him. "And just what is that supposed to mean?"

"You run around telling my business. That's what I get for trusting you with anything. You always were such a brat." Charles leaned across the table, raising his voice.

"I never asked you your business. You're the one who came to me," Simone said, her voice rising to meet his.

"You're my sister, I should be able to trust you."

"Everybody quiet," Joe said.

"You had no right to tell Tamara anything," Charles yelled.

"I didn't tell her anything, you moron," Simone yelled back at him across the table.

"I said," Joe spoke again raising his voice and banging on the table, "shut up!"

Everyone jumped, and the room fell quiet.

"I don't want this arguing in my house. If you feel the need to fight, I suggest you take it outside. Now!"

"Sorry, Daddy," Simone said, looking first at her father then at her brother.

"Will everyone excuse me?" Charles said. Rising from the table, he dropped his napkin on his plate and left the room.

• • •

"This certainly was an exciting evening," René said, as she entered the kitchen carrying the remainder of the dinner dishes.

Simone took the plates from her and started to rinse them in the sink. "A little too exciting, you might say," she said.

"What time is the movie?"

"Not for another hour. Karen and I will be leaving when I finish up here."

René nodded. She leaned against the counter watching Simone. "So Simone, what's gotten into to Charles?"

"I was wondering when you were going to get around to asking me that? I honestly don't know what's gotten into him. He has it in his head that I've set out to ruin his relationship with Tamara. I would never do anything like that."

"I know you would never do that and, deep down, Charles knows it, too," René said.

Simone sighed, shaking her head slightly.

"I don't know. You wouldn't think that from the way he's been behaving lately."

Simone told her sister what happened at the youth center and what happened when he arrived earlier that evening.

"Simone, you know how Charles is. He's always been one to be the center of attention when things are going good, but when things go south he's ready to place blame everywhere else. He was like that when we were kids. I wouldn't let whatever is going on with him bother you too much.

"Charles is, well, Charles. When he and Tamara work out their problems, he'll come back to you and apologize."

Simone wasn't so sure.

If Charles was right and Tamara had found out about Tanya, then things could get a lot worse. Charles was the type of person that if he were miserable, he was sure to make everyone around him miserable. And if you happen to be the cause of his unhappiness, you could bet your life that he would make you suffer.

"Okay," René said to Simone. "Now tell me what's going on with my little sister?"

"Nothing much," Simone said, pulling a piece of plastic from a roll of Saran Wrap and wrapping the leftover ham.

"There's something different about you," René said.

"Really?" Simone asked.

René nodded.

"Is it in a bad way?"

René was thoughtful. "No. In a strong way. You seem more confident."

Simone looked at the door and back at her sister.

"What?" René asked.

Simone smiled. "I think I'm in love."

"Oh, Simone," René said, reaching out and hugging her. "That's wonderful.

"Hey, slow down," Simone said, laughing. "I said *think*."

"Well you have to start somewhere. So have you told him yet?"

"No"

"Why not?"

"It's complicated," Simone said, picking at the plastic wrap on the ham.

"Alan is not complicated."

Simone looked at her sister saying, "It's not Alan."

"Huh?" René said with a look of surprise.

Simone shook her head as she spoke. "Alan and I have been dating for months and I like him. But I'm not in love with him."

"Then who?" René asked.

"A friend of mine. His name is Matt Turner," Simone said, feeling a smile spread across her face as she said his name.

René frowned. "Hmm, that name sounds familiar." She tilted her head to the side trying to remember where she knew it from. "Oh my gosh. Is that the guy that Mother has been complaining about?"

"Complaining?"

"Yeah, you know how she is. She says that he's up to no good. He's a bum and he'll ruin your life...Yadda yadda yadda," René said waving her hand. "So tell me about him."

"He's wonderful," Simone said, smiling. "He's sweet. Considerate. Funny. And he can sometimes be unbearably annoying and a pain in the butt," Simone paused. "He's white."

"Ah, interesting," René said, folding her arms. "Are you all right with that?"

"Sure, why would you ask?"

"No reason. It's just that some people have a problem with that. So is he behind the new and improved Simone?"

"New and improved?" Simone asked, laughing.

"Yeah, you know. There's a fire in you that wasn't there before."

"I don't know about that. But since meeting Matt, I do feel surer of myself, you know, like I can do anything."

"Well, it shows. So he doesn't know how you feel about him?" Simone shook her head. "Are you going to tell him?"

"No."

"Why?"

"Alan, among other things."

"But you just said that you didn't love him. Do you really think it's fair to Alan for you to be in a relationship with him and be in love with someone else?'

"No, it isn't," Simone sighed, tears pooling on the rims of her eyes. "Why does everything have to be so complex?"

René shook her head slightly, watching the sadness pass across her sister's face.

"Honey, love is never easy," she said as she stepped close and gathered Simone in her arms.

Chapter 15

Simone walked into the bedroom and dropped her gym bag on the floor. She was grumpy and tired. The evening that she had spent with Karen and Alan had worn on her throughout the day at work. Alan had been completely rude to Karen, and Karen had insulted him every chance she got. The only peace Simone had gotten was when the movie started and Karen was shoveling popcorn or Snowcaps into her mouth. Then Alan would whisper to Simone how totally appalling her taste in movies was.

When they left the movies, Alan was supposed to follow Simone to her house, but he told her that he was tired and decided to go home.

To Alan, the perfect idea of spending time together consisted of them sitting on her sofa with him reading a medical journal or technology magazine and her doing something equally quiet.

After the way he'd acted in the movie, Simone was so relieved that he decided to go home that she nearly jumped up and down while singing and dancing in the street.

She walked to the corner of the room and stepping on the scale she peered down. It showed 140.

"Nuts," she said, stepping off the scale.

She kicked of her tennis shoes and stepped back on. Again...140.

Groaning, she stepped off the scale again, quickly removing her sweatshirt, pants, and t-shirt. Stepping back on the scale, she gathered her hair in one hand to look down again. Finally, 139.

"Oh come on," she said, shifting her weight from one foot to the other with the hope that it would somehow change the reading. Still 139.

"Shit."

She stepped off of the scale, kicked it to the side and walked

across the room. Searching in her chest of drawers, she chose a pink t-shirt and white sweatpants.

After showering and dressing, she put her hair into a pony-tail and slipped on a pair of flip-flops before grabbing her keys and walking through the house to the back door. She walked to the end of the yard and opening the shed, took out sandpaper, rubber gloves, and a box holding six quart-sized cans of paint in various colors.

Setting the items on the porch, she walked around the side of the house to her car and untied the antique rocking chair that she had seen at a yard sale and just had to have.

"Do you need a hand?"

She jumped, turning quickly toward the sound of a voice.

"Hi," Matt said, grinning at her after seeing the startled look on her face.

"Hi, yourself." She smiled up at him. "What are you doing here?"

Matt's gaze dropped from her eyes to her shoulders to her breasts. Through the thin t-shirt she wore, he could see the outline of her nipples. He looked up quickly trying to ignore the heat building in his stomach and spreading to his groin.

"Um," he stuttered, "Uh, oh yeah, the fliers for the home. I had them printed earlier today...and um...thought I'd drop them off," he said, holding up the box.

"You should have called me. I could have stopped by your office and picked them up. It would have saved you the trouble."

"I don't mind." He shifted the box from one hand to the other. "I talked to this guy I know. He owns a hauling company. I asked him to save any decent furniture for us. So far he has seven twin beds and a couple of dressers. They're not much, but it's a start."

"Thanks," Simone said, smiling and stepping closer to him. She wrapped her arms around his neck and gave him a warm hug.

He brought his free hand up and placed it on the small of her back. His fingers brushed skin through the thin tee.

She immediately realized what she was wearing and stepped back abruptly, tugging uncomfortably on her short tee.

"I knew you couldn't resist me," Matt teased, trying to ease the awkwardness.

"Oh, please, you wish," Simone laughed, turning back to her car.

"Whatcha got there?" he asked, looking around her.

"An old rocker I picked up. Isn't it gorgeous?"

"Yeah, it's pretty cool." He nodded.

"I saw it outside of a thrift store on the way home and had to have it. I'm going to restore it and put it on the back porch."

"Here, take these."

Matt handed Simone the box of fliers and stepped around her, pulling out the chair allowing her to close the door. He followed her around the house watching her hips sway as she walked.

"Where do you want this?" he asked.

"Just put it there," she answered, pointing to the spot next to the paint and other things from the shed.

"Can I get you something?" she asked.

"Sure, whatever you have that's cold will be fine," Matt said, putting the rocker down and sitting on the porch steps. He looked around the well-groomed yard of evergreens and fall colored mums.

Simone walked out the back door carrying two glasses of iced tea. Sitting next to Matt she handed him one of the glasses.

"Thanks," he said, taking a sip of the tea.

"You're welcome," Simone nodded.

They sat in silence for a few moments, then Simone glanced at him watching his profile.

"Matt...may I ask you something?"

Matt glanced at her seeing her uneasiness.

"I don't know. Is it a question that I might not like?"

She scratched her nose and giggled. "No, it's nothing like that."

"Okay, shoot," he said and took a gulp from his glass.

"What do most men want in a woman?"

"What?"

"I don't mean any woman. I mean a woman they want to

have a serious relationship with. Sometimes I think that I'm not the woman that Alan wants. That he wants someone completely opposite from me."

Matt was quiet. He didn't know what to say. He didn't like Alan and he thought that Alan definitely didn't deserve Simone. He couldn't say that. He couldn't bring himself to be the one to instill more doubt in her mind and cause Alan any problems. Even though Alan was an asshole, he couldn't be the sort of man to break up someone's relationship. He looked down at his glass.

"Why would you say that?"

"It just seems as if he wants to be with me sometimes and other times he's withdrawn."

"Maybe he doesn't want to show you how he feels for fear of being hurt."

"I don't know if he's attracted to me," Simone said, biting her lip and turning away. She turned back to him to find his dark eyes caressing her softly.

"I find that hard to believe," he said, meaning every word. "Any man would find you attractive. I think that you need to talk to him and tell him how you feel."

Simone looked out at the yard, gently chewing her lip. She nodded more to herself than to him.

"I'm gonna tell you a little secret," Matt said, bumping her shoulder with his to get her attention.

"What's that?" she asked as he leaned close to her, his nose only inches from hers.

"You are truly the sexiest the woman I have ever met," Matt gently kissed the tip of her nose and rested his forehead against hers as he closed his eyes, taking a calming breath. Then he stood quietly and walked casually around the house toward his truck.

Once Matt left, Simone sat on the step for almost an hour thinking about her relationship with Alan. She weighed the pros and cons. The pros were that Alan was a very handsome, successful man with a bright future, whom her family, especially her mother, liked. Under the cons was that he wasn't Matt.

She didn't get that warm feeling when she heard Alan's

voice. Her heart didn't flutter when his hand brushed hers. He didn't make her laugh or find joy in simple things like Matt did. But, she reminded herself, Matt is only a friend. As long as he was seeing Cassie, there couldn't be a chance for them.

She shook her head. There could never be a chance for them. Why would Cassie give Matt up? He was wonderful, kind and considerate. And she was compassionate, sweet and gorgeous. Cassie was what a lot of men probably thought the perfect woman should be.

Simone looked at the sky as dusk started to settle and took a deep breath. No relationship was perfect. And if she did decide to break things off with Alan, she was going to do it knowing that she at least gave things a chance.

Nodding to herself, she stood and took the glasses back into the house. She put the box of painting supplies along with the rocker into the shed and went back inside the house to call Alan. She was going to give things an honest effort. She left a message on his answering machine at home and his cell asking him to come over for dinner. She told him that she had a special evening planned and that she couldn't wait to see him.

She made Supreme of Chicken with Black Cherries, set the table with her best dishes, lighted candles, and waited for his arrival. At 12:30 a.m. she woke up on the sofa and reached for the phone to check the caller ID. No missed calls. She cleared the table, threw the chicken away, turned off the lights and went to bed.

Chapter 16

"Where have you been keeping yourself?" Joe asked Simone as she walked into the living room. "Haven't seen you much this week."

"Just working," Simone said, kissing her mother and her father.

She sat down next to her dad on the couch.

"Alan and I had lunch together today," Debra said, not looking up from the newspaper she held. "He was telling me about this friend of yours — what was his name — Matt?"

Simone was silent. "Alan tells me that you've been spending a lot of time with this person." Debra glanced at Simone, watching her reaction.

"We just hang out sometimes," Simone said, her tone flat.

"Mmm. Is that so?" Debra scanned the page in the newspaper, then closed it slowly as she spoke.

"Well, why don't you bring him for dinner next week? Maybe Saturday? Since the two of you have become good friends I'd really like to meet him."

Simone looked at her mother suspiciously, but Debra's relaxed manner and warm smile gave nothing away.

"You know how I've always taken an interest in all of your friends. It's important to me."

"Okay," Simone said, nodding. "I'll see if he's free."

• • •

"Tell me again why your parents invited me to dinner?" Matt asked.

"You're my friend, and my Mother likes to try to get to know all our friends. Even though we've all grown up and have our own lives, I think it makes her feel that she's still a large part of it all."

Matt nodded.

"I hope that bringing these pies for dessert will be all right."

"You did not have to do that."

"I wanted to bring something. Ma taught us that you don't go to someone's house empty-handed."

Simone smiled, "I am sure the pies will be fine. Did you make them?"

"Mm hm."

"Looks good," she said, pinching a small piece of the crust and tasting it.

"Thanks, I have some extra strawberry filling. If you would like I could make a pie for you to take home later."

"No, that's okay, thanks anyway."

He nodded and turned to the refrigerator to put the bowl inside as strawberry filling splashed down the front of his tan shirt.

"Damn," he whispered, removing his shirt and t-shirt.

After rinsing as much of the red stain out as possible, he wrung out the water. He turned from the sink, looked up seeing her watching him. "I can't believe I did that."

Simone watched his muscular chest and arms flex slightly as he held the wet shirts. The crisp brown hair on his chest trailed from the tan mounds to the waistline of his pants.

Matt was quiet for a moment. "See anything you like?"

She hadn't realized he spoke until she looked up seeing him smiling at her.

"What?"

"You heard me," he said, grinning at her.

"No." She turned away.

"You want me. I can tell," he said, smiling broadly at her.

"Why would I want you?" she asked, turning back to him. "You are the most egotistical, ill-mannered, infuriating man I've ever met."

"I'm giving you a chance here. I'm yours for the taking," he dropped the wet shirt in the sink, walking close to her with movements smooth and catlike.

"Get away from me," Simone said, slightly startled.

She looked up at him, preparing to argue when he grabbed her arms, gently pulling her toward him and resting his hands on her hips.

"Your mouth says no, but your eyes say yes. I'll give you 10 seconds to get away."

Her mouth went dry and she couldn't move. All she managed to do was whisper, "Jerk."

"Too late," he said, pausing to gaze into her eyes. He smiled a small smile. Leaning forward, he ran his tongue across her lips and slid it into her mouth, kissing her deeply. She felt her knees buckle and was grateful that he was there to hold her up. She moaned as she leaned against him. Slowly she kissed him back. Seeing the dazed look on her face he drew back.

"You're so beautiful," he whispered, tilting her face toward him. His eyes met hers. "Sometimes you take my breath away."

Simone looked into his eyes. He seemed to be peering into her heart and her soul. There was a quiver in the pit of her stomach, her heart jolted, and her pulse pounded. She fought to get past the lump in her throat. Her mouth moved but only silence met her ears.

He stepped back abruptly as if he had just realized what he had done. Turning, he quickly left the kitchen.

Simone stood in the middle of the floor, dazed by the tingling in her lips as she slowly moved her hand to her mouth. She took a deep breath to calm her nerves and tried to steady her hands. After at least five minutes, she walked into the living room.

After going through the living room, Matt mounted the steps two at a time. He went into the bedroom, angrily opening one of the drawers of the dresser and grabbing a t-shirt. He slid it on and walked to the closet, snatching a shirt from the hanger without looking to see what it was. With every step he took his groin tightened painfully.

"Way to go, idiot," he mumbled, flopping down on the bed. He let his mind drift to work, sports, television — anything but the

woman downstairs that caused a fire in him so intense he could heat up the entire Western Hemisphere for a month.

He thought about her parents and the looks on their faces when he walked into their house with a boner, knowing it was because of their precious daughter. He smiled, that did it.

When Matt walked back downstairs, Simone was in the living room.

"Are you ready to leave?" she asked, her voice so calm she even impressed herself.

"Sure," he said, casually pulling on the clean shirt, "whenever you are."

• • •

"Debra, it means a lot to Simone that you invited her friend to dinner."

"I care about what's going on in her life, Joe."

He nodded and walked to his wife, taking her in his arms.

"Everything I do is to make her life better. I really only want what's best for her, contrary to what all of you believe."

"Debra, trust me, I know that." He pulled back and looked down at her. "And Simone knows that, too. Sometimes you're just a little hard on her."

"I know. I don't mean to be. I only want to help," Debra smiled up at her husband.

"She's an adult and she's a very intelligent young woman. She'll make the right choices for herself, I'm sure of it." He leaned close and allowed his lips to brush his wife's. "I'm going to set the table," he said, releasing her and leaving the kitchen.

Debra shook her head as he walked into the dining room to take the good china and flatware from the china buffet. She leaned against the counter and watched him busy himself setting the table.

At 56, he was still a handsome man. Butterscotch complexion and green eyes still turned many a woman's head to this day. He had passed his devastating good looks on to Simone. Along with his "the world can be a wonderful place" attitude.

Joe had always been such a romantic, she reminded herself.

If Simone and Matt seemed to remotely care for one another, Joe would be right there as their champion.

Alan had what she thought Simone deserved and needed in a husband. He was a good man, and Simone would marry him someday. She turned to the counter and looked out the window. She wasn't about to let some loser put a wedge between the two of them.

"I don't know what's going on, but I plan to put a stop to it," she whispered to herself.

• • •

"Hello?" Simone called from the foyer.

"I'm in the kitchen," Debra answered.

"Come on," Simone said, leading Matt through the 8-foot archway to the kitchen.

Debra stood at the counter arranging baby artichokes, asparagus and carrots in a roasting pan. She turned when she heard Simone and her guest approach the kitchen.

"Hi, Mom, I hope we're not late?"

"Ah, um. No, not at all," Debra said, watching the stranger standing next to her daughter.

"Mom, this is Matthew Turner. Matt this is my mother, Debra Porter."

"Mrs. Porter, how are you?" Matt said, extending his hand.

Debra looked at him as if she had seen a ghost. She looked from Simone to Matt before putting on her warmest smile.

"I'm very well, thank you. You?"

"Good, thank you," he said, handing her the pie plates.

"And what is this?"

"I hope you don't mind. I brought dessert."

"Matt made those pies himself," Simone said quickly. "He's a wonderful cook."

"Is that so?" Debra asked.

"I do okay." He smiled. "I made strawberry and peach."

"Did I hear someone say they had peach pie in here?" Joe said, walking into the kitchen. "That just happens to be one of my favorites," he said, smiling broadly.

"And this is my father, Joseph Porter. Dad, Matthew Turner."

"Nice to meet you, son," the elder man said, shaking Matt's hand.

"Thank you, sir. Nice meeting you, too."

"So, Matt. May I call you Matt?"

"Yes, sir."

"So, Matt, do you like sports?"

"What would life be without them?" Matt joked.

"A man after my own heart. Likes sports and can make peach pie." Joe let out a hearty laugh. "Let's you and I go into the living room. We can watch the game until dinner is ready."

Simone smiled at her father's openness, then turning to her mother she asked, "Mother, do you need any help?"

"No, I have everything under control. Why don't you go into the living room with your father and our guest?

Debra watched as Simone left the kitchen, a smile still on her face. When Simone was no longer in sight her expression clouded with anger. Turning around, she gripped the edge of the counter. She slowly looked at everything that she had set out and it all suddenly looked out of place. She busied herself straightening everything and putting it back in order. The way she had to put Simone's life back in order.

• • •

"So, Matthew, what do you do?" Debra asked, as they settled down for dinner.

"I do home improvement."

"Home improvement?" Joe said "I guess people test your skills like they do a doctor, telling you all their problems and trying to get free advice."

"Yes, I do get that quite a bit," Matt answered.

"Well, he can't very well be compared to a doctor," Debra said pleasantly. "I mean you hardly need a degree to hammer a nail."

Matt glanced at her, and she smiled sweetly at him, quickly

changing the subject. "Simone tells me that you two met when you had a car accident."

"Yes," Matt said, studying her.

"That's awful. She also said that you were in a coma for four months."

"Almost four and a half," Matt said.

"Debra, Matt might not feel comfortable talking about this," Joe said to his wife.

"Oh yes, I'm so sorry. How completely inconsiderate of me," Debra said, smiling compassionately at Matt. "Do forgive me?"

"No problem."

"It's no wonder the two of you became such good friends. Simone has such a good heart," Debra said.

"Yes, she does," Matt said, smiling in Simone's direction.

"She's the sort of person who will befriend anyone," Debra said.

"She's always there for the less fortunate. When she was a child she would bring home strays if I allowed it," Debra gushed. "She can always find the best in the worst sort of people."

"That's what makes her so unusual," Matt said, his eyes remaining on Debra. "She has a loving soul."

"She does that," Joe said proudly, looking at his daughter.

"Some might see that as a fault," Debra added.

Matt looked at Simone, who sat looking at her mother with quiet discomfort.

"How so?" Matt asked, glaring at Debra.

"Well," Debra spoke slowly, "in business it can lead to you not being successful. Everyone sees that you wear your heart on your sleeve and you become fair game for the competition."

"But she's not a business person," Matt said, defending Simone. "She's a person with a beautiful heart that she shares with the people she works with every day."

Debra met Matt's stare. Neither of them turned away. Both drawing invisible lines in the sand to mark their boundaries. Debra sucked her teeth gently.

"I hope you like roast leg of lamb?"

"Yes, very much," Matt said, trying to keep the venom from his voice.

Simone let the plate pass her as she opted for a salad.

"Simone, you're not eating?" Matt asked, as he watched her.

"Oh, I knew I forgot something," Debra said as she rose from her seat and went into the kitchen to bring back a plate with a small slice of lamb without the sauce on it.

Simone looked at her mother, then at Matt. She bit her lip, looking down quickly, but not before he saw the sadness in her eyes.

"That one's for you," she said to Simone.

Matt glanced at Debra.

"I'm sorry. I don't understand?" Matt hesitated, looking at Simone, confused. "Why aren't you able to eat the same thing everyone else is having?"

He saw the humiliation in her eyes.

Joe's head snapped in the direction of the comment. He slowly placed his fork on the side of his plate. Clasping his hands, he rested his chin on his knuckles as he watched the younger man.

His wife continued to speak, "Joe would you please pass the asparagus."

"Excuse me?" Matt said. "Why is Simone not allowed to eat the same thing as everyone else?"

"Because," Debra said, becoming annoyed "she's trying to lose weight."

"That's absurd. She doesn't need to lose weight."

"Mr. Turner, I don't see where this concerns you."

"Because," Matt said, becoming angry, "I don't like to see Simone hurt."

"If you cared about her as you say you do, then you would know that being overweight is not good for her."

"She's not overweight." Matt looked at the food on the table. "If you think she's not able to eat any of this, then why make it to entice her? Why not make something that we can all enjoy?"

"It is not to entice her," Debra said, her voice stern, "and we are not all on diets."

"So you humiliate her by singling her out verbally, by telling her what she shouldn't eat, and by preparing something different for her?"

The room fell silent. Clearing her throat, Simone stood, saying, "Matt, I think we should leave."

"Yes, Mr. Turner, I think you should leave," Debra said, emphasizing the word you.

Matt rose from his seat meeting Debra's challenging stare.

"Simone, I'm going to take you to dinner," Matt said, walking to her side and taking her hand.

"Good evening," he said to Debra.

Looking at Joe, Matt nodded. "Sir."

Debra looked at their joined hands and up at Matt.

He turned, leading Simone to the door.

"I have to get my purse. I'll meet you at the truck." Simone walked into the living room, picking up her purse.

"Simone," her father called from behind her.

"I'm sorry about this Daddy," she said sadly.

"There's nothing to be sorry about, baby girl," Joe spoke softly, walking to the window. He looked out the window to watch Matt standing next to his truck.

"He's an interesting young man. He seems awfully protective of you. A lot more than Alan, I might add."

"He's trying to be a good friend. And he means well. Really." She drew a heavy breath.

"I was afraid something like this would happen. I should have told Matt that Mother is always under the assumption that I should be dieting."

"Do you think that it would have changed his desire to protect you?"

Simone sighed, "Probably not."

Joe nodded. "I don't think so either," her father said, still looking out the window.

"For what its worth," he said, turning to look at his daughter, "I like him."

She smiled as she walked to her father and kissed his cheek.

"Thanks, Daddy."

Chapter 17

Joe walked into the kitchen carrying two of the serving plates from the dining room.

"Joe, I can't believe you just sat there and let that person talk to me like that."

"You didn't seem to need my help."

"That's not the point."

"Debra, I don't think he meant anything by it. I think that he feels he needs to protect Simone."

"Protect her from what?"

Joe remained silent.

She glared at him, banging the pot on the counter yelling, "Well?'

He sighed. "I believe he cares for her and wants to protect her. Even if he doesn't realize it."

She angrily bit the side of her mouth.

"I see. I don't think that their friendship is a good idea. It can only lead to trouble, don't you agree?"

"I don't see where there is a problem."

"That's absurd! How can you not see?"

"Well, they seem to understand and care about each other. Those are important things in a friendship."

"If he were a female it would be different, but his being a male," she said as she shook her head, "I don't know, it's just not right."

"Simone had several male friends over the years and you didn't seem to have a problem with any of them."

"This isn't the same. No, I don't like it. Not at all."

"Why? Because he's a different race?"

"Well, as a matter of fact, yes."

"What if he were Jamaican or from Trinidad or Tobago."

"That is totally different."

"How?"

"It just is. Don't be so naive."

"I'm not. We taught our children that everyone is equal and to treat everyone that way. And they do. So, if we tell Simone that we don't approve of her friendship with this man, then aren't we being like those people we abhor? The parents who say anyone can be your friend as long as you don't bring them home."

"Oh, please, that's different."

"How is that different?

"I cannot believe we're even having this conversation. I can't believe you're not on the same page as I am."

"Debra, they're friends for goodness sake. They're not planning on running away and getting married tonight."

"What if their relationship grows into something more? Tell me you wouldn't have a problem with Simone seeing that man!"

"I can't say that I would. If I have a problem with Matt because he's white, then I have a problem with my heritage as well. And that's not the case. And we've seen quite a few of Simone's boyfriends and I can say that I have never seen one of them look at her like this young man does."

"Lustfully?"

"No, complete admiration."

"Oh, my God — I cannot believe what I'm hearing."

"And if he is willing to stand up to you, he must have a strong personality."

She looked at him, waiting for him to elaborate on his comment.

"You can be a force to reckon with."

She squinted at him angrily, "Shut up and just leave me alone."

"Debra what I'm trying to say is..."

"Didn't I say to leave me alone," Debra said, not looking at Joe.

He stood slowly. "I'll be in the den reading."

"Yes, you do that," Debra said.

He turned to the door, then back to her, seeing the tightness of her jaw.

"I think something needs to be done," Debra said to Joe.

"Debra, I don't think there's anything to worry about. Please leave this alone. In the end, the only thing that will come from your interference is Simone's suffering.

• • •

"Are you sure you don't want me to make you something to eat?" Matt asked Simone.

"I'm sure. I just want to go home and get to bed."

"I'm sorry about what happened at your parent's house," Matt said, feeling guilty. "I really didn't want to upset your mother like that."

"Don't worry about it. She has a way of bringing out the best in some people. I'll call her later and smooth things over."

"I shouldn't have put you on the spot, though," he said, shaking his head. "You know, it's really surprising how your mother and my father are so much alike."

Simone looked at Matt, surprised at his statement.

"What makes you say that?"

"They're both controlling and think they know what's best for everyone. And they can be mean when they want to be."

"My mother is nothing like your father," Simone said defensively.

Matt looked at her.

"You father is rude and downright cruel. He says awful things to people. My mother is nothing like your father."

"How is she different?" Matt asked, tilting his head. "Is it the fact that she smiles at you when she insults you? That doesn't make her different. It just makes her better at what she does."

Simone met his curious stare.

"But your father is a racist."

"Yes, he is," Matt said, serious. "You will never hear me deny it, but your mother is racist, too."

"No, she's not."

"Yes, she is. I can tell by the way she looked at me."

"No, you misread her. My parents brought us up better than that. She has a strong personality, and you have to get to know her before you can tell what sort of person she is."

"She seems like a bitter, angry woman."

"My mother is not bitter or angry, and if she were she would have ample reason."

"And what would that be?" Matt asked, leaning on the counter and folding his arms.

Simone opened her mouth and let it snap shut. She put her hands on her hips, holding her head high.

"I don't have to justify anything to you."

"That's because you can't."

She looked at his complacent smile.

"Yes, I can." Her eyes shifted quickly as she tried to come up with a response, not wanting him to have the satisfaction of knowing he was right.

"Well?"

"I'll have to get back to you on that," she said, walking away quickly.

"Oh, no, you're not pulling that crap on me," he said, following her. "You're going to answer me."

She walked up the steps and into the bathroom with him in tow.

"You know I'm not just going to let this go without an answer."

"Do you mind?" she asked, stopping him at the door. "I have to use the restroom."

"Oh, yeah, that's convenient," he said, rolling his eyes slightly. "This conversation isn't over yet."

"Yeah, yeah, whatever," Simone said, waving her hand at him as he exited the bathroom and closing the door behind him.

She walked to the bathtub and sat on the side shaking her head. Searching her mind she tried to find the reason for her mother's anger. Then it came to her: Her mother didn't have a reason to

be angry. She had a wonderful husband, a family who loved her and a great career.

Many women would give anything to have that, but with her mother, it just didn't seem like enough. And as much as she hated to admit it, Matt was right about what he had said, he was right about her mother being bitter, and he was probably right about her mother being a racist. But she would never tell him that. She would strip off her cloths and run buck naked through Westfield Mall before she would admit to him that he was right, and see that smug grin of his.

Why do I let him get to me like this? Sometimes I could just kick him. She smiled shaking her head. And then other times she wished she could kiss him. She sighed, running her tongue across her top lip remembering when he kissed her. She shook herself attempting to erase the image and walked to the door, pressing her ear against it. Not hearing any movement, she opened the door and peered out, first to the left, then to the right. She walked quietly down the steps and across the living room. She grabbed her purse from the couch and walked to the door, opening it quietly.

"See you later, Matt," she yelled before stepping outside.

"I'm thinking you won't be going anywhere without these," he said, standing in the corner holding up her keys.

She looked at him and frowned.

"You still haven't answered my question yet."

"Sometimes you can be such an ass."

"And you're just figuring this out?"

Chapter 18

Slipping on her robe Simone rushed down the hall and peeked out the front door.

"Hi."

"Hey, you're not dressed yet."

"Yeah, I was running late leaving work. It won't take me long to get ready," she turned and headed down the hall.

"What time does the movie start?"

"At 6:45, but the comedy starts at 7:15."

"You got to choose last time. It's my turn, and I choose horror."

"Yeah, I figured as much," Matt grunted.

"Chicken," she said, as she made her way down the hall toward her bedroom.

"Yep, that's me," Matt yelled back, walking into the kitchen.

He looked in the cabinet for something to snack on while he waited for Simone. Picking up a bag of rice cakes and taking one out, he took a large bite and frowned.

"Damn," he said, closing the bag and setting it back on the counter. He reached into one of the overhead cabinets and took out a tumbler. He crossed the kitchen to the refrigerator and poured himself a glass of iced tea. Taking another bite of the rice cake, he took a gulp of iced tea to wash it down.

Hearing the doorbell ring, Simone yelled for Matt to get the door.

"Can I help you?" Matt asked the man standing at the front door.

The guy was at least three inches shorter than Matt with a cocoa complexion. He regarded Matt suspiciously as he stepped forward to enter the house.

Matt quickly stepped to his left, blocking the other man's way. The two men looked at each other for a long moment before the strange man spoke.

"Is Simone in?"

"Who shall I say is looking for her?" Matt asked, trying to remember where he knew the man from.

"Her brother," Charles said, slipping past Matt and walking into the house. He eyed Matt and then looked around apprehensively.

"Who are you?"

"Name is Matt Turner," Matt said, extending his hand toward Charles.

Charles looked down at the extended hand and put his hands in his pockets rather than accept the offer.

"Where's my sister?"

"We're on our way out to see a movie," Matt said, sliding his free hand into his pocket. "She's getting dressed."

He turned and walked back into the kitchen, leaving Charles standing alone in the living room.

When Charles entered the kitchen, Matt was sitting at the table slowly sipping his iced tea.

Charles opened the refrigerator looking for something to drink.

"Looks like she doesn't have anything but iced tea," Charles said.

"There should be soda in that small cupboard over the stove," Matt said casually.

"Thanks."

"No problem."

"You seem to be making yourself at home here," Charles said, as he took a cola from the cabinet, opened the can and drank it warm. He leaned against the counter, regarding Matt.

Realizing that Matt wasn't going to comment on his statement he asked, "So how long have you been dating my sister?"

"It's not what you think. Simone and I are friends."

"Now, you know, I get a different story from my mother."

"Excuse me?"

"Nothing," Charles said, shaking his head.

"Simone is my friend. Maybe the best friend I have."

"I'm just concerned about my sister. We all are. We only want what's best for her. And I don't want her to be hurt by anyone."

"You mean like you did," Matt said sarcastically.

"That's family business," Charles retorted.

"If Simone is hurt, then that makes it my business," Matt said sternly.

"Simone is a very smart, competent woman. What she needs is for her family to see in her what the rest of the world sees and appreciate her for it. She definitely deserves more from her brother than him being an asshole and treating her like shit."

Charles' jaw clenched as he glared at Matt.

"Matt, who was that at the door?" Simone asked.

"Hey, Simone," Charles said, smiling.

Leaning against the door frame, Simone folded her arms asking, "What's up?"

"Nothing," Charles said, shoving his hands in his pockets. "Umm, I was just wondering if I could talk to you. Alone." He glanced in Matt's direction.

Matt stood and crossed the kitchen to the sink. After putting his glass down, he turned to Simone. "I'll be outside when you're ready to leave."

"No," Simone said, shaking her head slightly, "Matt, you don't have to leave."

"Please, Simone, I need to talk to you. In private"

"You didn't want to talk to me in private the last time we spoke. You didn't have a problem talking to me in front of a couple dozen people," she said, tilting her head as she watched him.

Charles paused, nodding, "Fair enough. You're right."

He looked down, sighed, and looked back at her.

"I came to say that I'm sorry. For the things that I said and the way I've been treating you. I know now that none of this was your fault. You didn't tell Tamara anything. Tamara was finally able

to be in the same room with me long enough for us to have a mildly civil conversation, and she told me everything.

"It was all Tanya. She called and told Tamara about the affair and she set out to break up my marriage. And I let her. It's all her fault."

"You're right, it wasn't my fault. But it wasn't Tanya's either. This was entirely your fault."

"How?" he said, becoming instantly angry.

She held up her hand, silencing him.

"If you'll excuse me," Matt said, attempting to walk past Simone to give them some privacy.

"No," Simone placed her hand on Matt's chest, stopping him from leaving while she continued to watch Charles.

"Tamara is your wife. Tanya doesn't have to care about her. You do. If you hadn't let your hormones get the best of you, none of this would have happened."

Charles closed his eyes and he nodded slowly as he spoke, "You're right."

"All you want to do is blame someone else for the things that you did. I just happened to be caught in the crossfire. You're my big brother, and I've always looked up to you. To me you were larger than life."

He saw the pain on her face.

"You hurt me. Deeply," she whispered.

"I know, Simone, and I'm sorry. Can you ever forgive me?"

"Of course I do — or I should say, I will. You're my brother. You mean more to me than I can ever tell you, and nothing will ever change that."

She took a deep breath, standing tall.

"I love you, Charles. Now get out of my house."

He paused, unable to think of anything to say that would erase the past two months. He glanced at Matt and back to Simone. Nodding slightly he turned and left.

"You okay?" Matt asked, as he watched Simone's shoulder's slump.

She nodded.

"Are you still up to that movie?" she asked him, sighing.

"Do you still want to go? I'll understand if you want to be alone. Or, if you like, we could do something else?"

"No, let's just go to the movies," she said, biting the inside of her lip.

"Murder and mayhem?" he asked, hoping to cheer her up.

"No, I've had enough mayhem for one day. How about a comedy?"

Chapter 19

"Sarah's birthday is next week," Rebecca casually mentioned to Marty their daughter's coming birthday, as she turned the page in the book she held.

"I was thinking we could get her a vacuum cleaner. The last time we talked, she mentioned that she needed a new one."

"And just how much is this going to run us?" Marty asked, not taking his eyes from the TV.

"I don't know. I saw a really nice one with a hepa filter and extra attachments for around $150."

"That sounds like an awful lot for a birthday present. Why can't we just send her fifty bucks and be done with it?"

"I want to get her a vacuum cleaner."

"If you already made up your mind, what the hell are you talking to me about it for?"

Rebecca glanced at him.

"Because — I want to lend them some money, too."

"No," Marty said, quickly cutting her off.

"It's only for a short time. Vince's business isn't doing too good because of the weather and all. Sarah asked if we could lend them a few dollars until they get back on their feet. I was thinking maybe $5,000."

"What? Hell, no!" Marty yelled.

"Marty, they really need some help."

"I said no."

"Why not?"

"That boy shouldn't be sending his wife to beg for money from her family. He should be man enough to provide for his wife and kids."

"He doesn't even know Sarah asked me for the money. Sarah

says he's too proud for that. She says she'll pay it back over the next six months.

"Marty, I want to help her. She's our daughter."

Marty grunted or growled, Rebecca couldn't tell which.

"Good," she said, patting his arm. "I'll take part of the money out of the checking account and the rest from the savings account."

"She isn't getting a damn vacuum cleaner, too," Marty declared. "You tell her that $200 of that money is her birthday gift." Marty said, folding his arms and pouting.

"That's fine. As long as we have the money when Sarah comes for her visit."

"Coming here? Since when?" he asked, finally looking at her.

"Since I told you about it two weeks ago."

"I didn't hear you say anything of the sort."

"Thursday before last. We were sitting right here. I said 'Marty, Sarah's coming for a visit' and you said 'yeah, yeah, now hush.'"

"That had to be when CSI comes on. You know you can't talk to me when I'm watching my shows. I hope you didn't tell them that they could stay here. She can stay, but that boy can't."

"As a matter of fact, I did."

He cocked his head to the side, staring at her.

"Woman, what is wrong with you? They aren't staying here."

Rebecca sighed heavily.

"Don't worry, Sarah said she wouldn't stay here if I paid her."

"She said that?" Marty asked with a surprised and hurt look.

"She's so stubborn. Just like her father. What would you expect? She says that they're staying at a motel."

"Is she going to bring them kids with her? That little one's all right, but that older one," Marty said, shaking his head, "she has some mouth on her."

"Just like her mother and grandpa," Rebecca said, peeking at her husband over her reading glasses.

He grunted, "Yeah, if you say so."

"Well, since you're already bent out of shape, I guess you should know that Sarah, Vince and the kids are going with us to Helen's for Thanksgiving dinner."

"They aren't riding with me," Marty stated quickly.

"Marty, stop being like that."

"I'm just saying."

"You know Marty, the reason you and Sarah don't get along is because she's just like you."

"No, she isn't. If she was, she would do what was right. I never went against my father. He was a wise man, and I would have never turned my back on him for some outsider. Especially one that wasn't my own kind."

"Marty she didn't turn her back on you. She couldn't help who she fell in love with. And I sort of remember a certain someone courting a young lady when his father thought he should be with someone else."

"That was different."

"How so? It's the same thing. Your father thought that I wasn't right for you, thought I was too young and wouldn't make a good wife."

"We are together because we were meant to be together. Sarah's thing is totally different. She did this just to go against what I wanted, and you know that."

"Just like MJ did?" Rebecca asked.

He stared at her for a minute, then shaking his head he said, "I don't want to talk about this."

• • •

Matt opened the front door and stepped out onto the porch.

"Hey," he said happily, giving his sister a bear hug, picking her up, and spinning around as he held her. She squealed loudly, hugging him back.

Setting her down, he stepped back and looked at her. "You're a sight for sore eyes. I've missed you," Matt said.

"I've missed you too, little brother."

Matt stooped down to greet his nieces.

Standing, he frowned at the tall Latino standing on his porch and reached out nudging the man's chin. "Looks like you got a little dirt there."

"Ningún hermano que una barba. That's a beard. I'm all grown up now," the other man said, his accent heavy.

Matt grinned, shoving him. "Yeah, right." The two men started shoving each other playfully.

"Hey, you two, stop that," Sarah shouted.

"Aw, c'mon," Vince wined.

"Yeah," Matt said, trying to imitate Vincent.

"It's bad enough he acts like one of the kids at home. He can't be a kid with you, too."

Vince leaned close to her, whispering in her ear. "Usted didn't dice eso anoche…I'm not a kid where it counts."

She giggled, pushing him away. "Yeah, well, you two need to stop. I need you guys to watch the girls while I go see Ma and Pop. We need to have at least one adult in charge."

Matt raised his hand and waved it in the air. "Ooh pick me, pick me," he said, grinning at his sister.

She sighed, shaking her head, then whispered, "Oh, God."

• • •

After Matt showed Sarah which rooms they were using, he went down to the kitchen to prepare lunch for everyone. "Are the girls eating lunch with us?" Matt asked.

"No, we had a long flight. I put them down for a nap. They'll eat when they wake up." Sarah pulled a chair from the table and sat next to her husband.

"So," Matt said, "how's everything?"

"It's good," Sarah nodded, looking at her brother. "You look good."

"Thanks," Matt said as he smiled broadly, "I feel great."

Sarah smiled back at him. She leaned close to Vincent, saying, "Mi hermano tiene a una dama nueva, él está en el amor."

Vincent raised his brows asking, "Sí?"

"Sí," Sarah said, grinning at Matt.

"Hey, hey, stop that. English, people, English," Matt said, frowning, then grinning quickly.

"So, I hear you have a new lady friend?"

"Where did you get that from?"

"Ma says you really like this girl. What's her name? Simone?" she said, beaming at him.

Matt rolled his eyes, "Not you, too."

Chapter 20

"Goodness, Marty, why didn't you answer the door?" Rebecca asked, walking down the stairs.

"I thought you were gonna get it."

"You knew that I was upstairs."

"Hrumph," Marty grunted, hunching his broad shoulders. "Well, now you aren't."

Rebecca looked at him, sucking her teeth, before she went to the door.

"Sarah!" she squealed, pulling her daughter inside the house and giving her a long hug.

"Hi, Ma, how have you been?"

"I'm great now that I see you. I've missed you," Rebecca said, beaming at her daughter.

"I've missed you, too," Sarah whispered.

"Here, let me look at you." Rebecca stepped back looking over her daughter from head to toe. "You look wonderful."

"Thanks, Ma, so do you." She looked at her father sitting in front of the television set.

"Hi, Pop," Sarah said. She walked over next to him and bent to give him a small hug, noticing his attention never left the television set.

"Marty, turn that TV off. We have company."

"Sarah isn't company," Marty said, squirming as he tried to get comfortable in his chair.

"Matt got that chair for your father for Christmas last year. He loves it. Marty, why don't you let Sarah sit in your chair, so she can see how comfortable it is?"

"I don't see a shortage of chairs around here."

"Marty," Rebecca chastised him, crossing her arms over her chest.

"It's okay, Ma."

"Don't you think it would be nice to have a conversation with your daughter? You haven't seen her in months."

"We can talk during the commercials."

Rebecca unfolded her arms and walked across the room, taking the remote from the table next to his chair she turned off the television.

"Damn woman," Marty grumbled. "Man can't even have a peaceful afternoon in front of the TV."

"You can watch TV later. It's not going anywhere. Your daughter will only be here for a few days." Marty mumbled something under his breath.

"What was that?" Rebecca asked.

"Nothing," Marty mumbled.

Rebecca nodded, setting the remote on top of the television. "I'm going to get everyone something to drink." She eyed her husband looking at the television, then she reached for the remote and put it into the pocket of her apron.

Marty stood quickly, turning on the television.

Sarah laughed at him, shaking her head. "So, how have you been Pop?"

"Good."

"You been feeling OK?"

He nodded, then frowned, secretly hoping she would be quiet.

"How are things at work?"

"The same," he said.

She waited a few moments, then asked, "Don't you want to know how your granddaughters are?"

He looked at her and back at the TV. "How are the kids?"

"They're good. Vincent is doing well, too."

"I don't recall asking."

Sarah grimaced looking around the living room, then back at her father. "It would be nice if you pretended to care, after all, he is my husband, Pop."

Marty slid down farther in his chair. His only reply was a small grunt.

"I don't even know why I bother," Sarah whispered as she dropped down on the sofa.

A knock on the door brought Marty quickly to his feet. Marty rose from his seat, swiftly rushing to the door.

"Hey you, come on in," he greeted, pushing the screen door open and holding it for her. "You should have tried the door. It was unlocked."

"I didn't want to just walk in," Wendy said.

"Oh, don't be silly. You're family. You're always welcome here. Come sit with us," Marty took Wendy's arm, ushering her to his easy chair and letting her sit down. He sat next to Sarah on the sofa. He looked at his daughter, seeing the hostile glare she sent his way. He flashed her his best smile saying, "Sarah, look who's here."

"Yeah, I see, Pop. I have eyes," Sarah commented dryly.

"She stopped by just to see you. Didn't you Wendy?"

Sarah squinted at Wendy, suspiciously, "Is that so?"

Marty looked at his daughter, frowning. He looked from one woman to the other. "Becca," he yelled suddenly, "bring out an extra drink."

Sarah glared at her ex-sister-in-law, her expression not changing.

"Hello, Sarah," Wendy said, meeting Sarah's gaze and offering her a forced smile. "How have you been?"

"I'm good, Wendy," Sarah said. Casually folding her arms she cocked her head to the side asking, "So, how's tricks?" She smirked, watching Wendy as if she were waiting for an answer.

Wendy's mouth dropped open. "I still see you have your sense of humor considering the hard time you and Vince are having."

Sarah eyed Wendy and looked at her father who dropped his gaze and tugged on his ear. "Becca," he yelled again. "We could sure use those drinks about now."

Rebecca walked from the kitchen carrying a serving tray with four glasses of iced tea on it. She froze in her tracks when she

saw Wendy sitting in Marty's easy chair. Marty looked at her with what she liked to call his 'everything's working just like I planned' grin.

"Becca, Wendy stopped by to see Sarah. Don't you think that's sweet of her?"

Rebecca walked to the table and set the tray down. "Matt isn't coming. He's at home visiting with Vince and the kids."

Wendy looked from Marty to Rebecca. "I just wanted to see Sarah. I haven't seen her in such a long time and I thought we could have a nice visit."

"Sure you did," Rebecca said, glaring at Marty.

Marty quickly rose to his feet. "Well Wendy, maybe you can all go out to dinner. Sarah...and that boy...and you...and Matt. Becca can keep the kids."

"What?" Rebecca asked, turning to her husband with a look that asked, *since when?*

"I'm sure you won't mind keeping your grandkids for a few hours. Hell, I'll even pay for dinner."

Wendy smiled at Marty, "That sounds like a grand idea, but I don't..."

"Sure, that sounds like a good idea. Sarah would love to spend the evening with you. You all can have a nice dinner. It'll give you time to catch up. Wouldn't that be nice, Sarah?"

"We just caught up, and I've given up eating."

"See," Marty said, nodding. The he paused, looking at his daughter. "What?

"You know, eating," Sarah said casually, as she hunched her shoulders. "We gave it up a few months ago. Decided that we didn't want to indulge in a habit that we may not be able to keep."

Marty shook his head, turning to Wendy he said, "She's just kidding. You know how she is."

"No, I'm not," Sarah said, her tone serious.

"I think I should be going," Wendy stood abruptly.

"No, you just got here," Marty said.

"No, really Marty, I do have somewhere to be. I just wanted to stop by to see Sarah and say hello."

"Pop, I can't believe you would tell her my business."

"I didn't have to tell her — seeing who you married — it was just a matter of time. A blind man would have seen it coming."

"Just when I thought things could possibly change, that you could eventually turn into a human being, you say something like that. Damn."

"You watch your mouth girl. I'm still your daddy."

"Yeah, go ahead and rub that in."

"You two, stop!" Rebecca said in frustration.

"You hear that, Becca?" Marty said, pointing at his daughter. "That's where your granddaughter gets that smart-ass mouth."

Rebecca walked to the television set, pushed the off button, and turned to her husband. "Marty, I need to ask you something," she said, folding her arms, "and I want the truth. Why was Wendy here?"

"I told you, she wanted to see Sarah."

"They don't even like each other," she said, shaking her head not buying what he had said.

"But they're family and even if they aren't all hugs and kisses — family is family."

Rebecca examined him closely. She turned to leave the room, then turned back to Marty.

"How did Wendy know that Sarah would be here?" She eyed him suspiciously.

"I don't know? Maybe she was in the neighborhood and saw Sarah come in the house."

"In the neighborhood, huh? Sure she was. Well the next time she just happens to be in the neighborhood and stops by, when she leaves, she'll be taking you with her."

"What the hell is that supposed to mean?"

"Figure it out," Rebecca stated, storming from the room.

Chapter 21

Matt slipped the dark blue sweater over his head as he walked into the kitchen. He opened the oven door and checked the sweet potato pies. The sweet aroma of sugar and cinnamon drifted toward him. Grabbing the potholders, he took the pies from the oven and set them on the cooling rack. Reaching for the phone, he dialed Simone's number.

"Hello," she whispered.

"Hey, did I wake you?"

"No, not really. I was just resting."

"I just called to say, 'Happy Thanksgiving'."

"Thanks. You, too."

"Are you headed over to your folks?"

"No, I'm staying in today. I'm a little under the weather. I have a bug."

"I'm sorry to hear that. How long have you been sick?"

"A couple of days. I'm getting over it though."

"So you guys are in for the day?"

"I was going to run out and get a few things later."

"What do you have to get?"

"I need some more Vicks Dayquil and probably a few more boxes of tissues."

"Maybe you shouldn't be going out. Can't Alan go out and pick it up for you?"

Simone was silent.

"He is there with you?"

"No, I'm alone, but I'm okay. I'm sure I'll be fine tomorrow. What are your plans for the day?" she asked quickly, changing the subject.

"I have plans to go and see my aunt in Pennsylvania. Each year the family rotates to a different home for Thanksgiving and

Christmas. This year my aunt Helen was the winner," he paused, "or the loser, depending on how you want to look at it. And lucky me, I get to drive all the way to Uniontown, Pennsylvania, with two little girls that I'm sure cannot hold their water more than an hour."

Simone laughed. "That all sounds like fun, even the pit stops. Hold on for a sec." She moved away from the phone and Matt heard several sneezes. "Sorry. Have a great time and have a safe trip."

"I will. And you take care of yourself."

"Thanks."

• • •

Matt hung up and glanced around the kitchen. He didn't like that Simone was sick and home alone on Thanksgiving. And where was Alan? What sort of man would leave his woman alone and go off with his friends or family while she was sick, especially on a holiday. Why wasn't he taking care of Simone? You can bet she would be there to take care of Alan's sorry ass. Matt shook his head in disgust muttering, "Asshole." Then he picked up the phone and called his mother.

• • •

Simone answered the door wearing dark blue flannel pajamas. Her hair was in a braid hanging down her back and it looked like she hadn't combed it in the last 24 hours. Her face was puffy. Her nose and eyes were red. Matt's heart melted. He wanted to take her in his arms and hold her tight. "Hey, what are you doing here?" Simone asked, surprised to see him.

"Taking care of you, of course," he said, walking past her. In his arms he carried two grocery bags. Simone closed the door and followed him into the kitchen.

"I thought you were headed to Pennsylvania?"

"Change of plans." He looked at her, smiling at the amazed look on her face. "Why don't you go take a hot bath and relax while I fix you something to eat?" Matt said.

Setting the bags on the counter, he started removing the contents. Taking out a 2-liter bottle of ginger ale, a mixed variety of

fruits, and several baggies of vegetables, he went to the refrigerator and put everything inside. He removed several cans and set them on the counter.

"I thought that Sarah, Vince and the kids were riding with you?"

"I talked to Ma. She's letting Sarah drive her car."

"Matt, this is really wonderful of you and I really appreciate that you would do this for me, but I don't want to ruin your holiday. Why don't you just let me do that? You go and spend the day with your family."

"No," he stepped toward her, "I'm where I want to be. Now about that bath?" he said, ushering her from the kitchen.

• • •

Forty-five minutes later, Simone walked out of the bedroom wearing red pajamas and a bright yellow robe, her freshly washed hair hanging loose down her back.

Matt had made a centerpiece using multi-colored gourds and Indian corn, adding several orange and yellow flowers. Around the centerpiece, he had placed eight brown-sugar-and-spice scented candles. Simone noticed what a cozy feeling the light gave the room. Matt had set places for the two of them.

"Feel better?" he asked as he came out of the kitchen.

"Much," Simone said. She glanced at the coffee table and saw a box of Dayquil and two boxes of tissues. She smiled as she walked to the dining room table and sat down.

"Here you are, my lady," Matt said using a terrible English accent. "Thanksgiving dinner is served." He placed a bowl of turkey noodle soup in front of her. "We have turkey, peas, carrots and pota-toes." He went back into the kitchen and brought out two glasses of cranberry juice. "Can't forget the cranberries and pumpkin pie." He looked at Simone and saw the tears welling in her eyes. "Hey, what's wrong?"

"Nothing," she quickly wiped her eyes, shaking her head. "It's just...thanks."

"No problem," he said, as he took her hands and gently kissed her knuckles.

• • •

Sitting on the sofa Matt and Simone watched "It's A Wonderful Life." When a commercial came on, Matt asked Simone if she was comfortable and if she needed anything.

"If you don't mind, I'd really appreciate a blanket and pillow," she replied.

Matt went into the bedroom and took one of the pillows and a blanket from the bed. Before leaving the room, he picked up the brush from the dresser. When he returned to the sofa, he helped Simone down to the floor in front of him, putting the pillow behind her back and draping the blanket around her.

Matt gently brushed her hair, his fingers softly massaging her scalp as she watched George Bailey run to the bridge telling Clarence that he wanted to live again. She watched intently as Bert the policeman approached George and George threatened to hit the cop again.

"I love this part," she said, and softly recited with Jimmy Stewart, "My mouth's bleeding, Bert! My mouth's bleed...Zuzu's petals! Zuzu's...they're...they're here, Bert! What do you know about that? Merry Christmas!" Then she gently leaned to her left, resting her head on Matt's knee.

Setting the brush on the seat next to him, Matt continued to stroke Simone's hair. He closed his eyes. His heart fluttered and felt heavy at the same time; he knew that he was madly and hopelessly in love with this woman. A woman with the most loving spirit and compassionate heart he'd ever seen. And she could never be his. An overwhelming feeling of sorrow filled him. He took a deep breath, storing this precious moment in his memory forever.

Chapter 22

Rebecca was full of excitement. She sat across from Matt at his kitchen table waiting for Sarah to come downstairs. They had spent Thanksgiving night in Pennsylvania with Marty's sister and they didn't have a chance to go Christmas shopping on Black Friday. It was not the first Saturday after Thanksgiving that thrilled Rebecca. It was that her daughter was going shopping with her for the first time in two years. Matt had his bills spread out on the table as he wrote checks. "Ma, you seem as if you're going to burst."

Rebecca beamed at him. "I feel like it. I love Christmas shopping. Since Sarah moved away, it's just didn't seem the same. I'm so happy she's here. I've really missed her."

Matt smiled at his mother. Rising from the table, he moved to the counter to prepare them each a cup of coffee. Rebecca looked at the bills he had spread across the table. "Matt, you didn't sell that condo yet?"

"No, I have a realtor all set to list it. I just haven't moved all the extra stuff out."

She tilted her head watching him and he knew that look. Sighing, he said, "Ma, I'm over Wendy. Really I am. I just can't seem to let go of the past. It's that one last piece."

"Matt, sometimes it's hard to let go."

"I know it doesn't make sense but I just can't seem to do it."

• • •

Running from the kitchen to the living room, Simone turned down the radio, grabbing the phone on the fourth ring. "Hello."

"Hi, Simone."

"Hey, Tamara, how have you been?"

"I've been good. How about you?"

"Okay."

"I'm sure you're busy."

"Not really, you're giving me a break from my Saturday morning chores."

The other woman was silent for a moment.

"Simone, I need to ask you something."

Simone closed her eyes...*damn*...she sat down, nervously twisting her ring around her finger, dread building with each passing second. "Ah, sure."

"I want to know about Charles and Tanya?"

Shit, shit, shit, Simone thought to herself. First she splashed bleach on her favorite red sweater and then Alan called to demand that she have brunch with him and his parents the next morning. And now Tamara. *This day just keeps getting better and better and better.* "Tamara, why would you be calling me asking about Charles and Tanya?"

"Because she's your friend and Charles all but told me that you knew." Simone was quiet. "Simone, I love you like a sister and I know you love me. Please don't lie to me."

Simone paused. "Tamara, I do love you and I swear I would never do anything to hurt you, but I don't think it's fair of you to put me in this situation. Regardless of what Charles has done, he's still my brother."

Tamara didn't respond for a long while. "Simone, did you know that he was seeing her?"

"No," Simone said. The other woman heaved a heavy sigh.

"Thanks, Simone, I'll talk to you later," the other woman said and she hung up abruptly.

The doorbell rang startling from Simone from her thoughts. She strolled to the door, peeked out the window, then smiled.

"Hey, girlfriend."

"Hey," Simone said, embracing Karen, "I'm glad you stopped by. I could use some company."

"I'll bet you will never guess what I found in your drive way?"

"Not the neighbor's puppy again?" Simone said, stepping onto the porch.

"Nope, a full-grown woman," Karen said, grabbing René's hand and pulling her close.

"Hey you, what brings you by?"

"Max is away on one of his business trips, and I have the whole day free. I thought, what better way to spend it than with my favorite sister."

"I'm your only sister," Simone said with humor in her voice.

"Just a technicality."

They both laughed as Simone gave her sister a hug and ushered both women into the house.

"New hairstyle?" Simone asked, admiring her sister's hair.

"Yeah, I thought it was time for a change."

"Girl, you're looking at her. Don't you notice anything different about me?" Karen asked, her hand on her hip. Simone turned to her, assessing her appearance.

"No," she said, smiling.

"Girl, don't play with me."

"Well," Simone said, placing her finger on her chin, "I can't really say that you look like the same old Karen to me." Karen sucked her teeth and Simone grinned.

"You finally got the color contacts."

"Yeah, you like?"

"Looks great. How do they feel?"

"The first few days I caught hell. I dropped one down the drain the first night I took them out. That bitch at The Vision Center jinxed me by telling me that a lot of her customers drop one down the drain when they first start wearing them. When I saw that thing go down the drain, it was like watching a movie in slow motion. And while I watched it slip down the drain into the abyss, all I could hear was her voice." The three women laughed as they made their way farther into the living room. René and Karen sat on the sofa with Simone sitting across from them on the armchair.

"What the story with the pr… I mean Alan?" Karen asked, grinning.

"Who cares about how Alan is," René said before Simone had a chance to answer. She crossed her legs and leaned forward. "What I want to know is how Matt's doing?"

Simone smiled. "He's all right, too."

"Mmm...he's more than all right," Karen said, fanning herself.

"So you've met him?" René asked Karen. Karen gave Simone a 100-watt smile.

"Oh, I sure did. Simone didn't tell you what happened?"

"What happened?"

"It was nothing," Simone chimed in quickly.

"Let me tell you. Our little Simone went out with Beverly and me and got pissy drunk."

"No, not Simone?"

Karen nodded, still grinning.

"Simone!" René said, looking at Simone in disbelief.

"No, I didn't," Simone quickly denied.

"Yes, she did," Karen said just as quick. "René, you should've seen her. She was talking all loud. Can you imagine that mousy voice saying 'I'm not going to let Debra push me around anymore' and 'I'm not standing for it'? She even tried to dance!"

"Oh — that had to be priceless."

"She did this little twitchy thing with her head and her arms. It was a sight."

"You both know that I can't stand you, right?" Simone said dramatically.

"And by that time she was so drunk she could barely stand at all."

René laughed uncontrollably, turning to look at Simone.

Simone rolled her eyes. "Seriously, it wasn't like that."

"She was so drunk she called Matt and, when he heard she was drunk and at some bar, he came running."

"And I wasn't pissy drunk," Simone put in, her lips pursed as she crossed her arms.

"What?" Karen shot a questioning look at her. "Say that again?"

"Okay, maybe I was a little."

"The next day she told me she couldn't remember anything that she did the night before. Now tell me, was that drunk or was that pissy drunk?" Karen asked René.

"I'm not a professional on the subject or anything, but it sure sounds like she was pissy drunk to me," René said in a sing-song voice.

"Whatever," Simone said, playfully rolling her eyes.

"And guess what Matt calls Simone?" Karen said, batting her eyes at Simone. "His angel." She smiled broadly. "Isn't that cute?"

"He doesn't call me that."

"Yes, he does, I heard him myself," Karen teased. "He has the hots for you!"

• • •

Twenty minutes later, there was a knock at the door. "Be right back?" Simone rose from the sofa and looked out the window. She was surprised to see Rebecca Turner and another woman. "Hi Mrs. Turner," she said as she opened the door.

"Hi, Simone. I hope this is not a bad time."

"No, come in." She let the women enter the house. When Rebecca entered and saw the other women sitting on the sofa, she apologized.

"You have company. I'm sorry, I should have called first."

"That's all right," Simone assured her. "What can I do for you?"

"It was nothing. I just wanted you to meet my daughter, Sarah Rodriguez."

"Nice to meet you, Sarah." Simone reached for Sarah's hand.

"Nice to meet you, too, Simone. I've heard so many good things about you." Simone turned from the door.

"This is my friend Karen Edwards and my sister René Evert.

"Karen, René, this is Matt's mother, Rebecca Turner, and his sister, Sarah."

"Hi," they both said, waving from the sofa.

"Can I get you anything?"

"No, thank you. I have to drop Sarah off at the mall. I have Marty's truck. I was going to go over to Matt's old condo to move a few of his things out. I just wanted to stop by to say hello."

"You didn't tell me you were going to do that," Sarah said, looking at her mother.

"I just decided to do it this morning. It'll only take me a couple of hours and then I'll meet you back at Matt's house."

"No, Mom, you shouldn't be doing that alone. I'm sure he'll get around to doing it eventually."

"I know he will, but he has so many things on his mind, and I don't mind doing it," Rebecca said.

Sarah pressed her lips together. "Well if you insist on doing this, I guess I should help you."

"If you need help, I'm there," Simone volunteered.

"Hey, I'll help, too," René called from the sofa. Simone smiled back at the two women.

"Not me," Karen said, quickly waving her hand.

• • •

"I wouldn't mind if you helped a little," Simone said, passing Karen a glass and some newspaper.

"Yeah?" Karen sat on the kitchen counter casually swinging her legs. She took the paper, wrapped one glass, crossed her arms, and continued to swing her legs as she spoke, "Hey, did you know Tanya quit last week?"

"No, I didn't know. Did she say why?"

"Nope, just up and quit. Not one word. No notice or anything. Have you heard from Charles?"

Simone sighed. "He and Tamara are living apart. Charles told Tanya that he would take care of her baby but he didn't want to spend time with either of them."

"That's so ignorant," Karen said. "It's not the child's fault."

"I know. I tried to talk to him, but you know he's selfish."

"Sooo," Karen said, grinning. "When are you and Matt going on a real date?"

"We're not."

"Why not?"

"Because."

"*Because* is not an answer."

"Karen, we've been over this before. I'm still seeing Alan. We have a relationship, and it wouldn't be fair."

"No you are not." Karen pointed a finger at Simone. "Your mother is seeing Alan vicariously through you. You're just going along for the ride. You don't have a relationship with him. You told me yourself you hardly like him."

"I don't know if I said those exact words."

"Close enough. Tell me — do you get excited when you know he's coming to pick you up? Do you think of him all the time?"

"Those are not things that are important in a relationship."

"That's not you talking. That's Debra. Come on, Simone, anyone that sees you and Matt together can tell he cares for you." Karen sighed dramatically. "I guess you two are the only dopes that can't see it."

"Girl, stop," Simone whispered.

"You know I'm right. What are you scared of? If I had that fine man ogling over me, I would throw him on my bed and wear him out," Karen said, wiggling her butt on the counter.

"Wear who out?" Sarah asked, walking into the kitchen.

"Nothing," Simone said, eying Karen.

"Yeah, it's nothing," Karen said. She watched Simone put the last glass in a box and pick up the box to carry it from the kitchen. She jumped from the counter and followed Simone into the living room.

"I think that about does it," Rebecca said, walking back into the condo after putting the last box in the truck.

Simone, René and Sarah stood looking at an overstuffed sofa that had been reupholstered with what had to be the ugliest fabric in the world.

"Do you think he wants this thing?" Sarah asked, nudging the sofa with the toe of her shoe.

"I believe so. I think he loves that ugly monster," Rebecca said, patting the round back.

"Why?" Sarah said, frowning.

"He said it holds sentimental value."

"It should hold the sentiment of what not to put in your house," Karen said from the spot she had bonded herself to after moving two boxes.

"It really is hideous," Simone said, looking at the blue and brown paisley monster. "So what do we do with it?"

Rebecca brushed a few stray hairs from her forehead. "I guess we can take it to the house and let him decide what to do with it."

"Do you think we can get it down the steps?" René asked.

"We can, with the five of us helping," Simone said, looking at Karen. "Karen do you think you could give us a hand?"

"Hey, I don't do manual labor. Why do you think I got a job sitting on my ass?"

"If you help, we'll feed you," Simone said, knowing just what to say to get her friend moving.

Karen quickly jumped to her feet. "Why didn't you say that in the first place?"

Rebecca laughed, saying, "That's the fastest I've seen you move today."

"Never let it be said that Karen Edwards would let the opportunity for a free meal get past her." The women laughed and gathered around the sofa.

After fifteen minutes, they were able to get the sofa into the hall and halfway down the steps. Simone and Sarah lost their footing, slipped and dropped the sofa. They heard a loud crunch and looking under the bottom they saw that two of the legs were broken and the center of the base was cracked.

"Oh, shit," Sarah whispered, looking at the other women, "what are we going to do?"

"I don't know. It's halfway down now. It wouldn't make

much sense to take it back upstairs. I think we should just take it to Matt's house," Rebecca said, her eyes large and innocent.

"Matt is going to be pissed," Sarah said.

"No, he won't. It was a mistake," her mother insisted.

Sarah just stood shaking her head. "Doesn't mean he won't be pissed."

"Well, we can't change it now. It's done already and we might as well keep on moving it," René said.

"What do you think Simone?" Sarah asked, looking at her.

"I think your mother's right. We can't leave it here, so we might as well take it to his house."

"No, I say we take it to the dump and tell him someone stole it from the curb while we were in here packing up everything else." Sarah said quickly.

"He'll never believe that. Who would steal that ugly thing?" René said, shaking her head.

"He wanted it. Who's to say there's not some other knuckle-head out there with the same awful taste?" Sarah said. Rebecca laughed, shaking her head at her daughter.

"What do you think Karen?" Sarah asked, looking at Karen, who was standing on the other end of the sofa. Karen scratched her head looking puzzled.

"Damn, I hope this doesn't interfere with lunch."

• • •

Matt spread jelly on the bread as he smiled at his 4-year-old niece, Sadie. She sat at the kitchen table drawing in her sketchpad, chattering away, her chestnut-brown hair framing her small round face. Matt peeled a banana, sliced it and placed it on the sandwich.

"Uncle Matt, do you know what D-A-M-N spells?" she asked.

"Yeah," he answered, glancing at her curiously. "Why?"

"Because my friend Stacy spelled it, and my teacher, Mrs. Gilmore, said it was a bad word?"

Matt smiled and nodded. "Yes, it's a bad word."

"Mrs. Gilmore said that only bad little girls say bad words and if they do, they have to sit with soap in their mouth."

"Oh yeah?" Matt thought that was harsh treatment for a 4-year-old.

"And that the little girls will just cry and cry," Sadie continued, "because the soap is so nasty, and they will never say a bad word again."

"Is that so?"

"Yup," she said, looking at Matt, her eyes bright. "Humph, Mrs. Gilmore don't know Sadie likes soap. Sadie thinks soap is mmm-mmm good." She smiled broadly, displaying deep dimples.

Matt laughed, shaking his head.

"Hello?" He heard his mother's voice call from the living room. He placed the plate in front of Sadie, then walked into the living room. His mother, sister, Simone, Karen, and another woman he'd never met stood in the middle of the floor holding boxes. "Where do you want these?" Rebecca asked him.

"What is all this?" Matt asked, surveying the box in his mother's arms.

"The stuff from the condo," she said, meeting her son's gaze.

Matt shook his head slightly as he walked to his mother, taking the box and kissing her on the cheek. Then, whispering, "Thanks," he walked back to the sofa. "You can just set them on the floor in front of the couch and I'll take care of them later."

"We sort of…," Rebecca started when Sarah cut in.

"Matt, what were you going to do with that old beat up sofa in the apartment?"

"I don't know?" he said, hunching his shoulders.

"You just bought that one," she said gesturing toward the brown leather sofa in his living room.

"You certainly don't need two."

"Yeah, but the old one is nice. It's really comfortable." He paused. "I guess I could take it over to the church and give it to charity," he said.

"You know what?" she said, smiling at him. "We have it on

the truck already, so don't worry about it. We'll take care of it for you."

"I can drive it over there now," he stepped toward the front door.

"No, don't worry about it," Sarah said, turning Matt and pushing him toward the kitchen. "We have everything under control."

"All right," he said, slightly suspicious of his sister's eagerness. "Thanks. I think." Sarah looked at Simone, smiled and winked.

• • •

"Matt, thanks for inviting us to dinner," René said, scanning the menu.

"No problem. Thanks for helping my mother earlier today." Matt, Simone, Karen, René and Vince sat at one of the tables in Parthenon's Greek restaurant.

"Everyone better know what they want because I'm starved," Sarah said, searching for the waiter. After everyone placed their orders, they all made small talk over their salads. A short time later their food was served and Sarah entertained everyone with stories of life with Marty Turner.

"Simone?"

Simone glanced to her right to see Alan standing over her. "Hi, Alan." She wiped her mouth quickly, and standing, she let her lips lightly brush his. Then she quickly introduced Alan to Sarah and Vince. Alan nodded to them, not acknowledging Karen or Matt.

Walking around the table, Alan gave René a quick kiss on the cheek. "How in the world did you end up with this bunch?"

"What are you doing here?" Simone asked as she sat down.

"I'm here with a few of my colleagues," he said, glancing down at Simone's plate and giving her a disapproving look.

Karen saw the look on his face and quickly asked, "Alan where are your friends? I might know them."

"I'm sure you don't. You wouldn't be on their level," Alan answered.

"Alan!" Simone chastised him quickly.

Karen gave him her *oh no you didn't* look, but before she had a chance to say something, Matt said, "I don't suppose she associates with assholes much, unless you want to include yourself."

Karen grinned at Matt, saying, "Oh, I like you."

"Turner, do you have a problem with me?" Alan asked, his tone light.

"I've been trying really hard to like you, but you're not making it easy for me."

Alan walked back to Simone's side. "Frankly, I don't give a damn if you like me or not. I'd much rather you didn't like me, that way we both know where we stand. When Simone ends your friendship, you'll know exactly why." Though Matt remained seated, he clenched both fists. He wanted to leap across the table and strangle this ignorant asshole, but he stayed calm. "Soon Simone will realize that you care nothing about her and that you are probably just trying to get what any man wants from a woman."

Matt stood abruptly, leaning over the table and facing Alan, "I happen to have Simone's best interests at heart," Matt said. "I respect Simone as a woman and a friend. Can you say the same?" Matt leaned on the table so hard that it moved slightly.

Karen grabbed her plate pulling it closer. "If you guys spill my food, I am not going to be happy."

"I've shown her nothing but respect," Alan said, poking his finger into Matt's chest a little harder then necessary.

"That's not what I've seen," Matt disagreed.

"Why don't we take this outside?" Simone said, already standing, pulling Alan's arm, and leading him to the door.

"Simone, I don't want you seeing this man again," Alan stated, glaring at Matt.

"Simone and I will see each other whenever we damn well please. Not you or anyone else can do anything to change it." The waiter stepped close to Alan's side and calmly suggested the two men leave the restaurant.

Alan disregarded what the man said. "Oh, we'll see about that." Alan walked back to the table and picked up Simone's coat and purse. "Simone, we're leaving."

"No Alan, I'm not leaving," she said quickly, extracting her things from him.

"Yeah, she's not going anywhere with you," Matt said smugly.

Simone looked over her shoulder at him. "Shut up, you've caused enough trouble." Matt smiled sheepishly at her, then bit the side of his mouth.

"You had better stay away from Simone," Alan threatened.

"Or you'll do what?" Matt asked softly. "Are you threatening me? Because, I've been itching for a fight for weeks now. You want to accommodate me?" Alan glared hostilely at Matt, his jaw clenched.

René stood quickly, pulling Simone to her side. Sarah stood too, grabbing Matt's arm. Karen and Vince were still watching and eating as if the whole show was for their entertainment.

Chapter 23

Lying across the bed, Matt thought about the evening's events as he stared up at the ceiling. Why did he have to go out of his way to piss off that jerk? He wanted to protect Simone, but the only thing he succeeded in doing was pushing her to defend Alan. He picked up the cordless phone to call her and changed his mind, putting the receiver back on its base. He groaned and brought his arm up, covering his face. He listened to Sarah down the hall bathing the children. He missed having other people in the house. He was glad he had convinced his sister and brother-in-law to stay with him instead of a hotel. "Sadie, stop licking the soap," he heard Sarah shout. He smiled to himself, sighed and picked up the phone.

Simone laid her book on the nightstand and rubbed her tired eyes. She reached for the ringing phone. "Hello."

"Hey, are you busy?" Matt asked.

"No."

"Feel like talking for a while?"

She let out a slow breath. "I guess so."

He waited a moment and said, "I'm sorry about what happened at the restaurant. I don't know what came over me." She remained silent. "You still there?"

"Yeah, I'm here."

"I just wanted to apologize. I really am sorry."

"Okay," she whispered.

"Will you forgive me?"

"Yes, I guess so."

"Are we still friends?" he asked.

"Of course," she said, sighing.

"So what are you doing?" he asked with a lighter voice.

"I was just reading."

"Do you feel up to company?"

"It'll take you forty minutes to get here," she said.

"I don't mind if you'll wait up," he said, closing his eyes hoping she would say yes. Simone looked at the clock, which read 10:45 p.m.

"I don't know," she said.

"Come on, it's Saturday night. I could stop and pick up some ice cream and cookies. Maybe rent a couple of movies. We could binge all night, and I won't tell a soul," he said, trying to convince her. Simone smiled to herself.

"Okay, that sounds fun."

"Great," he said, standing up quickly, "see you soon"

"Hey," Simone called before he could hang up.

"Yeah."

"Can you get peanut butter cookies, too?"

"Anything you want, Angel."

Matt walked bristly across the room and opened one of the drawers of his dresser. He pulled out a pair of gray sweat shorts and a white tank top. He dressed quickly and slipped on a pair of beach sandals. He met Sarah on his way down the hall.

"Hey, where are you off to?"

"I'm going out for a while."

• • •

Picking up the DVD's on the seat next to him, Matt dropped them inside the shopping bag he'd gotten from the all-night super-market. After getting out of his truck, he walked briskly up the front steps and knocked on the front door.

"Come on in," Simone called from inside the house. Pushing the door open, he walked into the living room. Simone had removed the pillows from the sofa and lined them on the floor in front of it. Then, using the pillows from her bedroom and the guest room she piled them behind the sofa pillows for them to rest their backs against. She had moved the television and DVD player to the floor in front of the pillows. She walked out of the kitchen wearing hydrangea-pink shorts and a matching t-shirt.

"I made popcorn," she said, smiling at Matt. He gulped a few times trying to swallow the lump in his throat.

"Hey," he finally said. She walked to the pillows sitting in front of the television. She looked up at him, confused.

"What's wrong?" she asked.

"Nothing," he said, walking toward her.

"Sit down," she said, reaching for the bag that he held. He stood watching her, his eyes never leaving her face. He studied her, her soft hair hanging loosely around her shoulders, falling forward when she leaned over and dug into the bag. "What did you get?" she asked. He didn't answer. She looked up at him. "Did something happen on the way over here?" she asked, concerned.

"Uh, no, I'm sorry. I got rocky road and butter pecan." He stared down at her, still unable to move.

"Mmm. I like both of them. Which do you want?"

"We can share," he said. She set a spoon and the pint of rocky road on the pillow where he would be sitting and looked up at him again.

"Well, are you going to watch the movie standing up?"

"Uh...oh...no...of course not."

"Then sit down," she demanded. He moved the ice cream from the pillow and sat next to her.

"What are we watching?" Simone asked.

"I got three different movies. First we have the psychotic chaos of "Texas Chain Saw Massacre," "The 40-Year-Old Virgin" for the comedian in all of us and "Sweet Home Alabama" for the hopeless romantic. Your choice."

"I vote for murder and mayhem first," Simone said, raising her hand and waving it like a child. Matt grimaced and shook his head laughing.

"Murder and mayhem it is." He reached in the bag, took out the movie and moved to the television, squatting down in front of it. He popped the DVD inside the player and pushed the start button.

Simone watched his movement. Her eyes traveled down his broad back to his firm round hips and muscular thighs. He looked

back, meeting her gaze. She smiled nervously, looking away. His lips twitched and a slow smile spread across his face.

"Were you checking out my butt?" he asked, amused.

"Yeah, right," Simone said, forcing herself to laugh. "You wish." She took the top off of the butter pecan ice cream, shoved the spoon in and scooped out a huge mouthful. Matt watched her blush and he chuckled as he moved back to his spot next to her on the pillows.

Halfway through the movie, Matt found himself grimacing at all the gore. He looked over at Simone. "Whew, why do you like this crap?"

"It's fun to be scared sometimes," Simone said.

"I'm assuming you never had nightmares as a kid?"

"Boy, I lived with Debra Porter for 19 years. I would have welcomed nightmares when she was on a rampage," Simone said, never taking her eyes from the television. Matt laughed. He found it amusing that she was so gentle and sweet, but liked watching movies that made his hair stand on end. She looked at him. "What?"

"Nothing," he said, still smiling. "I want to apologize again for my behavior this evening."

"I forgave you earlier," she said, turning back to the television.

"You sure?" he asked.

"I'm positive. Unfortunately, I have a soft spot for jerks," she said, smiling to herself.

"I'm glad because I wouldn't want you to be angry with me."

"Mm-hm."

"That restaurant was pretty good. How was the fettuccini?"

"Why do you always have to talk during a movie? I'm trying to watch this," she said, pointing at the television with a fist full of popcorn.

"Do you want me to be quiet?" he asked, mischievously.

"I would appreciate that," she said, then yelled, "Run!" at the young woman on the television.

"I'll be back, I have to use the restroom," Matt said, getting up and walking down the hall.

Simone waved at him, still looking at the television. She reached for the remote and turned up the volume. After a few moments, she heard what she thought were footsteps creaking on the porch. Reaching for the remote, she put the movie on pause, listening. All was quiet. She pushed play again and turned her attention back to the television. Then she heard what sounded like a tap or scratch at the front door. She stopped the movie and stood up, creeping to the door. Peering out of the window, she didn't see anyone. Turning on the light, she looked out on the porch, scanning the yard, but not seeing anything. She turned the dead bolt and reached for the light switch, paused, and decided to leave the porch light on. She thought she saw a shadow move past the window.

"Matt? Are you all right?" she bit her lip, looking down the hall toward the closed bathroom door. A sudden tap at the window caused her to jump and she turned toward the window. Nervously, she glanced over her shoulder down the hall toward the bathroom. Maybe she should go and check on him. She heard tapping at the window again. She heard what sounded like loud drums and realized it was her heart beating. She took a deep breath to steady her nerves and reached for the curtain. She looked down the hall once more wondering what was taking Matt so long. *What if a psycho got into the house! What if he got Matt and he's waiting for me!* She looked at the window and squealed at the slight tap. With trembling hands, she pulled back the curtain and peered out the window. She didn't see anything. Closing her eyes she took a calming breath. When she opened her eyes someone was staring at her from the other side of the window.

She screamed, releasing the curtain and running to the sofa. Grabbing one of the throw pillows, she screamed, "Matt!!!!" at the top of her lungs. She sat in the corner of the sofa bringing her knees to her chest and hugging the pillow before she stopped screaming abruptly.

"What the hell?" She dropped the pillow and raced to the window. She drew the curtain back to see Matt with his face pressed

against the glass. She hit the window screaming "You!" He walked to the front door laughing uncontrollably. She went to the door and opened it letting him in. "You are such a jerk!" she screamed.

"I thought you like being scared?" he asked, still laughing.

"Only when I watch it on TV or in the movies, not in real life! What if I'd had a heart attack?"

"Then I would have given you CPR."

"Not if you couldn't get in," she said, going back to the television and flopping down on the pillows.

"I'm sorry," he said, laughing. "It was a joke." Simone looked at him and started laughing.

"You scared me half to death," she said. "I'm going to get you back." He sat down next to her.

"How?"

"I don't know? But I will," she said, taking a handful of popcorn and throwing it at him. He studied her face. He reached up and took her chin in his hand. Leaning close, he brushed his lips against hers. He drew back, looking into her eyes. He slowly slipped his arms around her, unsure why he sensed that any sudden movement would scare her away.

"You are so beautiful," he whispered, "I thought that the very first time I saw you." He leaned close, kissing her again. This time he allowed his tongue to slip past her lips, tasting her. His heart raced and he could hear his blood rushing in his ears. He drew back, his breathing labored.

"I'm sorry about that," he said, looking into her eyes.

"Don't be," she whispered. Their faces were just inches apart.

"I've been doing a lot of things I can't explain today," he said, resting his forehead against hers.

"No, I wanted you to."

Choosing his words carefully he said, "Simone, I know you think of me as your best friend, but I've never wanted a woman more than you. Ever. Do you want to be with me?"

"Yes," she said, moving closer. She timidly ran her hand along his chest. He moved her hands to the hem of his shirt, urging

her to help him remove it. As she slipped it over his head, he gently eased her blouse up. She reached for his hands. "No."

"Why?"

"I feel self-conscious. No one has ever seen me before."

"Alan has never seen you?" She averted her gaze, shaking her head. He drew in a deep breath, bringing his hand up stroking her cheek. "You're gorgeous." Tears escaped the rims of her eyes to run down her jaw. "What's the matter?"

"Nothing."

"Yes it is. Tell me?"

"No one's ever said that to me before."

"Maybe I need to tell you more often," he said, looking at her longingly. Opening his arms, he let her come to him. She slowly moved forward allowing him to embrace her. She closed her eyes as his mouth tormented the flesh behind her ear. She drew back, looking deeply into his eyes.

"I don't know what to do. You'll have to show me," she said, struggling to hold back the tears that were streaming down her cheeks. He gently stroked her cheek, brushing away her tears. He kissed her again, placing his hand on her leg and moving it slowly up her thigh. Gently, he massaged her through the thin material of her shorts. She moaned slightly as he slid his finger inside her shorts and into her moist opening. His heartbeat quickened as he felt his manhood grow harder than he could ever remember. He slowly eased her down, moving next to her. Resting his weight on his elbow, he looked down at her. The passion he saw moments ago was gone. It has been replaced with uncertainty.

"Oh my God," he whispered, his mind speeding back to the things she had said to him. *No one's ever seen me before...I don't know what to do...you are going to have to show me.* He looked down at her and asked, "Are you a virgin?"

She bit her lip hesitantly, "No, of course not." He looked down at her, her green eyes looked up innocently at him.

"Shit," he said, sitting up and pulling her with him.

"What?" she asked, alarmed. "Did I do something wrong?"

"No," he yelled, immediately softening his tone. "No. We can't do this."

"But I want to," she said, placing her hand on his chest.

"No," he said, moving farther away from her. "Simone, talk to me. Something's not right."

"I don't know what you mean?"

"You said that Alan has never seen you naked and that you didn't know what to do. That sure sounds like a virgin to me."

She sighed. "Okay, Alan and I have never been intimate."

"What?"

"I told him that I wanted to wait until I was married."

"But you said…"

"I know what I said and I'm not."

"So how long has it been?"

"A few years."

"A few years? What, three?"

"No…a little longer than that."

"Four…. Five…?" When she didn't respond, he said, "You need me to keep going?"

"More like nine."

"Nine years, no way! You're trying to tell me that you haven't been with anyone in nine years?"

"My first time was when I was in high school. I thought that I was in love with him. I mean…it's a long story."

"But nine years. That would have made you?"

She took a deep breath before speaking. "Seventeen. I was seventeen my first time and my only time."

Matt's mind raced. Her only time was nine years ago when she was a kid. After, she decided that she wanted to wait until she was married. "I don't understand, why now?"

Simone bit her lip. Did she want to tell him how she felt? What if he didn't take her seriously? Worse yet, what if he didn't feel the same way about her? "I just decided not to wait any longer."

Matt shook his head. "You've waited a long time for this. It should be special."

"It will be special if it's with you."

He was quiet for a few moments. He needed to think. "Oh man," he whispered, "what have I done?"

"You're not attracted to me. That's it, isn't it?" Simone heaved a sigh and turned away from him.

"Hey, that is not true," he reached for her, but she shrugged off his touch.

"I'm fine. I just want to be alone and I'd like you to leave, please."

He sighed, reaching for his shirt. Then he looked at her.

"Can you look at me, please?" he asked. She turned to him angrily swiping tears from her cheeks. "I'm sorry," he said, wiping away the remaining tears. He stood quickly, sliding on his shoes. "I'll come by in a few days to get the movies." He walked to the door and turned back to her. She sat on the floor looking lost. "Are you going to be all right?" he asked. She could only nod. "I am not doing this to hurt you. You'll never know how much I want to be with you. I just don't want you to regret being with me. You chose to be celibate for so long, which has to be tough. I just think that now that you've decided to make love it should be with someone you love," he turned, walking out the door.

"But I love you," she whispered, so low he didn't hear her.

• • •

Matt jumped, seeing a figure standing at the bottom of the steps. He looked over at the clock. It read 4:30 a.m. "Hey," he said to Sarah.

"What are you doing down here beating the hell out of that punching bag this early in morning?"

"I couldn't sleep," he said, turning back to the bag.

"Obviously," she said, walking farther into the basement gym. She sat on the weight bench next to where he was pounding the bag. "Who are you so pissed at?" she asked.

"What makes you think I'm pissed?" he asked, out of breath.

"You did the same thing when we were kids. Whenever dad would push you to the limit, you would go the basement and beat

the hell out of that stupid burlap sack. I used to think you pretended it was Dad."

"No," Matt said, still punching, "I never pretended it was Dad. I use to pretend it was me and I was toughening myself up." Sarah shook her head at her brother.

"If it were me — that would have been an exact replica of dad," she looked at him. "So am I to assume that the bag is you?" she asked Matt. He didn't answer. He just hit the bag harder. "Okay, what did you do to warrant such an ass-whipping?" He stopped and looked at her. Then he walked to the bench where she sat. He picked up a towel and wiped his face. "Well?" she asked, raising a brow as she waited for him to answer.

"I think I might have ruined any chance I may have had with Simone."

"You really like her don't you?" Sarah asked. He sighed looking up at the tile ceiling.

"I think I'm falling in love with her," he said more to himself.

"I know, I can tell," Sarah said. "Mom can tell, too. That's why she wanted me to meet Simone." Matt looked down, his eyes meeting hers. She saw a sparkle she hadn't seen before.

"I've never wanted anyone or anything so badly in my life," he said.

"What about witchy...I mean Wendy?" Sarah said, smiling, apparently amused at her own humor.

"Not even Wendy. No one makes me feel like Simone does."

"Well, then," his sister said, "go for it."

"You make it sound so easy."

"It is. You just have to make it happen."

"It's not that easy. There are so many factors," Matt said.

"Like what?" she asked.

"Like her mom and Pop. That guy we saw earlier this evening."

"Ah," Sarah said, nodding. She now understood why Matt was so rude to Simone's friend at dinner that night. "You can win

over her mother. As for the other guy, just eliminate the competition," she said matter-of-factly. "And as for your father," she always referred to Marty as "your father" when she spoke about him to Matt in a negative way, "good luck to you on that one. Guess you could hold your breath and wait until he comes around. That'll probably be when hell freezes over. But I say if you really want her, then you make her yours."

Matt looked at his sister, admiring how she always thought you could do anything if you set your mind to it.

"Thanks, Sis."

Chapter 24

"Good morning," Alan mouthed, peeking into Debra's office.

She smiled brightly at him, nodded and waved him inside the office. After a few minutes she wrapped up her phone call, giving him her full attention.

"Well, good morning," she said cheerfully.

"I received a message that you wanted to see me?"

"Yes, sit down." Alan sat in the plush armchair in front of Debra's desk. She took off her glasses, meeting the young man's gaze. "How are you Alan?"

"I'm very well, thank you. And yourself?"

"I could be better." She glanced down and sighed heavily. With the index and middle fingers of both hands, she deliberately massaged her brow, giving her statement a more dramatic affect. "That's what I wanted to talk to you about," she continued. "It's Simone."

He raised his brows in surprise, "What seems to be the problem?"

Debra met his steady gaze. "I think that she's becoming disillusioned with your relationship." Alan made no comment. He just sat silently waiting for Debra to elaborate. "I don't mean to pry, but, as her mother I feel I need to ask you this." She paused, crossing her arms and resting them on the desk. "Where are the two of you in your relationship?"

"I don't know if I understand what you mean?" he said slowly.

"I mean, have the two of you spoken of making a serious commitment to each other, a commitment such as marriage?"

Alan moved nervously in his chair. "We haven't progressed to that stage yet." Debra rose from her desk, walked to the office

door and closed it. She returned to her desk and sat on the edge, crossing her arms.

"Tell me, what do you think of this Mathew Turner?"

Alan was silent for a moment, "Simone speaks highly of him."

"No," Debra said, shaking her head slightly and keeping constant eye contact with him. "I mean, what do you think of him?"

Alan placed his elbows on the armrests, steeling his fingers under his chin. "I don't care for him. I don't care for the way he behaves toward Simone."

"Meaning?"

Alan thought for a moment. "I believe that he wants more than friendship from Simone. I mentioned this to her, and she assured me that this was not the case."

"I've had the pleasure of meeting Mr. Turner and I have no doubt that he has more than friendship on his mind."

Alan glanced out the window. "I know that she spends a lot of time with him. But you know how she is. If she thinks that this man is her friend, she won't have a problem spending time with him." He turned back to Debra.

"Yes, I know that, and that's exactly what I'm afraid of. I think he'll take advantage of her. She's too trusting for her own good."

"Turner and I have had words, though I don't see where it has done any good. Maybe I should have a talk with him again?"

"No, I really think that Simone doesn't know where the two of you stand. If she did, then I'm sure she would be pursuing your relationship a little more." Alan watched Debra, not liking the direction the conversation seemed to be heading. "It's the uncertainty that has her so standoffish." Debra saw what looked like doubt in Alan's eyes. He didn't say it, but she believed he thought that there was more to Simone's unwillingness to move any farther in their relationship. She pushed on. "I know that you two don't have much in common as far as goals," she said, sighing, "but in time, with your guidance, Simone can get on the right path and see past her idealistic

views of changing the world. The two of you can have a wonderful life together. You can have the lives you deserve."

"So how do I to convince Simone of this?" he asked casually, wiping his palms on his pants and hoping that she didn't notice.

"We need to rid ourselves of Mathew Turner. I have an idea that will do that and bring Simone closer to you at the same time." She sat in the seat next to him. "Simone's birthday is coming up and we're going to have a birthday party for her. This is what you're going to do..."

• • •

After hanging up the phone, Alan leaned his elbows on his desk and put his face in his hands. He wasn't looking forward to this evening. Telling someone that you really cared about them was hard. Telling that person that you were planning to marry someone else would be unbearable. But it had to be done. He had let this thing go on long enough, and now it was time to end it. It would be much easier if he didn't care so damn much for Dana.

• • •

Alan turned off his car and got out slowly. Breathing deeply, he walked onto the porch. After ringing the bell, he waited for Simone to answer the door. "Hey Alan, I didn't expect to see you?"

"Simone, we need to talk," he said, stepping inside the house. "It's about one of the kids at the center. Mari Hernandez. She tried to commit suicide tonight."

Chapter 25

Reaching for the alarm clock, Matt pressed the button and rolled onto his back. He stayed in bed with his eyes closed for a few more minutes. Then, getting up quickly, he walked into the bathroom. He stripped off his clothes, stepped into the shower, and turned on the cold water to wake him up. After dressing, Matt walked into the kitchen, grabbed his thermos from the top of the refrigerator and left the house.

He drove downtown to the Einstein Bros. Bakery, arriving just as they opened. Taking the thermos he went inside. He selected a blueberry bagel for himself and one sesame and one chocolate chip for Simone. Then he had them fill the thermos with decaf coffee. Afterward he walked a few blocks, stopped at a florist shop and picked out two dozen of their best pink and white roses.

Once he got back to his truck, he placed everything on the seat next to him and reached over to open the glove compartment, taking out a small box wrapped with pretty blue paper. He fingered the silver ribbon, picturing the sparkle in Simone's eyes as she opened the gift and looked at him with pure pleasure. He smiled to himself and put the box on the seat next to the roses.

He drove to Simone's house. Stopping at the corner a few houses down as he prepared to turn onto her street, he saw Simone and Alan getting out the car. Matt paused, watching as they walked onto the porch and stopped at the door, talking. Matt put his truck in park and waited. Alan leaned down, kissing Simone gently on the lips, then turned and headed toward his car. Simone waved at Alan and waited as he pulled away from the curb. Alan headed in the opposite direction from where Matt's truck was. Simone waited until the car was out of view before going inside.

Matt watched the taillights of the car disappear. He glanced back at the house and sighed. Then propping his elbow on the arm-

rest and bringing his right hand to his face he massaged his eyes. He sighed heavily. Shifting the truck in gear, he drove home.

• • •

Matt argued with himself on whether he wanted to go to Simone's birthday party. After deciding not to go, he changed his mind at least a dozen times. Matt finally showered, dressed and left for his parent's house. "Are you ready to leave?" Matt asked, as soon as he stepped inside the house.

"Good evening to you, too," Rebecca said, frowning at her son.

"Sorry," he mumbled, shoving his hands in his pockets. "Hey, Ma."

She nodded slightly, asking, "Is everything all right?"

"Yeah, everything's just peachy," he said, tight lipped.

"Something's bothering you. What's wrong?" She turned to her son, waiting for him to answer her.

"Ma, I really don't want to talk about it," Matt said quickly. Rebecca opened her mouth preparing to say something when Marty stormed into the room.

"Well if we have to go, then let's go and get it over with," Marty grumbled. Matt looked at his father, his eyebrows raised.

"You're going?"

"I have to," Marty said, looking at his wife. "If I don't, I'll have to fix my own supper for the next week." Rebecca picked up the gift from the table.

"Damn," Marty grunted. "For crying out loud, we have to take a present too?" Rebecca shook her head as she pushed him toward the door.

As he sat in the cab of his truck listening to his father gripe about being forced to wear a tie. Matt wanted to turn the truck around and go home. He knew he was making a mistake. He knew it when he took a shower and got dressed. He knew it while he sat in his driveway in the truck for twenty minutes before he started the engine. He wasn't ready to see Simone, not now. Not when he

knew that she had chosen to be with Alan. He tried to convince himself that it didn't matter to him. That it wasn't his business, but he couldn't erase the image from his mind of Simone kissing Alan. He couldn't let go of the anger.

"Did you see the game last night?" Marty asked, leaning around Rebecca to see Matt.

"No."

"It was pitiful, just pitiful. Edgar and some of the boys are gonna try and get tickets for the next game. Wanna come?" Marty watched Matt's face, waiting for an answer. "Matt?"

"Marty, leave him alone. I don't think he's feeling very well," Rebecca said. Knowing Matt's mood, she thought it best to keep her husband from noticing it.

"What, you got a bug or something? 'Cause if you do, we should go back home. We don't want to be spreading it to all them folks," Marty said eagerly.

"No, I'm fine," Matt said, gripping the steering wheel.

"What's wrong with you?"

"There's nothing wrong with me."

"Oh, I see what it is," Marty said, studying Matt. "You and that gal had a fight." When Matt slowed at a red light, he reached for the radio and tried to tune out his father. As Los Lonely Boys sang about "Heaven," the light turned green and Matt pulled off. Marty reached for the radio, turning it off.

"So what happened? What did she do?" Marty asked.

"She didn't do anything."

"She must have done something for you to be mad at her."

"I'm not mad at her."

"If you aren't mad at her, then who the hell pissed in your cornflakes?" Marty asked, raising his voice as he spoke.

"Ma?" Matt said, glancing pleadingly at his mother.

"Marty, shut up," she said.

"Why are you telling me to shut up? He's the one with a bug up his ass."

"Leave him alone!" she ordered her husband.

Marty grunted, folding his arms. "You know what? I'm get-

~ 232 ~

ting real tired of you people thinking you can tell me what to do." He turned away and looked out the window.

• • •

Matt parked a few doors down and on the opposite side of the street from the Porters' home. He put the truck in park and looked at the house with all of its festive lights. He could tell his mother was watching him closely. He tried offering her a smile, hoping that she would believe that all was well, but he couldn't quite pull it off. "Why would these people invite us to their home, anyway?" Marty said, breaking the silence.

"Simone is a friend of the family and it's her birthday. It's going to be fun," Rebecca said, trying to lighten the mood.

"Yeah, I'm sure it's going to be a barrel of laughs," Marty said as they got out of the truck. They crossed the street, walked down the sidewalk, and up the walkway toward the house. "I hope they don't play any of that there jungle music," Marty said quickly.

"Pop. Behave," Matt whispered, cutting his eyes at his father.

"What?"

"You know what!" Matt said.

"I'm just saying," Marty said, hunching his shoulders, as they mounted the steps. Matt shot him a warning glance as he stepped to the door and rang the bell.

A moment later, Simone opened the door. She stood for what seemed like an eternity to her, which was actually only a moment, taking in Matt's appearance. He wore a black turtleneck tucked inside dark bluejeans and a black leather jacket. His hair hung loose around his shoulders and Simone thought she had never seen him look more handsome. "Hey," she finally spoke.

"Hey," he said, shifting his weight from one foot to the other.

"Well, shit," Marty grumbled loudly, "are we invisible or what?" Rebecca elbowed him in the side.

Simone turned to Marty and Rebecca, "Hi, Mrs. Turner, Mr. Turner."

"Hi, Simone," Rebecca said. Simone opened the screen door allowing the Turners access to the house. Rebecca gave Simone the gift she held with its pretty lavender paper and bright white bow. She reached for Simone, giving her a hug. "Happy birthday."

"Thank you," Simone said, smiling.

"You look sooo pretty," Rebecca raved. Stepping back, she held Simone's arms out to her side, looking at her winter-white mohair turtleneck and white wool slacks. "Doesn't she look pretty Matt?" Rebecca asked looking at her son.

"Yeah, Ma, Simone always looks beautiful," he said, meeting Simone's gaze. She smiled nervously and turned away.

"Come on," she said, "let me introduce you to some of the other guests." She led the Turners around the living room and introduced them to various family members and friends. She led them to her parents last. "Daddy, Mother," she called as she approached. "Mr. and Mrs. Turner, these are my parents, Joseph and Debra Porter."

"Very nice to meet you," Rebecca said, shaking first Debra's then Joe's hand.

"It's so nice to finally meet you," Debra said. She looked at Matt. "Mathew."

"Mrs. Porter," Matt said, nodding slightly. Joe stepped around his wife, taking Matt's hand.

"Matt, my boy, how have you been?"

"Fine, sir. And yourself?"

"Wonderful. Made any peach pies lately?"

"No, but I was thinking of making a couple next weekend. Maybe I could drop one off for you."

"Sounds good," he said, patting Matt's shoulder. "So how about those Ravens?"

Matt laughed, "I try not to think about them." They both laughed and Marty stepped closer. Hearing talk of sports, he joined the conversation. Debra chatted politely with Rebecca and excused herself by saying that she and Joe had to greet some of the other guests.

"Can I get you anything?" Simone asked Rebecca and Marty.

"No," Rebecca said, "you're the birthday girl. I should be serving you."

"Why don't we go together?" Simone said. She looked at Marty. "What would you like Mr. Turner?"

"What do you have?"

"We have punch, soft drinks, wine, or I could fix you a mixed drink."

"Now you're talking. I'll take a rum and coke," Marty said grinning.

"No," Matt said quickly, shaking his head and looking at his father. "I'll have coke. He'll have the same." Marty rolled his eyes at Matt, shoving his hands in his pockets.

Rebecca followed Simone into the kitchen and returned shortly with three glasses. Matt glanced in the direction of the kitchen and asked, "Ma, was Simone in the kitchen alone?"

"She was when I left."

Matt nodded, setting his glass on one of the many coasters scattered through the room and walked into the kitchen. He stopped in the doorway, watching Simone. She was standing at the counter peeking inside the cake box. Reaching inside, she scooped some of the frosting from the cake with her finger and poked it into her mouth before closing the top. This was the first time that he had seen her with her hair up. Ringlets of auburn hair curled around her face and at the nape of her neck. Matt thought to himself that she truly looked like an angel. He took a deep breath to slow the racing of his heart before stepping farther into the kitchen. She looked over her shoulder and, seeing him, she smiled.

"Hey."

"Hey. I wanted to say 'happy birthday'."

"Thanks."

"How are you?"

"I'm a little tired, but I'm good."

"So, I'm guessing you didn't get much sleep late last night?" he asked sarcastically.

"No, I didn't."

"I have something for you." He reached into his pocket and

pulled out the small gift. Stepping closer, he handed it to her. "I hope you like it." She took the box, tearing off the paper and opened it. Inside was a multi-gemstone bracelet.

"It's beautiful," she said, "thank you."

"You're welcome. I stopped by your house to give it to you this morning," he paused.

"I was there until eleven. I didn't hear you knock."

He was quiet, becoming instantly angry remembering the vision of her kissing Alan. His expression revealed no emotions, but his eyes burned with fire.

Simone tilted her head, confused. "Is something wrong? What's going on?"

He searched his mind, trying to come up with something to say, anything but what came from his mouth. "I didn't want to disturb you. You looked as if you were in the middle of something pretty deep." *Change the subject* the voice in the back of his mind warned.

"What are you talking about?" she asked, puzzled by his tone.

"Nothing," Matt said, shoving his hands deep in his pockets.

"No," she said as she walked to the doorway, leading to the other part of the house and closed the door. "If there's something going on, I'd like to know. Is there something you want to say to me?"

He turned away.

"Matt?"

"Did you sleep with Alan?" he cringed after he said it.

"I can't believe you would even have the audacity to ask me that."

He turned back to her, folding his arms and holding his head high.

"Well, did you?"

"Where is this coming from?"

"It doesn't matter. What matters is your answer."

Simone searched his face. "Matt, you need to go home," she

said softly. Tears welled in her eyes so quickly that she didn't have a chance to fight them back.

"Did turning you away...push you into his arms...into his bed?" He was angry, not at her, but at himself for asking her. Angry because he was the cause of the tears streaming down her face. "I know you don't love him. If you just wanted someone to be with... to have sex with...you should have said so."

"Screw you," her voice squeaked. Matt laughed at the sound in spite of himself.

"You know," he replied, his voice much lower than before. "This is none of my business. You're a grown woman. You can do whatever you want"

"Matt, go home. I don't want to talk to you." She turned her back to him. "I don't want to see you."

He paused, watching her. "Is that what you want?"

"It's what I want," she said, swallowing back the lump in her throat. He turned, heading through the house, weaving through the other guests as he made his way to the front door. He walked outside, leaving the door ajar.

Simone let out a small sob and leaned against the counter for support. *How could he say such things to her? Could he think so little of her that he would think she would sleep with Alan just to satisfy a sexual desire?* She let out a small sob, then jumped and turned to the sound behind her.

"I'm sorry," her father said, "I couldn't help but hear."

She looked away, brushing tears from her cheeks. "How much did you hear?"

"More than I should have," he said, then walked to her, taking her in his arms. She let the river of tears flow. "Everything will be fine," he cooed.

"Daddy, everything's such a mess. Matt has everything totally wrong and I don't know where it's coming from."

"He's jealous and he's a man. We sometimes let our emotions rule us...like you women do...we just handle it differently. You go. Find him and talk to him."

"I can't leave. Mother did all this for me and she'll be so upset."

"You let her know that you have to leave. I can take care of the rest," he drew back, looking at his daughter. "He loves you. I can tell. And you love him. Don't let a misunderstanding come between you." Simone nodded, wiping away her tears.

"Thanks, Daddy. I love you."

"I love you, too, baby girl."

Chapter 26

Getting into his truck, Matt rested his forehead against the steering wheel. He felt as if the world were closing in around him. *Why did I have to say those things? Why did I have to attack her like that?* The pain in his heart felt as if a hand were squeezing it and ripping it from his chest. He took a deep breath, trying to calm his racing heart. He needed to sort all this out and figure out what was wrong with him. "Damn it," he whispered, he already knew what was wrong. He was pissed off and jealous. He couldn't bear the thought of Simone being with Alan. He couldn't bear the thought of her being with any man but him.

He wanted to tell her how he felt, but what if she didn't feel the same way? He had to do something. Part of him wanted to run away and get away from everything. Another part of him wanted to take her in his arms and make her want him as much as he wanted her. What if she was so angry that she wouldn't forgive him?

He felt so many confusing emotions, and dammed if he didn't feel like crying. He shook his head, rubbing his eyes, trying to ease the tears he felt just below the surface. *When she told me to leave I should have said no. I should have stayed and talked to her... should have told her that I was sorry for being such a jerk...sorry for causing her pain.* He got out of the car and walked back up the walk toward the house.

• • •

Alan met Debra's gaze from across the room. Debra smiled, then nodded. Alan rose from his seat, setting his plate on the table next to him. He looked around the room searching for Simone. She was headed toward Debra. He crossed the room, quickly taking her hand, "Simone, do you have a minute?"

"Alan, I need to talk to you too, but I can't right now. I have to leave."

"It will only take a moment. Come with me." He led her to the center of the room. "Excuse me everyone, can I have your attention, please," he said loudly. Simone looked around seeing all eyes on them. She felt a sense of dread.

"Alan, I don't think this is a good time," she said, trying to pull her hand free of his.

"I want to say something," he said, facing Simone.

"Alan, don't," she said, placing her fingers on his lips trying to stop him and taking a step back. He grasped her hand, holding her to him.

"Simone, I want everyone here to know that I really care for you..."

• • •

Matt stepped inside the house, stopping in mid-stride and watching in disbelief as Alan took Simone's hand. "Like your mother pointed out to me before," Alan continued, smiling down at her. "We might have different ideas of careers, but we have a lot in common."

"No!" Matt bellowed, causing everyone in the room to turn in his direction. He walked across the room, meeting Alan's surprised gaze.

"What?" Alan stood stunned, not sure what to say.

"I'm sorry, man. This isn't about you," Matt said. He turned to Simone and looked deep into her eyes as he took her hand. "Simone, please, give me a chance."

"A chance for what, Matt?"

"A chance for us. Together." His voice was soft and unsure. "You are the most beautiful, desirable, loving woman I've ever met. Everything about you is perfect. The way you scratch your nose when you're nervous and the fact that you shared your lunch with the kid down the street when you were ten, even though your mother told you not to."

"You remember that?"

"I remember everything about you." Matt felt a lump in his throat. He slowly reached up, allowing his fingers to gently stroke her cheek. Simone gazed deep into his dark eyes. Alan watched the look that passed between them.

"Alan, do something!" Alan heard a whisper. He glanced to his right, startled and surprised that Debra was at his side so quickly. Alan stepped closer to Matt.

"Just what the hell do you think you're doing?"

As Matt looked into Simone's eyes, he saw his future. Everything he could ever want and everything he would ever need. "Something I should have done a long time ago," Matt said, not looking at the man next to him. "I love you, Angel. I can't live without you. Please give me a chance?"

Simone smiled up at him, "All you had to do was ask."

"Wait one damn minute," Alan yelled.

"Oh, hell, no," Marty stood, preparing to rush across the room.

"Marty, sit down," his wife demanded.

"I am not going to let this happen."

"I said sit down or I swear on my life, when we get home I will pack my bags and leave." He looked at his wife in disbelief, then across the room at his son making what he thought would be the worst mistake of his life. He eased himself down in the chair, angrily tightening his fists.

"Simone, what are you doing?" Debra asked. "You can't be serious. What does this person have to offer you?"

"Debra, calm down," Joe said, taking his wife's arm.

"No!" she yelled at her husband, snatching her arm away. "You can't be with my daughter," Debra yelled at Matt. "I forbid it!"

"Oh no you don't," Marty said, rising from his seat this time. "You can't tell my boy who he can and can't be with."

"Mister," Debra turned to Marty, pointing at him. "You need to mind your own business," she said, still yelling.

"This is my business. Whoever Matt dates is his concern, not

yours. And I'll be dammed if I'm going to let you or anybody else stand in his way," Marty said, hiking up the front of his pants.

"You, look here," Debra said, stepping in front of Marty. "You people are lucky my daughter would even give your son the time of day."

"Yeah, right lady. Time of day, my ass. She follows him like a little puppy...always sniffing around. You need to keep her on a leash."

"Marty!" Rebecca yelled.

"I mean it," he said, cutting his eyes toward his wife. "She's like a dog in heat."

"How dare you. You people would be lucky if an ounce of my daughter's class and brains rubbed off on you," Debra said, flailing her arms around.

Matt leaned close to Simone. "Let's leave," he whispered. She looked at her mother and back to Matt. "Come on, if we're lucky, they'll kill each other."

"What about your mother and my father?" Simone asked him.

"She's used to this. She'll leave before any shrapnel hits her, and I can almost bet your father knows how to dodge the bullets, too." Matt took Simone's hand, leading her to the front door.

"Simone, just where do you think you are going?" Simone heard her mother call. She stopped at the coat closet long enough to get her coat and purse. Her mother was still ranting as they stepped out onto the front porch away from all the commotion.

Matt turned to her. "I think it's time we had a formal date," he brought her hand to his lips, kissing it. "Miss Porter, would you please have dinner with me tomorrow evening."

Simone smiled at his formalness. "Yes, Mr. Turner, I would love to."

Matt grinned at her, then glanced back inside the house. "I probably should go back inside and rescue Ma."

"I think so."

"What are you going to do now? I mean, I sort of killed everyone's party mood."

"Not mine," Simone said, smiling up at him.

"Are you sure?" Matt stepped closer to her and placed his fingers under her chin.

"Positive," she answered. He turned her face up to him and brushed her lips with his. He pulled back, his eyes piercing. Standing on her toes, she slipped her arms around his neck and parted her lips as he took her mouth.

"I'll see you," he said, watching as she walked to her car and got in. He waited for her to pull out of the driveway before going back inside the house in search of his parents. The room was all abuzz and everyone turned when he entered. The room fell quiet. He looked around not seeing Simone's parents or Alan. He found his mother whispering to Karen and his father sitting in a chair not far away with a beer in his hand. Matt walked over, oblivious to the eyes that watched him. "Ma, are you guys ready to leave?"

"Where's Simone?" Rebecca asked.

"She was tired. She went home."

"You go ahead and leave. Your father and I can get home."

"I'll take you," Karen spoke up. Then she stepped close to Matt, kissing his cheek and patting his chest saying. "Good job. You have a real gem there. You better take good care of her."

"I know. I will," he assured her.

Chapter 27

Although Matt woke at 5 a.m., he stayed in bed thinking of all the things he wanted to do before his date with Simone. At 5:45, he finally got out of bed knowing there was no way he was going to go back to sleep. He cleaned his bedroom and the bathroom. After doing two loads of laundry, he checked the time. Seeing that it was only 8:15, he tapped the clock to make sure it wasn't broken.

At 9:30, he drove downtown and went to one of the men's shops to buy a new suit and tie. On his way back, he stopped at the florist and ordered a dozen red roses sent to Simone. He bought a single white rose, taking it with him for that evening. He walked to his truck, got in and placed the rose on the seat next to him. He reached over and turned on the radio to one of the local jazz stations. His cell phone rang. Turning down the radio, he reached for the phone. "Hello"

"Where the hell have you been? I've been calling you since last night," Marty gruffed.

"Hey, Pop, I was busy. What's up?"

"Busy with monkey business I bet. What the hell is going on with you boy?"

"What do you mean?"

"You know what I mean. What is going on with you and that gal? What was that bullshit about you saying that you love her and all? Have you lost your damn mind?"

"I'm not going into this with you, Pop," Matt paused, "and what was all that stuff you said about not being able to tell me who I can and can't be with?"

"I wasn't going to let one of them think they can talk to you like that! Boy, you're making a fool out of yourself."

"No, I'm not. Pop, this is none of your business."

"What about Wendy?"

"What about her?" Matt shouted.

"She's your wife."

"Ex-wife," Matt corrected, angrily gripping the steering wheel, causing the truck to swerve and narrowly miss an oncoming car. His heart raced as he felt a sense of deja vu. Knowing he shouldn't be driving at that moment, he put on his right turn signal, merged into the right lane and pulled into a 7-Eleven parking lot.

"You and Wendy were good together. You should be able to work things out."

"No we can't, or have you conveniently forgotten that she's living with another man?"

"So you turn to this gal just to get back at her?"

"This has nothing to do with Wendy, and it's none of your business."

"Yes it is. This can only lead to trouble. It's going to be just like it was with your sister. I can feel it. She goes against me and marries a spic. Then you turn around and get yourself a nigger. Boy, think before you make the biggest mistake of your life."

"Marty, what are you doing?" Matt heard his mother yell in the background.

"Becca, someone has to do something." Matt heard a muffled sound.

"Matt, your father has to go," she said, hanging up the phone. Matt took a deep breath realizing he was still a little shaken from the near-miss accident. Closing his eyes, he laid his head against the headrest, breathing slowly.

• • •

When Rebecca walked into the living room she froze in her tracks. She couldn't believe the things her husband was saying to Matt. She had asked him to promise her that he would not interfere. He would not do anything to come between Matt and Simone. He swore that he wouldn't. Now here he was doing just that! She stormed across the room and snatched the phone from him. After speaking to Matt, she hung up.

"I'm not finished talking to him yet," Marty yelled at her.

"You told me that you wouldn't interfere in Matt's relationship."

"I'm not."

"What do you call this?"

"Like I said, someone needs to talk to him and that's all I'm doing, talking."

"It didn't sound like you were just talking to me. It sounded like you are saying awful things about Simone and Vincent."

"Someone needed to tell him the truth. You won't."

"This is his life. If you don't stop what you're doing, you are going to start a battle that will end in you losing your other son."

"That will never happen."

"Marty, don't be stupid. It already happened. Twice, I might add. It'll happen again. Simone is a wonderful girl and if she makes our son happy, then so be it."

"Well, I won't stand for it," Marty said, folding his arms tightly across his chest. Rebecca slowly sat on the sofa next to him.

"What about Marty Jr.?" She watched him, waiting for an answer. "When he brought Alex home to meet us, I was so surprised. I shouldn't have been. Deep down, I think I always knew. But that's beside the point. When he told us that he was gay, I didn't expect it, but I loved him because he was my son and I accepted it. Then you turned your back on him and treated him like he was less of a person. You called him 'fag' and 'queer' and all those other terrible names... you and your stupid friends. They would always torment him at the plant and you never said a word. He would come home and talk to me about it because he knew he couldn't turn to you. He once told me that he took the job at the plant because he thought that was what you wanted. Did you know that? He thought that he could earn your respect that way," she said, her tone bitter.

"One day he told me that they put something awful in his locker. He wouldn't tell me what it was, but I can only imagine. That was when he decided he was going to move away. He wanted to get away from you and your evil kind. Before he and Alex could find the peace that they deserved, he died in that car crash. I never told you this, but I blamed you."

"That wasn't my fault. It was that drunk driver's fault."

"It was just as much your fault as the man driving that other car," Rebecca said tearfully, pointing a slim finger at her husband. "If you hadn't driven him from our home, then he wouldn't have been on that road heading east and he would still be here. Then, you forbid Sarah to see Vincent. She ran off with him and went all the way to Texas to get away from you," she stood, raising her voice. "And by God, I will not let you chase Matt away, too."

"Don't be so dramatic, woman. He isn't going nowhere," Marty grunted. Rebecca squared her shoulders as she spoke to her husband.

"Marty, I'm going to Texas."

"What for? Sarah just left to go back home."

"Not to visit. To stay."

"Now who's being stupid?"

"You still are," she yelled. "You don't see what you're doing. You don't see how you've ripped our family apart. You drove our oldest son to his death, turned our daughter against you, and now you are going to chase Matt away with your hatred. I'm leaving and I won't be back unless you change."

"Change what?"

"Change the way you treat Matt's relationship with Simone and change the way you treat Vince."

"I don't need to change."

"That's your choice. I feel sorry for you. Unless you do, you're going to be a very lonely man. You'll be without your children and you'll be without me," she said with finality. He grunted, getting up quickly and walking to his easy chair where he flopped down. Reaching for the remote, he turned on the television and turned up the volume. She watched him for a moment, then went upstairs and into the bedroom, closing the door behind her.

• • •

Karen answered her phone. "I need your help," Simone cried, not bothering to say hello.

"I was wondering how long it would take you to call me," Karen said, laughing.

"Where are you?" Simone asked.

"Believe it or not, I had an appointment to get a manicure and pedicure this afternoon, and I canceled it. I'm on my way to your house."

Simone breathed a sigh of relief. "Thanks."

"Be there soon."

• • •

Simone stood in Lord and Taylor's, looking at herself in the full-length mirror. "Don't you think this dress is a little risqué?" She asked, pulling at the cleavage of the dress she wore. The silver mesh halter dress, embellished with black beads and embroidered appliqués, showed off her curvy figure. Simone tried to adjust the front by pulling the straps around her neck.

"Don't do that, that's how it's supposed to be," Karen said, smacking Simone's hand and grinning. "I like it. It's hot."

"But, is it too hot?" Simone asked, looking worried. "It shows a lot of cleavage and I don't want to give him the wrong impression."

"It can never be too hot. This is exactly the impression we're going for. You look great. I'll do your hair. He's not going to be able to keep his hands off you." Simone smiled at her friend. "So, what has Debra said about what happened?" Karen asked.

"I haven't talked to her yet. She called me every 15 minutes last night and every half-hour today so far. I haven't answered my cell and I've been letting the machine pick up at home," Simone said, still looking in the mirror.

"I'm sure she's had a cow by now," Karen said, laughing at the image.

"No," Simone said, "more like a herd!"

Karen chuckled, shaking her head.

Karen walked to a rack and picked out a sheer shawl that matched the dress Simone wore. Walking to Simone she wrapped it

around her shoulders. Karen stepped back, looking at the outfit Simone wore. "Perfect," she said, now all we need are some hot shoes.

• • •

Marty glanced at the clock on top of the television set just as he heard Rebecca walking down the steps. "What are we having for supper?"

"You'll have to fend for yourself," she said.

"What the hell is that supposed to mean?" he asked, looking in her direction. He looked at the suitcases she held in her hands.

"Just what it sounds like. You have to fend for yourself."

"Where do you think you are going?"

"I'm going to Texas."

"Yeah, right," he said, chuckling. "If this is some trick so you can get me to do what you want, it isn't gonna work," he shouted, reaching for the remote and turning the television up a little more.

"Bye, Marty," she said, walking to the front door. She set both suitcases down long enough to get her coat out of the closet before walking out the front door. He watched her close the door, then got up quickly, walking to the window and peeking out. She set her bags down, one on each side of her, buttoned her coat and folded her arms.

"Just what I thought," he whispered. "You want me to come running and beg you not to go. But it isn't happening." He went back to his usual spot, flopped in his seat and waited. After another ten minutes, he took another look out the window. He watched as Rebecca got into a cab. She never once looked back at the house. "She'll be back. She isn't going nowhere. Just like a woman to take things too far." He went back to his seat and waited for her to come back and make his supper.

Chapter 28

Rebecca had to force herself not to look back at the house to see if Marty was watching. She was going to follow this through. She was going to Matt's house to spend the night and catch a flight from Baltimore to Texas in the morning.

"Ma, are you sure you want to do this?" Matt asked his mother. He walked onto the porch, taking her bags from the taxi driver. He set the bags inside the door and paid the driver.

"Yes, this time your father has gone too far. I don't like the way he talked to you today, and I don't like the way he treats Simone. Not to mention the fact that his own daughter won't even speak to him. It's a shame," she said, shaking her head. "I told him I wouldn't be back until he changes."

"What if he won't change?" Matt asked her.

"Then I won't be coming back."

"You can't be serious?" he asked, surprised at her answer.

"Yes, I am. I already talked to Sarah and they would love to have me stay with them to take care of the girls."

"But what about Pop?"

"He made his bed — now he can lie in it."

Matt couldn't believe what he was hearing.

"Ma, I'm sorry — this is entirely my fault."

"No, it's not. You can't help who you fall in love with. I can tell you love Simone. I knew before you even admitted it to yourself." Matt crossed his arms as he watched his mother. "Don't give me that look," she said, scolding her son playfully. "Whenever she's around, your face lights up, and you come alive. Not even Wendy had that effect on you, and you thought she was the love of your life." Matt laughed at his mother's ability to read him. "I think Simone will make a good wife and an even better mother."

"You never said that about Wendy."

"You didn't ask what I thought about Wendy."

"If I had, would you have said the same?"

"If you remember, I asked you if you were sure you were doing the right thing. You never asked me what I thought of her."

"Maybe I should have asked you what you thought."

She smiled. "Maybe you should have."

Matt laughed quietly. "Let me take your bags up. I'm supposed to pick up Simone at 6, but I'll call her and let her know that something's come up. I'm sure she'll understand."

"Don't you dare," Rebecca said quickly. "You and Simone need to spend some time together. I'm a big girl and I can take care of myself."

"Are you sure?"

"Yes, honey, I'm sure."

He picked up her bags and was halfway up the stairs with them when the phone rang.

"Can you get that for me?" he asked.

Rebecca walked to the phone, lifting the receiver.

"Hello."

"Hello, may I speak to Matt please?"

"Simone?"

"Yes?"

"This is Rebecca. Are you all right?"

"Sure, I'm fine, Mrs. Turner"

"It's just your mother was a little upset yesterday and I was concerned. I don't mean to pry."

"No, you're not prying. I haven't spoken to her yet, but I'm sure everything will be okay."

"Good. If you need me, I'm here for you," Rebecca said.

"Thank you."

"Matt just went upstairs. He should be down in a moment."

"Okay." There was an uneasy silence.

"Simone?"

"Yes."

"Can I ask you something?" Rebecca paused. "It might be

too personal, and I'll understand if you tell me to mind my own business."

"Sure. Go ahead," Simone said.

"How do you really feel about Matt? I want to hear you say how you feel."

"I don't know if I can tell you how I feel about Matt. I haven't even told him yet."

"Yes, you're right. I understand."

"I can say that when I'm with him I feel things I've never felt before," Simone said, then took a deep breath and continued. "I'm happy and strong. And I feel like I can conquer the world."

Rebecca smiled to herself, saying, "It sounds like you love him."

"With every part of my soul," Simone admitted. "I hope that what I'm saying doesn't bother you?"

"No, it makes me happy, Simone. Thank you," Rebecca said.

"For what?"

"For loving my son in spite of who his father is."

Chapter 29

Simone took a hot bubble bath, adding scented oils to the water, hoping it would help ease her nervousness. Sitting up, she pulled the stopper and let the water run down the drain. She toweled off and put on her robe. She stood in front of the mirror opening her robe, hoping to see herself the way Matt would. She smoothed on vanilla-jasmine body oil and sprayed the same scent on her pulse points. Slipping on her dress, she turned to the side, surveying the way the opening revealed the honey-colored length of her leg and thigh. Going to her dresser she sat down and applied her makeup. Then she put on her onyx earrings and the bracelet Matt gave her for her birthday.

Meanwhile, Matt looked in the rearview mirror to check his reflection before getting out of the truck. He felt nervous, like this was the senior prom and he was the same old shy Matt Turner, but he was taking out the hottest girl in school. He tugged at his tie uncomfortably as he rang the bell. When Simone opened the door he opened his mouth to speak, but froze staring at her in shocked silence instead. "Wow," he finally spoke, "you look fantastic."

"Thanks," she said, not sure what to do next. She turned and walked inside. He followed her in, closing the door. He quickly kissed her cheek and gave her the white rose.

"Thank you, Matt," she said, shyly taking the rose. She held it to her nose, inhaling the fragrance before putting it in the vase with the roses that were delivered earlier. "Do we have reservations somewhere? Should we get going?" Simone couldn't believe how nervous she was.

"Yeah, but we have a half-hour. We'll be on time."

• • •

Once seated inside the restaurant, the waiter brought them

their menus. "How did everything go with your father? I'm sure he was upset."

"No — not especially." Simone pursed her lips and raised her eyebrows.

"Okay, maybe he was a little upset. But he'll be fine. He still hasn't let go of the idea that Wendy and I will get back together again."

Simone looked down, switching the order of her silverware before speaking. "Is there any chance of that happening?"

"No. What we had is long over."

"But do you still have feelings for her?" Simone asked nervously.

"Wendy was different. She was unobtainable. Every guy in school wanted to be with her, but she chose me. "

"You wanted what you couldn't have?" she questioned. She didn't say that she was referring to herself, but Matt understood what she was asking.

"No, I was a boy from a working class family. She came from a different class and a different world. I was like a child who wanted what all the other boys wanted and couldn't have."

"Oh," she said, looking down at her place-setting. Matt reached across the table and tilted her chin upwards with his index finger bringing her gaze to meet his.

"That was when I was a boy. I'm a man now and I know what I want, and the only person that I want now — or ever — is you." She reached for his hand and brought it to her lips, kissing it. He slowly stroked her fingers asking, "Have you talked to your mother?"

Simone sighed. "She's been calling me all day. I'm really not looking forward to talking to her."

"I'm sorry," Matt said.

"No, it's not your fault. I just need to talk to her and make her understand that I make my own decisions."

"She's not going to like that," Matt said.

"Maybe," Simone said, "but she can't change it."

"My day has been rather eventful, too," Matt said. "My

mother is going to Texas — indefinitely." He paused, clasping his hands under his chin.

"I'm sorry that she has to go through that," Simone said sadly.

"Yeah, me too."

• • •

When they arrived back at her house, Simone reached inside her purse, removing her keys. Matt took them and opened the door for her. "Thanks," she said, taking the keys and walking into the house.

"I had a really good time."

"I did, too," he said, suddenly feeling nervous again.

"So," he said, shoving his hands in his pockets.

"So," she said, fidgeting from one foot to the other.

"Would you like to come in for a while?"

"Sure," he said quickly, walking inside. She took off her coat, hanging it across the back of the arm chair, and dropped her purse on the table.

"You really do look beautiful tonight," he said.

"I was a little nervous about the dress," she said, looking down at her outfit. "I was thinking that it was a little too much."

"No," he said, his eyes remaining on her face, "it's perfect. Just like you are." She cocked her head, watching him. He walked to her. "You really don't know how beautiful you are, do you?" he said, lifting her face to meet his.

She laughed and nervously turned away.

"Come here," he said, taking her hand and leading her to the armchair. He sat on the arm, pulling her to stand in front of him. "You're beautiful. Everything about you is beautiful. Your face," his fingers, stroked her cheek. "Your heart ... ," his fingers traveled from her cheek to her neck and down to her collarbone gently brushing the spot between her breasts, "... and your magnificent, sexy body." His hands traveled down to her hips where each hand gently massaged as he spoke.

"Every man at the restaurant envied me. They all wanted to

be me just so they could spend a second with you. And lucky me, I get to be with you forever."

Tears welled in her eyes. She leaned close, kissing him. "Thank you," she said.

"You don't have to thank me for telling the truth." He brought his hand back up, running his finger along her jaw. "When I was in the coma, do you know what brought me back?" She shook her head. "You did. I heard your voice and I came back with the hope that I would have the chance to be with my angel." He pulled her close, kissing her. Through the thin material of her dress he could feel her nipples harden against his chest.

"I want to be with you," she whispered against his mouth. He kissed her jaw down to her neck where his warm breath lingered for a moment before traveling back to her jaw. He pulled back, watching her intently as he slowly slid her dress from her shoulders allowing her full breasts to spring free. His hands slid across her silken belly, up along her ribs and gently outlined the circle of her breast, his eyes never leaving hers. She breathed lightly between parted lips as shivers of delight from his touch embraced her. His eyes traveled down to her golden orbs and she moved slightly, letting her dress slide from her waist to the floor, revealing a black low-rise lace thong.

Matt's breath caught in his throat. "You're more gorgeous than I could have ever imagined," he whispered, his heart beating wildly. He closed his eyes, calming himself to keep from losing control. When he reopened his eyes, Simone was studying him. She reached up, grasping the cord that held his hair in a place, slid it down, and watched his hair fall around his shoulders. He smiled at her, letting his lips brush hers. He lightly kissed her collarbone, allowing his tongue to make its way down the slope of her breast to the tip of her nipple. His tongue swirled slowly around the edge of the taut peak before he gently drew it into his mouth.

Simone inhaled deeply as Matt pulled her closer. Her knees felt weak and she wrapped her arms around him for support. He pulled back and quickly stripped off his jacket, tie and shirt. He led her into the bedroom, sat her on the end of the bed and stooped to

remove her shoes. He kissed her ankles, slowly moving up her calf, up to her thigh to the black satin material. She tried to move to the center of the bed. "No," he held her in place, "stay there." Kneeling on one knee in front of her, he slipped his fingers inside the top of her panties. With her rising slightly, he slid them from her hips. He took her mouth, ravishing it hungrily. Leaving her mouth, he gently kissed her neck down to her left shoulder and to the mounds of her breasts. Her body trembled as his tongue brushed against her hardened nipples. He suckled her nipples, first one then the other. Drawing back, he met her hungry gaze.

She brought her hand up, tracing her finger along his browline, down his strong jaw to his lips. "You have beautiful lips, so soft and sweet," she whispered. The look she gave him made his blood race. She leaned close, kissing him and moaning gently.

He laid her back, making his way to the warm spot throbbing for attention between her thighs. He gently licked the outside folds. Hearing her gasp, he then slid his tongue deeper. As her gasps turned into moans, he ate like a man receiving his last meal. His desire built with each moan and whimper she made. Standing, he pulled his t-shirt off, his hair spilled around his shoulders. Simone thought that she'd never seen a more gorgeous sight.

Reaching into his back pocket, he pulled out his wallet and removed a condom. Giving her a sexy smile, he gripped the packet between his teeth while throwing his wallet over his shoulder. His hands gradually moved to his slacks. He slowly unfastened them to let them slide leisurely from his hips. Simone sat up reaching for him as he moved toward the bed. Taking her hands he slipped the condom into her palm and guided her hands to him. She opened the pack and he took her hand, guiding her as she slid the condom onto his engorged shaft. Leaning forward, she pressed a row of kisses along the muscles of his stomach, her tongue sliding around his nipple and her fingers wrapped around his thick length. She simply held him for a moment, enjoying the feel of him. A moan erupted from deep within Matt's chest as he slipped his hands around Simone's waist, holding her firmly while he sank slowly and deeply into her moist, welcoming heat.

Once he entered her, her intense heat engulfed him, nearly throwing him over the edge. He paused, giving her body time to adjust to his. He began moving slowly, and she gasped as her body tightened, clamping around him, hot and needy. He threw his head back, clenching his teeth to control himself, and she rose to meet him. She moaned, calling out his name, and he sank himself so deep inside of her he felt they were one. Matt held to his control until he felt Simone slip over the edge and, as she cried out, he joined her.

• • •

Matt's steady breathing was soothing to her. She rested her head on his chest, looking at his sleeping face. "What are you doing?" he asked, his eyes still closed.

"Watching you sleep," she said lazily.

"Mmm," he murmured as he slowly ran his hand up and down her arm. "I have to leave," he said, opening his eyes and meeting her gaze. "Mom's leaving for Texas in the morning and I want to see her off." Simone nodded her understanding. "Can you come with me?" he asked.

"To the airport in the morning?"

"No, home with me tonight. I don't want to leave you. I want to spend the night with you." Simone hesitated.

"What about your mother."

"What about her?"

"I don't know? She might not be comfortable with me staying with you."

"I'm a big boy. I think I can have an overnight guest," he said, laughing. Simone sat up and swung her legs off the bed. "Hey, where are you going?"

"I'm getting dressed," she said.

He reached for her, pulling her toward him. "Not just yet."

Chapter 30

Creeping down the stairs, Wendy quietly opened the front door heading toward her SUV. Opening the back door of the vehicle, she put the small suitcase inside. Then she walked around to the driver's side and slipped behind the steering wheel. Starting the vehicle, she drove away without seeing Jamison watching her behind the heavy curtains in his office window.

• • •

After dropping off Rebecca at the airport, Matt and Simone went back to his house. They were in the kitchen just finishing lunch when Simone stood up and took Matt's hand. "Let's take a nap," she said, grinning and pulling him from his seat.

They walked through the living room toward the stairs when the doorbell rang. Stopping on the bottom step, Matt leaned down to whisper in Simone's ear, "They'll go away." When they reached the top landing, the intruder rang the doorbell continually. "Damn it," Matt cursed as he quickly walked down the stairs with Simone following him.

"Geez, Wendy."

"Hi, Matt," she said, biting her lip.

He ran his hand through his hair, sighing. "What can I do for you?"

"I was wondering if we could talk." She stepped forward toward the entrance of the house. Matt blocked her way.

"About what?" Matt asked. Wendy glanced around him at Simone. "Anything you have to say to me you can say in front of Simone," Matt said defensively. She looked at him, then back at Simone.

"It will only take a moment, I promise," she said to Simone.

Simone nodded. "Sure, no problem. I'll be upstairs."

. . .

Jamison opened his safe and removed his gun, sliding it into the back of his pants under his jacket. He looked over his shoulder at Adrian sitting in the chair across from his desk. He looked for any sign of nervousness: a tick, sweat on his brow, something to show that he was scared. The only thing he saw was the same calm and collected Adrian, sitting with his long legs stretched out like he didn't have a care in the world. Jamison walked to the bar and picked up the whisky decanter with his shaky hands. He forced the shaking to stop, hoping Adrian hadn't noticed. Pouring a double, he downed it in one gulp. Turning to Adrian, he said, "I'm ready."

They left the office heading down the hall toward the front door. Adrian saw in his peripheral vision Sunee standing in the corner and looking as if she wished she could disappear. Adrian glared at her briefly before following Jamison out of the house.

. . .

Matt tapped on the door to his home office. "C'mon in," Simone said.

"You okay?" he asked.

"Mmm-hmm." Simone was sitting behind his desk writing furiously on the pad.

"I know her coming here bothered you. I'm sorry."

"No, not at all. I know you two had a life together," she said, not looking at him.

"You seem a little upset."

"No," she said, as casually as she could, rolling her eyes. "I'm fine." Matt laughed, walking to the desk and snatching the pad. "Give that back!" She rose from the chair as he held it high over his head out of her reach.

"No," he continued, laughing. "Not till you talk to me."

"All right," Simone said, folding her arms, "I was jealous! Are you satisfied now?"

"Do you want to know what we talked about?" Matt asked, dropping the pad on the desk.

"No!" she said, pouting and folding her arms, feeling completely ridiculous.

"You lie." He grinned. She sat down, watching him. Her arms still folded. "She told me that she thinks she made a mistake ending our marriage."

"Oh, yeah. That made my jealously subside — just like that," she said, snapping her fingers.

"Do you want to hear the rest?"

"Do I dare?"

"I told her that her leaving me was the best thing that ever happened to me. If she hadn't, I would have never met my beautiful angel. I told her that I was totally and madly in love with you."

Simone bit her lip as she smiled at him. "Yeah, you better had. I'd hate to have to hurt you."

Matt grinned. "Could you do that later anyway?"

She laughed. "You're bad." Matt sat on the end of the desk and she rose from the chair to step between his legs and wrap her arms around his neck.

"Wendy's still here."

"Is everything okay?"

"I'm not sure. I don't think so. I'm going to see if I can find out what's going on."

Simone nodded. "Well, in that case, I should probably go and talk to my mother."

"Do you want me to go with you? I can ask Wendy to come back later or to wait until we come back." Using the back of his fingers, he gently brushed her cheek.

"No, I'll be fine."

"It might be better if we face her together."

Simone shook her head. "This is my battle."

Matt cringed, angrily saying, "It shouldn't be a battle."

"I know. I don't think that this is really about you. I think it has more to do with me doing something different than what my mother wants. I can handle it."

"Are you sure?" he asked.

"I'm sure." He reached inside his pocket, pulling out his truck keys and giving them to her. "I'll be back in a couple of hours," she said, taking the keys.

"When you get back I'll have dinner waiting," he said, tilting her head up and kissing her. "I love you."

She smiled up at him. "I love you, too."

• • •

Sunee ran up the stairs of the factory, slipping into the back door. Seeing her husband's friend and co-worker, she looked around nervously before waving him over. "Sunee, what is the matter? You look as if you have seen a ghost."

She shook her head briskly. "More like the devil. I need to see my husband. Can you find him?" He nodded, taking her arm and leading her to a corner so their foreman wouldn't see her. A short while later she saw husband.

He glanced around to be sure no one was watching them and he led her outside. "Sunee, what are you doing here? Why are you not at work?"

"Kiet, I don't know what to do. I hear Mr. Jamison today. I hear him tell his friend that he going to kill Miss Wendy and her ex-husband."

"Sunee, I told you to keep quiet. We don't want trouble."

"But Kiet, I see him put a gun in his pocket. He's going to kill these people now." Her husband shook his head, giving her a stern look. She bit her lip, then added, "Mr. Jamison friend, he was there too. He saw me. He know I hear everything."

"Are you sure, Sunee? Maybe you just think he saw you?"

"No, he look right at me. Mr. Jamison knows where we live and we don't have money to hide. What we gonna do?" Her husband rubbed his hand across his face.

"Sunee, we don't know these people! What are we to do — go to the authorities with no names — nothing but the word of a crazy woman?"

She reached into her pocket, slowly pulling out a folded

piece of paper. With a trembling hand she gave it to her husband. "Ms. Wendy left a book. I take her ex-husband's address."

Her husband watched her. After a few moments, he took a deep breath and nodding, he said, "We go to police."

• • •

Using her key, Simone let herself into her parents' house. She walked through the house looking for her mother and finding Debra and Joe in the back yard. Debra looked up when she heard movement behind them. Simone walked over to Joe.

"Hi, daddy," she said, giving him a quick peck on the cheek.

"Hi," he said, taking her hand squeezing it.

"I'm so pleased you have decided to grace us with your presence," Debra said sarcastically.

"Hi to you, too, Mother."

"Where have you been?" Debra demanded.

"I was with Matt," Simone answered.

Debra grunted her disapproval. "I can't believe you," Debra said, shaking her head in disgust.

"Why would you ask me if knowing the answer would upset you?" Simone asked.

"I have no idea. Maybe I was hoping that you would have come to your senses and gotten as far away from that person as possible."

"What do you have against Matt?" Simone demanded, sitting in one of the patio chairs.

"A lot."

"Like what?"

"He's not Alan, for one."

"And I'm glad of that," Simone said sarcastically.

"Alan's a wonderful man," Debra said.

"Then you go out with him," Simone added. She looked at her father. "Sorry, Daddy."

Joe shook his head and waved his hand. "Don't worry about

it. I think I'll leave you ladies alone to work this out." He rose, walking into the house.

"Simone, he'll ruin your life. He's using you."

"I love him, and he loves me," Simone said. Debra sat forward dropping her head into her hands.

"Simone, you're so naive. You are not in love. You are in lust. And this man cannot possibly love you."

"Mother, how could you possibly know how we feel about each other?"

"Okay," Debra said, raising her hands, "let's just say for the sake of saying it, that he does love you. Then what? So you love him. What sort of life can he give you?"

"Jesus. Mother, give it a break," she said, rising from her seat.

"Simone," Debra said, "what has come over you?"

"I'm tired of you trying to run my life and telling me what is best for me. I'm an adult. I can make my own decisions. I love Matt and I've chosen to be in a relationship with him." She turned and walked toward the gate.

"We are not done here, young lady!" Debra called to her.

"Yes, we are."

Simone walked to Matt's truck, got in and drove away.

• • •

"Wendy, when he hit you the first time, you should have gone to the police," Matt said from his seat on the sofa.

Wendy sat next to him, wringing her hands and rocking nervously. "I know, but I was afraid. What if he kills me?"

"Is he really capable of that?"

She nodded reluctantly.

Matt shook his head, saying, "Wendy, what have you gotten yourself into?"

"Matt, I'm so scared. I know I shouldn't have come here, but I didn't know where else to go or what else to do. You were always there for me when I needed you. I guess a part of me would like to think that you will be there forever."

Matt didn't want to hear her statement. "Wendy, I'll help you as much as I can."

"I just wish… I wish I could go back and change things. I wish I could go back to the safety of us."

"You know what's funny, Wendy? Even after all we've been through, I still love you. I'm just not in love with you. I don't know if I ever was." He sighed. "I think I was in love with the idea of being in love with you."

"Matt, you took care of me and always made sure I got what I wanted."

"Wendy, love is more than that. It's laughing together and crying together. It's accepting each other's shortcomings and loving that person just the same. That's what Simone and I share. Even though I can be an asshole sometimes, she loves me anyway." Wendy was about to say something when someone knocked on the door. "That must be Simone. She's back early." Opening the door Matt came face to face with the devil.

• • •

Parking the truck, Simone walked briskly to Alan's front door and rang the bell. He opened the door with a huge smile on his face, and Simone watched as it slowly slipped away. "Hey," she said.

"Uh, Simone, hi. I didn't expect to see you," Alan said, stepping outside the door and closing it behind him.

"I know I shouldn't have come without calling," Simone said "but I didn't know if you would see me and I had to talk to you. I had to let you know how truly sorry I am for…"

"Baby, is that the pizza delivery?" Simone heard someone say from inside the house as the door opened. "Oh, uh...sorry," The person standing next to Alan said. Simone looked at Alan and at the man standing next to him.

"Hi, I'm Simone," she said with a questioning look. She looked at Alan's attire. He was shirtless and wearing dark blue silk pajama bottoms. The other man also wore pajamas. His wore gold silk shorts, but he wore a matching top. Simone's brow furrowed as

realization set in. Her mouth became dry and she felt her eyes tear up. She backed up, turned and quickly walked from the porch.

"Simone, wait!" Alan called, running barefoot to catch up with her.

She looked at him. "Alan what the hell is wrong with you? Why didn't you tell me that you're…gay?"

"I'm not gay."

"Are you seeing that man?"

"It's not what you think."

"Are you seeing that man!"

"Simone, calm down," he said, reaching for her and looking around.

"Hell no! Don't touch me and don't tell me to calm down. I asked you a question and I want the truth."

"I don't know where to start."

"You could start off by saying 'Simone, I'm gay!' "

"Simone, I'm not gay. It's just a fad. Before we got married, I would have gotten it out of my system."

"Alan, I don't think this is something you just get out of your system. I can't believe you led me to think you wanted to have a relationship with me when you were seeing someone else. A man!"

"Simone, aren't you being just a bit melodramatic?" Alan said in his normal patronizing voice.

"Fuck you," Simone yelled even louder. "Don't you dare tell me I'm being overly dramatic when you were pretending all this time to be straight."

"Me? You were running around with Turner behind my back. You make me out to be the bad guy? Going to the movies and out to dinner. Hell, you spent more time with him in the last two months than you've ever spent with me."

"I wasn't sleeping with him," she paused. "Is that why you never wanted to touch me?"

"No! I wanted to wait until we were married. I was going to leave the past behind me. By us waiting, we would have had a fresh start."

Simone looked at him like he had gone mad. "I came here

to apologize to you for what happened. Stupid me, I thought you deserved better." She walked to the truck and opened the door.

"Simone, please?" Alan rushed to the truck. "Please?" He heaved a heavy sigh, "I'm sorry."

Simone watched him closely. "Alan, why didn't you just tell me? Why didn't you just tell me the truth? "

"I couldn't risk your mother finding out."

"She would have never heard it from me. This would have saved us a lot of trouble. We were pretending to be a couple for months."

"We were a couple."

"No, Alan, we weren't." She paused, then looked up at the house and saw the worried look on the other man's face. He tried to smile at her, but he just looked more worried and anguished. She met Alan's steady gaze. "Alan, don't pretend to be someone you're not. I've done that most of my adult life and I can tell you, it's hell. Do you love him?"

Alan looked down, not wanting to meet Simone's gaze. Then he looked around nervously, taking a heavy breath, he let it out slowly, as if with the single breath he let go of a huge weight. "I think so."

Simone watched him for a moment, for the first time seeing the real Alan. "Good." She smiled and then kissed his cheek. "I hope he makes you happy."

She looked toward the house again and watched the man standing in the window. He was holding his arms protectively around his waist. She smiled at him and waved. He waved back and she slipped into the truck.

"Simone," Alan called before she backed out of the drive. She looked up at him. "Are you sure you want to do this."

"Do what, Alan?"

"Be with Turner."

"Yes, I am. I've never been surer of anything in my life." He looked down, then back at her, nodding.

"I hope things work out for you. I really do," he said, backing away from the truck. Then he turned and headed toward the house.

Chapter 31

Simone parked Matt's truck between the two vehicles sitting on the parking pad in front of Matt's house. She recognized the SUV as Wendy's, but the other vehicle was unfamiliar. She walked onto the porch and using Matt's key she let herself in. "Matt I'm back." She called from the living room. Matt walked briskly from the kitchen.

"Simone, go home," he said, his voice hurried. "Take my truck and leave." Simone stood rooted in her spot. That's when she saw the other man standing behind Matt. She leaned slightly to her left trying to get a better look at him. She met Wendy's gaze and saw a look of sorrow on her face. Matt moved over slightly, blocking Simone's view. "Simone, go home now. I don't want you here. Get out!" Matt's voice boomed.

"Matt, I don't understand. Why are you doing this?"

"This is the way it has to be. Don't ask any questions."

Her lip trembled slightly and tears immediately welled in her eyes. She raised her chin. "Fine," she angrily swiped the tears from her right cheek. "I'll just get my things," she said and started toward the steps.

"No!" Matt said abruptly. "I said get out. Now!" Simone glared at him.

"Too late." The man standing behind Matt stepped around him allowing Simone to finally see the gun that he held. "She's not going anywhere," he said as he moved toward Simone.

"No!" Matt crossed the room quickly, putting his body between Simone and the man standing before him.

"Matt, what's going on?"

Matt turned to face her, pulling her in his arms. "Why didn't you just leave, baby? Why didn't you just listen?"

• • •

Marty walked onto the porch. He reached for the doorbell and paused. Then he walked to the window and looked in. There was Matt, sitting on a kitchen chair in the middle of the floor. Simone was sitting on the sofa. "Damn," he grunted and walked to the end of the porch, sliding his hands in his pockets and looking around the front yard. After a moment, he looked over his shoulder at the door and then walked over and rang the bell. The door opened slightly. He hesitated, pushing it open farther and walking into the house. He looked at Matt. He saw Matt's ankles were tied and then Marty realized his arms were also tied. He quickly looked to his right, seeing a strange man standing next to the door, grinning at him. "What the hell is going on here?"

"Glad you could join the party, old man."

• • •

"Did you find anything to tie these two up with?" Adrian asked Jamison, as he walked down the stairs pulling a reluctant Wendy behind him.

"A couple of telephone lines and some extension cord." Adrian nodded, taking one of the cords to tie Simone's arms and using another to tie her legs.

After tying Marty up, Adrian went to search the house for whatever valuables they could find. Jamison took Wendy into the kitchen. Marty glowered at Matt. "What kind of shit have you gotten yourself caught up in boy?"

"Pop, be quiet. I'm trying to think."

"No, I want to know what the hell is going on here. I told you if you didn't change the way you've been acting you were going to regret it. Now look what happened. I told you that gal was nothing but trouble," he thrust his head in Simone's direction. "That's what you get for not listening to me. All of those people are nothing but trouble." Simone looked at him, not responding, but instead closed her eyes.

"Pop, I said shut up."

"Boy, don't talk to me like that."

"Do you want to know who those people are? One of those

guys is Wendy's boyfriend. He's got it in his head that I want her back and has decided to get rid of me and anyone else who happens to be here. Now will you shut the hell up?"

"You hear how he talks to his father?" Marty asked Simone, his eyes as big as fifty-cent pieces. "You woulda thought I brought him up better than that."

"We need a plan," Matt said.

"What?" Marty asked.

"We need a plan," Matt said to himself.

"Yeah, yeah, good thinking," Marty nodded, shifting in his seat. "What are we going to do?"

"Maybe you could pretend you are having a heart attack. They might untie you and you can get the gun away from one of them. I'm thinking the little guy. He seems a bit naive and you can probably subdue him."

Marty stared at him, his mouth agape. "Me? I know you don't mean me?"

"Yeah, you can do it, Pop. I know you can."

"Boy, is that the best you can come up with?" Marty asked, stunned. Looking toward the ceiling he said, "Oh, sweet Jesus, we're going to die."

• • •

Adrian walked down the stairs carrying Simone's overnight bag, which he had emptied and filled with whatever valuables he could find. "Hey man," he called to Jamison in the kitchen, "did you find anything else?"

"No." He walked out of the kitchen holding Wendy's hand. "Nothing worth the effort." He pushed Wendy farther into the living room.

"Jamison, please don't do this. I'm sorry if I hurt you. I love you — you just scared me," Wendy begged.

"You were going to leave me for him."

"No, I wasn't"

"I saw you put your suitcase in the car." Wendy bit her lip

anxiously. "I'm not going to let you hurt me. I'm not going to let you kill me like my mother killed my father," Jamison said.

"Baby, please," Wendy cried, trembling. "Please." Jamison glanced at Adrian.

Adrian shook his head, "Come on man. We need to take care of this and get out of here." Jamison nodded.

"Finally," Adrian said, pulling his gun from under his jacket. Everyone started talking at once. Jamison seemed frazzled by the chaos, but Adrian was very calm, thriving on everyone's fear. He walked to Matt. Matt froze in a momentary state of shock. His mouth was suddenly dry. He couldn't move, couldn't think. He looked over and saw his father thrashing in his seat. He could hear Simone gasp, and let out a loud shriek, and Wendy, sobbing, pleading with Jamison.

"Shut up!" Jamison yelled. "Just everyone be quiet. Let me think. Adrian, wait a minute." He looked at Wendy. She seemed to be hyperventilating. "I don't know about this. We're going to have three bodies murdered executioner style. In these parts, that's not common."

Adrian looked at Jamison and sneered. "Three? Don't you mean four?" He thrust his hand in Wendy's direction. Wendy looked at him with her eyes large. Immediately her legs gave out and she sank to the floor.

"What time is it?" Marty said suddenly.

"Why, you got a date or something, old man," Adrian asked laughing.

"If you untie me, I'll show you an old man," Marty said, glaring back at him. Adrian laughed harder. "I can't stay here. I'm gonna miss 'Law and Order.' It comes on soon. If I miss it, I'm going to be pretty upset."

From his spot next to Matt, Adrian looked at the older man, chuckled and shook his head. "You're a funny old dude, but missing your television show is going to be the least of your worries." He then turned his attention back to Jamison, saying, "Come on, man, let's do this." He smiled at Matt, aiming his gun at the right side of his head.

"Wait, man," Jamison said quickly.

"Please don't do this," Simone pleaded and began to cry. "Please don't kill him. I'll give you anything if you let us go. I have some money in my savings account and a few savings bonds. Please."

Adrian laughed maliciously, dropping his arm to his side.

"I think we should rethink this whole thing," Jamison was saying. Adrian held his hand up, stopping Jamison from speaking. He walked to Simone and squatted down in front of her. "You're begging for his life? What are you willing to give in return?" Simone looked at him, her fear visible. "Are you willing to die in order for him to live?"

As her lip trembled, she looked over at Matt and their eyes locked. Tears filled her eyes and she nodded, whispering, "Yes."

"Come on, man," Matt started fighting in his chair, trying to get loose. "Leave her alone, she doesn't have anything to do with this." Matt turned to Jamison saying, "This is between you and me."

Adrian looked back at Matt and at Jamison, who was crouched down holding Wendy in his arms. "I don't know man. He might be a hard act to follow."

"Jamison, stop him," Wendy begged. "Please, if you love me, you won't let him do this. Stop him and we can leave now. We can go away where no one will ever find us. I promise." Jamison looked at her, seeing the fear and sincerity in her eyes. Adrian stood quickly, raising his gun at Simone, preparing to shoot her.

This can't be real, Marty thought, *I see this kind of stuff all the time on TV, but people can't do this sort of thing in real life.* He felt like he was having a bad nightmare and wasn't able to wake up. But it wasn't a nightmare. It was real, and these guys were going to kill them. He watched Simone as tears filled her eyes, and his heart skipped a beat. He watched as she nodded and whispered *yes*. It all seemed surreal to him. He opened his mouth as the guy stood raising his gun, pointing it at Simone. "No," was all he managed to yell.

"Adrian, drop the gun," Jamison said, pointing his gun at his friend.

Adrian's jaw clenched. "Are you really that stupid? At this point, you're going to let these people go. They'll go to the cops quicker than you can bat an eye." Matt, Marty and Simone started talking at the same time. "Shut the fuck up," Adrian yelled.

"Wendy and I are leaving. We'll leave the country if we have to...start over. We can all leave. They don't have to mention you. They can say it was all me."

"You're pointing that gun at me...you better kill me. Because if you don't, I'm definitely going to kill you," Adrian said, his voice almost a whisper. He swung around, pointing his gun at Jamison as shots rang out. Before the loud bang of the gunfire faded, Jamison dropped next to Wendy with a red, gaping hole in his chest. Wendy wailed, pulling him into her arms as Adrian turned his attention back to Simone.

"Freeze, drop the gun!" Adrian turned, looking down the barrels of four police officers' guns. He hesitated. "Don't make me do it," one of the officers warned. Adrian's eye twitched slightly. Slowly, he raised his hands, grinning and letting the gun dangle on his finger.

• • •

Matt closed the door behind the last of the police officers. He turned to watch Marty and Simone trying to clean up the blood. He heaved a heavy sigh of relief. Wendy had left with the ambulance, going to the hospital with Jamison. Matt didn't know anything about gunshot wounds, but he didn't think Jamison was going to make it. Matt walked to where his father and Simone knelt on the floor. "You okay, Pop?"

"Yeah," Marty nodded, standing. Matt pulled Simone up, took her in his arms and held her tight. Marty bit his lip and asked Simone, "You all right?"

Matt released her, and she turned to Marty. "Yes, sir, just a little shaken up." He stepped closer to her, reached out and put his arm around her shoulder. Then he pulled her close to him and kissed the top of her head. "You did good. You know, if you're going to be

part of the family, you need to know how to cook. I tend to piss the missus off a bit, so I might be stopping by for supper pretty often."

Simone smiled up at him and said, "That will be fine."

Epilogue

Matt turned up the television volume, trying to tune out the commotion buzzing around the living room. His nieces, Sadie and Amanda, sat on the floor to his left debating the colors that were appropriate for the turkey's feathers in the Thanksgiving coloring book. His parents, sister Sarah and brother in-law Vince sat at the dinning room table playing scrabble. They were having an animated discussion on whether or not a certain word was in the dictionary. And his beautiful wife, Simone, sat on several pillows on the floor between his legs. It's A Wonderful Life blared from the television adding to the confusion.

Matt watched Simone as she gently massaged her round belly. She was determined that their daughter would be a professional soccer player, but Matt argued that their son would be the best kicker the NFL had ever seen. Matt gently ran his fingers through Simone's hair, and she slid down, resting her head on his knee.

For three years in a row, Simone's mother refused to come to their home for Thanksgiving dinner. Simone's father, Joe, and her siblings would stop by for dessert, but Debra would never come. Matt knew how much it hurt Simone, and he wished with all his heart that he could do something to change the way Debra felt about him, but as hard as he tried she remained hostile toward him.

"C'mon, Pop, that's not even a word." Sarah sighed in frustration.

"Yes, it is."

"Noooo, it's not."

"Yesss, it is," Marty protested, arranging the scrabble tiles to spell 'didgaeat.' He grinned at his daughter, saying, "Simone lets

me use that word all the time, and this is her house so I can use it if I want to."

"Oh, for crying out loud!" Sarah said, throwing her hands up.

"I love this part," Simone said, snuggling closer to Matt as she softly repeated Jimmy Stewart's dialogue, "My mouth's bleeding, Bert! My mouth's bleed…Zuzu's petals! Zuzu's…they're…they're here, Bert! What do you know about that? Merry Christmas!"

Matt leaned forward and wrapped his arms around Simone. His lips brushed her temple.

"I love you," Simone whispered.

"I love you, too," he said, and he knew that he would forever love his angel.

If you enjoyed reading *My Angel*, you'll also like *My Everything*, Denise Sketon's first novel:

At the age of 20, Benjamin Harrison's father dies, leaving him to provide for his mother and sister. Years later, his sister is in need of a bone marrow transplant, and Ben seeks the help of Meyer's Investigations to find an unknown sibling to save her. His immediate attraction to the sexy female P.I. sets things in motion, and their relationship blossoms.

Adventursome private investigator Deanna Meyers senses her attraction toward Ben, but she is reluctant to date him after seeing what her best friends go through with their own interracial relationships.

Ben's ex-girlfriend Janet and Dee's cousin Terry have one thing in common. They both want Dee out of the picture. But only one will go to any lengths to make that happen. Even kill.

Here's how you can order books directly from Denise Skelton:

Denise Skelton

P.O. Box 60

Lutherville, MD 21094

United States

Please add $2.50 for shipping and handling for the first book and $.75 for each additional book. Maryland residents, add appropriate sales tax. No cash, stamps, or CODs. Canadian orders require $5.00 for shipping and handling and must be paid in U.S. dollars. Prices and availability are subject to change. Payment must accompany all orders.

Name: _____

Address: _____

City:_____

State: _____ Zip: _____

E-mail: _____

I have enclosed $_____ in payment for the checked books(s).

❏ *My Angel*

❏ *My Everything*

For more information, check out www.deniseskelton.com.